From #1 N
Carlan, discover ... .gc Auction: Book Three

You can now dive into the Kindle Vella phenomenon with over 2 MILLON READS. This saga has ranked #1 for over a full year and continues to break records each month as America's favorite serial. Each book contains more than 10% new content that includes two never before scenes from some of our favorite couples.

What would you do for three million dollars?

Four young women enter into a clandestine auction to be married to the highest bidders. For no less than a million dollars a year, for three years, each woman will do what it takes to secure her future. Entangled in a high-stakes game of money, lust, power, and the hope for absolution, this group of women becomes a sisterhood unlike any other.

Once chosen by a man she's never met and agrees to marry sight unseen...there is no going back. Hidden secrets, wicked desires, fiery couplings and intense family drama are all part of the deal when you willingly enter into The Marriage Auction.

You may now kiss the bride...

THE MARRIAGE
AUCTION

Also from Audrey Carlan

The Marriage Auction
Book 1
Book 2
Book 3
Book 4

Soul Sister Novels
Wild Child
Wild Beauty
Wild Spirit

Wish Series
What the Heart Wants
To Catch a Dream
On the Sweet Side
If Stars Were Wishes

Love Under Quarantine

Biker Beauties
Biker Babe
Biker Beloved
Biker Brit
Biker Boss

International Guy Series
Paris
New York
Copenhagen
Milan
San Francisco

Montreal
London
Berlin
Washington, D.C.
Madrid
Rio
Los Angeles

Lotus House Series
Resisting Roots
Sacred Serenity
Divine Desire
Limitless Love
Silent Sins
Intimate Intuition
Enlightened End

Trinity Trilogy
Body
Mind
Soul
Life
Fate

Calendar Girl
January
February
March
April
May
June
July
August
September
October

November
December

Falling Series
Angel Falling
London Falling
Justice Falling

THE MARRIAGE
AUCTION

BOOK THREE

By Audrey Carlan

The Marriage Auction: Book Three
By Audrey Carlan

Copyright 2021 Audrey Carlan
ISBN: 978-1-957568-50-8

Published by Blue Box Press, an imprint of Evil Eye Concepts,
Incorporated

Editor: Jeanne De Vita
Cover design by Asha Hossain

Episode 67

Desperate Times, Desperate Measures

JOEL

"He's dead." My cousin Bruno's voice was a throaty rumble through the phone I clutched to my ear. Not thirty seconds ago, he had woken me from an intense dream about Faith, the girls, and me at the Maldives resort I owned. The cobwebs cleared as I glanced at the clock. It was just after four in the morning.

"Who?" I whispered as I attempted to detangle myself from a very clingy Faith. My fiancée seemed to have octopus tentacles in sleep. No matter where I was, she'd find a way to curl her limbs around my body. Shockingly, I'd never slept better. Alexandra, my late wife, hadn't been a cuddler during sleep. I was surprised to learn that I enjoyed being pressed up against a woman's body all night.

"Luther, the man I had on Robert Marino this evening," Bruno grated, clearly frustrated.

I slid out of bed and waited to speak until I'd gotten inside the master bath and had shut the door, doing the math as I did so. Las Vegas was ten hours behind Santorini, Greece.

"Explain," I growled, pressing my ass against the vanity and rubbing at my tired eyes. The marble counter chilled me straight through to the bone.

"Every day I do my standard check-ins. Luther didn't respond to the five o'clock call. I sent a couple of men out to look into it, and they found him. His throat was slit right where he sat in the driver's seat of his car."

"Fuck!" I ground down on my molars. "And Faith's father?"

Silence.

Bruno didn't say a single word. It was as if all the air was immediately sucked out of the bathroom. My lungs constricted, and I gasped for air.

"I'm sorry, Joel. He's gone," Bruno stated flatly.

"What the fuck do you mean *gone*, Bruno?" I seethed.

"I no longer have eyes on him. He's disappeared. His car is still parked near the burned-out remains of his restaurant. Last information we had was that Luther had tracked him from The Alexandra to the restaurant. That's where we found Luther. He would have followed at a distance, as ordered. Luther was one of my top guys. Ex-Marine. Special Ops training. The scene inside the car was ugly. Whoever killed Luther did so without being detected."

"And you have no trackers on Faith's father?" I asked, already anticipating his answer.

"His cell phone was found crushed on the ground near his abandoned vehicle," Bruno confirmed.

"Jesus, Bruno. What the hell? How am I supposed to go into my room, wake up Faith, and tell her that the man I had guarding her father is dead and her father is missing?" I bit out.

"My father is missing. Who's dead?"

The one voice I did not want to hear spoke from behind where I was leaning over the counter, my phone pressed tightly to one ear. I looked up and gazed straight into the now pale face of my intended.

I closed my eyes and took a breath before focusing on the matter at hand once more.

"And the other target?" I clipped, my gaze never leaving Faith's beautiful one in the mirror's reflection.

Her bottom lip trembled, and her eyes turned glassy as they filled with tears.

"I don't know," Bruno choked out.

"You don't fucking know!" I roared, my anger lit like a stick of dynamite. All my fear and hate toward Aiden Bradford and the vile things he'd done ignited and coalesced into a mighty explosion I could no longer contain. I grabbed the ceramic soap dispenser and chucked it at the long mirror across from me. The mirror and the dispenser shattered, pieces of both falling to the concrete floor in reflective shards and broken chunks. A gaping hole the size of a baseball splintered out from the mirror, the glass cracking in every direction in a starburst pattern.

Faith called my name, but I ignored her.

"How am I to keep my family safe? I trusted you, Bruno! You had one job. One fucking job. To protect Robert Marino at any cost."

A sob tore through Faith as she crossed her arms over her chest, rubbing them while hugging herself. She stood barefoot at the threshold of the bathroom and our bedroom in a pink satin camisole and shorts set, shaking with what I knew had to be fear.

I needed to pull my shit together and do it quickly so I could take care of her.

"And that cost was the life of a good man, Joel. I'm on it." His tone was confident and in charge. Something I usually appreciated about my head of security.

"I want information on where Mr. Marino is the minute you have it," I barked and then ended the call.

I stood panting, feeling like a fire-breathing dragon ready to burn down the world with my flames. I'd messed up. Gone too soft on Aiden Bradford, expecting we could hit him where it hurt a man like that—in his pocketbook. Apparently, that hadn't been enough. He'd need a much firmer hand. I knew only one man who could and would go as dark and deadly as I wanted if I gave him the go-ahead. And he owed me two more favors.

Diego Salazar, my non-friend compatriot who ran the Latin Mafia. He'd gotten the job done when Aiden had taken Eden. With me being here and with Faith's father missing a continent away, I would need his expertise again. This time, I'd have zero guilt about cashing in one of my favors.

"Come here, darling," I called to Faith.

My love was a bullet ready to release as she ran to me, her arms flying around my shoulders, her chest slamming against mine. "H-he has my dad, doesn't he?" she croaked.

I wrapped my arms around the woman I loved and held her tight, tucking my face against her neck and breathing in her comforting coconut-and-citrus scent. I allowed all that was her essence to soak my skin and nerve endings, calming me from the outside in.

"We're going to find him," I murmured against her skin, a promise as much a prayer to God Himself that he'd let me be capable of fulfilling such an oath.

Her body convulsed in my arms as another sob ripped through her frame.

I could physically feel her pain seeping into my soul.

I held her for a long time, long enough for her tears to abate and her body to stop shaking.

"I'm sorry I lost it. I shouldn't have allowed my anger to get the best of me. It won't happen again," I reassured her, holding her close.

"It's okay. I understand." Faith pulled her upper body back, our bottom halves still pressed tightly together. "I have to go home," she stated so low I could barely hear her.

But I did hear her. And I hated every single last word.

I shook my head. "It's too dangerous."

"It's me he wants. He'll kill him, Joel. He will take my father's life to get to me. I couldn't live with myself if that happened."

I licked my dry lips and set my forehead to hers. "He's already taken the life of one of my men. The man I had trailing your father... He slit his throat. Ex-military, Special Forces. A heavily trained, skilled, and armed man. I can't willingly put you in that kind of danger."

"Joel, I can't sit here and do nothing. I have to try and speak to Aiden. Get him to release my father. An exchange, something." Her nails dug into the skin of my shoulders as her voice rose. "It's the only way."

"Give me a little time, Faith. Trust me to find a way to get him back. I did with Eden when he took her, remember?"

She frowned and nodded.

"I understand how much this hurts. If it was my mother, I'd want to burn the world down, but we have to be smarter than him. We can't just knee-jerk react to his antics. The man has no morals. He beat up your father. He kidnapped your niece. He set fire to your family's restaurant. He killed a good man."

"And now he has my father. There's no limit to what he might do..." she pleaded. "If I could just see him face-to-face, maybe I could reason with him."

I pressed two fingers to her lips. "There is no reasoning with a delusional, murderous psycho, Faith. And more than that, your father made me promise to take care of you. To not bring you back to Las Vegas. To keep you as far away from Aiden Bradford as humanly possible."

Tears filled her eyes once more as she shook her head. "It's the only way. Use me to get to him. Whatever we have to do. I cannot live like this anymore, Joel. Fearing that he'll take me, Eden, or my father. Hurt, maim, or kill one of us. It has to stop. When is enough truly enough?"

I closed my eyes and sighed. Her breath was warm against my face as a myriad of tumultuous thoughts came and went in a flurry of activity. My mind was assessing and discarding ideas faster than I could really hold on to them. Weighing the pros and cons of every possibility as long as they did not include Faith being anywhere near that madman.

I kept coming back to Diego. In my mind, he was the only way to rid the world of the shit stain that Aiden was to everyone. But at what cost? Conspiracy to commit murder wasn't a decision I was capable of making lightly. And yet, I wasn't sure I had any other choice to get Robert Marino back safely, while also ridding Faith's and Eden's lives of the scum.

"I'm going to find a way to make things right. To rid all of us of Aiden's wrath once and for all," I said.

"You have to take me home. I need to be closer."

"Absolutely not," I growled.

She tried to push away, but I held her fast. "Faith, I've asked you before to trust me, and what did you do? Almost got yourself kidnapped right alongside Eden. I'm asking you now, as the man who loves you, as the man you admitted just yesterday you are in love with, to give me a little time. Please," I begged.

Begging wasn't something I ever made a habit of, but for this woman, to keep her safe, I'd pull any tricks I had out of my hat. If I needed to get on my knees in order to convince her, I'd drop down right here on the cold concrete floor.

Thankfully, I didn't have to because Faith leaned forward, lifted her head, and took my mouth in a soft kiss. I didn't take it further, content to simply touch her sweet lips.

"Okay. I trust you, Joel."

If we weren't in the middle of an emergency, I'd have lifted her up, taken her straight back to our bed, and shown her physically how much her gifting me her trust meant to me. Alas, I settled for another peck of her lips. After, I intertwined our fingers and led her into our closet.

"Let's get dressed. I've got some calls to make."

She nodded numbly, seeming to move on autopilot, as though her thoughts were a million miles away—likely on what Aiden was currently doing to her father.

I slipped on a pair of loose house pants and a T-shirt. When Faith had finished putting on a pair of yoga pants, a tank, and a cardigan, I once again took her hand with mine and led her through our room and into our quiet home. Everyone else was still asleep and would be for a while longer.

I led her to the living room where I lit the gas fireplace and she took a seat on the comfortable couch, pulling her knees up and to the side. I took the throw blanket hanging over the arm and covered her legs with it.

"I'll get you some tea," I offered.

She nodded, her gaze lost to the flames across from her.

After setting her up with tea, I kissed her forehead. "I'm going to be in my office. Come get me if you need me, okay?"

As I was about to leave, she grabbed my hand and squeezed it, her gaze lifting to mine. "Find my father, Joel. Save him. Whatever it takes, please save him."

"I will. I swear it," I vowed, knowing that was a risky move but committing myself to the task anyway. "Whatever it takes," I added.

Unfortunately, *what it would take* might make me a criminal—just like the man we were trying to escape. Briefly, I wondered if in this case two wrongs actually would make a right.

I left Faith to stew in her thoughts as I stormed to my office, shut the door, and immediately picked up the phone to dial Bruno.

"Anything?" I asked the moment he answered.

"One of my guys hacked into the traffic cam systems surrounding the restaurant. We have the entire thing on film. Aiden was there, Joel."

"You're kidding?" I ran my hand through my hair and

rubbed at the tension at the back of my neck.

"After one of his men got the drop on Luther, he exited the car and approached Robert himself. The old man went for him, Joel. Had him on the ground in two seconds with his hands around his neck. The guy who killed Luther came up behind them and clocked her father on the head with the butt of his gun. Then, together they lifted him unconscious into a blacked-out SUV."

"Where did they take them? His casino?"

"No, worse. An abandoned section of west Las Vegas. We haven't nailed down the exact location, but we have video feed all the way up until there literally aren't any more cameras. It's a bad neighborhood. I've got every guy I have heading that way. Still, I'm not sure it will be enough."

"I know a person we can get some muscle from." I sighed and put my thumb and index finger to my throbbing temples. I didn't want to have to call in this favor, but I was at a loss.

"We're going to need any help we can get," Bruno stated sharply.

"Fuck, I didn't want to call him again," I hissed.

"Desperate times, desperate measures. He killed Luther...my friend." I could hear Bruno tapping his chest when he said the word *friend*.

"I know. I'll be in touch," I said and hung up. Immediately, I checked my contacts and pulled up the one number I'd never wanted to call again.

"*Amigo*, I did not expect to hear from you so soon," Diego Salazar stated straight away.

"I had hoped not to need your unique services again."

"Unique services. I like the way you phrase things, Castellanos." He chuckled, but I had no humor to give in return.

"He's taken my future father-in-law," I stated flatly, letting Salazar fill in the blanks of what I wasn't saying.

"The *cabrón* my boys messed up? El Diablo owner?" he

confirmed.

"That would be the same one. In retaliation for what your boys did to him and the child we rightfully returned to her family, he burned down my father-in-law's Italian restaurant, killed one of my men, and kidnapped my fiancée's father."

"That place was connected to your family?" he asked. "We heard about that fire. Figured it was an accident since the owner was well-known and well-liked in the community. Great Italian food. Ate there many times myself, *amigo.*"

"In so many words, yes. I claim them as my own. Aiden Bradford has rained Hell upon my fiancée and her family for far too long. I am done."

"What do you need?" Diego got down to business.

"Everything you've got." My nostrils flared as I imagined Aiden torturing Faith's father. Kidnapping Eden. Raping Faith. "I want it messy," I confirmed, no longer feeling any guilt as the reminders of all he'd done to Faith and her kin weighed down on my shoulders.

"It will be done," Diego answered.

I updated Diego on the finer details, providing Bruno's information as a direct contact and the general location where we expected to find Aiden and his men.

When I hung up the phone, I looked out the window, seeing nothing but an endless expanse of blue water. It was then I finally smiled.

Aiden Bradford was a dead man.

Episode 68

Too Much Information

RUBY

I woke to the feeling of the bed dipping next to my legs. I opened my eyes to find Nile grinning. "It's about time those beautiful eyes made an appearance."

I frowned and glanced around the room, noting there wasn't a speck of daylight to be found.

Nile put his hand on my hip and rubbed back and forth. "How are you feeling?"

"Um, a little out of sorts, but good." I yawned, covering my mouth with my hand.

"You must be peckish. I'll have the governess put together a meal for you," he offered.

"What time is it?" I asked and blinked against the sandpaper crustiness of my eyes.

"Half past six," he said.

Six in the evening? Damn, I'd been asleep for most of the day. After he'd gone down on me, I'd used my hand on him and then promptly crashed. I didn't even remember him leaving the bed to clean up or anything.

I reached out and fingered the tie that hung from his neck. He was dressed in a pristine tailored suit that looked scrumptious on him.

Feeling bold, I pushed up to a seated position, curled my hand around the back of his neck, and pressed my lips to his. He wrapped his arm around my shoulders, holding me close as our lips said what I wasn't able to yet.

I'm glad I chose you.

I made the right choice.

We'll find happiness together.

He groaned and kissed his way down the column of my neck and back up. "I want nothing more than to pull back these covers and devour you whole, my darling, but your sister is asking for you," he murmured against my skin.

That's when it all came back.

My mother had tried to kill my sister.

My sister was here in England, probably scared out of her mind.

I flung off the blankets and bolted out of bed. I stood there, bare-ass naked, as I searched the ground for the dress I'd worn. I spied my lace panties and lifted up the shredded material. "Really?" I held them up just like the men back home did when they'd caught a huge fish on the river.

He adjusted his cuffs, pulled out a cloth from his pocket, and started to clean his black-rimmed glasses. "It had to be done." He gave me a sly, sexy smirk.

If I wasn't so worried about Opal, I'd have jumped him, tarnishing his coiffed hair and perfectly put-together appearance. From the way he was eyeing my naked body, I thought he might enjoy that option immensely.

I shook my head and continued searching the room for my dress. I found it dangling off the corner of the bed.

With the speed of a rattlesnake striking, I tugged on the dress and pushed my messy bedhead out of my face, finger-combing it the best I could.

"How do I look?" I asked, flustered.

Nile's lips twitched. "Good enough to eat. Oh wait, I've already done that. Most certainly wouldn't mind seconds." His eyes heated, and he licked his lips.

I glared and pointed a finger at him. "This is not the time to make me want to jump your bones."

He chuckled. "Anytime you want to try, I'm a willing tribute."

I lifted my head to the ceiling and groaned. "What am I going to do with this playful side of you?"

"Jump my bones?" He reiterated my words.

I couldn't help but laugh, half exasperated, half entertained. "Where's my sister and do I have time to grab a pair of panties?"

"Absolutely not. I rather like the idea of you walking around my home with easy access to the very delectable part of your anatomy that I've recently become quite fond of." He approached and took my hand. "Come. I'll take you to Opal."

I threaded my fingers through his, and the second our palms touched, my entire body warmed. This new connection we were forming was more powerful than I'd anticipated. When I chose Nile, I assumed we'd have plenty of fun in the sack, attend fancy events together, and do whatever it was rich people did with their time when they weren't at work. Now I began to wonder if we were better suited than I'd originally imagined. I figured only time would tell, and we had three years ahead to figure it all out.

For the first time in a long time, I was finally excited about the possibilities the future held for me, for Opal, and for the Pennington brothers.

As we walked through the entrance to the sitting room, a glimmer of light from the lamp on a side table sparkled against something on the ground. I stopped and bent over, grabbing the engagement ring I'd picked out from Tiffany's before we'd left Las Vegas.

It felt like an eon ago.

Nile flinched when I showed him the ring.

"Are you having second thoughts?" he whispered at first, his tone growing in volume.

"No, but it is a very pretty ring, and extremely expensive. I shouldn't have tossed it like I did, but I was trying to make a very important point."

"One you absolutely made. Beautifully, I might add." He smirked.

I smiled at his praise. "Give me your hand."

He lifted his hand, and I put the ring in the center of his palm before curling his fingers around it.

"Please make sure he gets it back." I patted his closed fist. "And don't throw it in his face or be mean about it." I prodded the center of his chest. "Be nice."

He promptly put the ring in his inner jacket pocket. "I shall do my best."

I rolled my eyes. "I guess that's all I can hope for."

"Indeed."

Nile led me through the house and into the formal dining room where I'd had my first round of etiquette training. Low and behold, there were Opal and Noah, sitting side by side at the large table. Opal's gaze lifted to mine, and she gave me big eyes which in sister-speak meant, "I don't know what's happening." Noah snarled as his gaze flitted to Nile and me holding hands.

The governess breezed in wearing a slick as shit tweed pencil skirt with an off-white silk blouse that had a big, oversized bow tied at the neck. The sleeves were bulbous and flowy and gathered at the wrist, where a series of delicate buttons kept the fabric neatly tucked.

"I'm glad you could make it," the governess announced as she set a bottle of wine on the table near the head seat.

Nile ushered me toward the chair that the governess had been about to sit in.

"Ms. Bancroft, I believe my fiancée should sit to my right, wouldn't you agree?" Nile cocked a brow.

Her head lifted, and she put her hand to her chest as though she was taken aback. "I hadn't realized a decision had been made regarding your impending nuptials."

"It has been decided. Ruby and I will wed by month's end," Nile announced to the room at large.

We hadn't spoken about the wedding specifically, but the official time according to the contract we'd both signed was running out. And I needed a lot of money in order to pay for Opal's schooling, especially with the change from the podunk school back in Mississippi to the exorbitant expense of a school like Cambridge here in England.

As I passed by the governess, she looked me up and down. I was barefoot and wearing the same simple dress I'd had on earlier when Opal arrived.

"I see you didn't take the time to change for dinner. A Pennington woman always dresses according to the event she is attending." She tsked with disapproval.

I ran my hand down my hair that was more like a rat's nest than the sleek sheet of blonde I preferred. "Yeah, well, I'm not a Pennington yet, so I'm going to sit down and have dinner just as I am. Rumpled dress and all."

Once we sat down, I leaned over the corner of the table, and Nile did the same.

"She'd lose her mind if she knew I wasn't wearing any panties," I whispered and winked at my fiancé.

He pressed his lips together for a moment and grinned devilishly, saying, "She'd be positively scandalized."

"Good. Maybe I'll tell her," I teased, lightening the mood.

"Tell me what, Ms. Dawson?" she asked in that posh British tone that spoke of judgment and disdain.

"Just that I'm happy to be here with all of you," I said while giving Nile a coy smile. "Thank you for preparing dinner, but you really didn't have to go to such effort for us. We would have been happy with a PB & J."

"Oh my God, what I wouldn't give for a PB & J," Opal hummed, closing her eyes. Noah focused on Opal's face and grinned.

"Never had it," Nile announced, fluffing his napkin and laying it across his lap.

Not one but two servers dressed in penguin suits carried two plates apiece. They set one down in front of Opal, then me, and then served Ms. Bancroft and Noah. Nile waited for his dinner to be delivered, so I kept my hands in my lap, as did the rest of the party. I distinctly remembered the governess teaching me not to start eating until after all the guests had been served.

When Nile got his plate, Ms. Bancroft lifted her fork. I copied the utensil she chose, and she gave me a nod of approval. That slight nod was enough to have me bouncing in my chair and digging into the feast on my plate.

"Nile, is there any way I can change your mind about the wedding date? It's going to be hard to invite everyone who is anyone to this event on such short notice," Ms. Bancroft stated.

I frowned, holding a lump of mashed potatoes loaded on my fork above my plate. "Everyone who is anyone? What does that mean exactly?" I asked.

"Means you're about to have a bunch of stuffy British folk attend your wedding, Ruby Roo." Opal pointed her fork at me.

"Ms. Opal, it's rude to point your fork at someone. Please refrain from doing so at the dinner table, dear," the governess chided.

I chuckled under my breath as Opal hung her head. "Sorry, Ms. Bancroft." She kept her face down, but I could see the giant smile she was hiding.

"Well, I don't care what kind of wedding we have. Do you, Nile?" I reached out and put my hand over his wrist.

He tilted his head and stared at me in a way that felt much like awe and wonder. "No, darling. Whatever you and the governess decide will be fine with me."

"That's all good and well, my boy, but on such short notice, I don't know how many royals will be able to attend. Not to mention all the celebrities you work with on your musical scores," Ms. Bancroft added. "It's going to be harrowing getting a proper designer here to fit your bride and her sister in time."

Nile shifted his hand and held mine. His eyes stayed on me while he spoke to her. "I'm sure you'll make it a beautiful affair. I have complete faith in you." He finally turned his head. "This is the first time you get to plan a wedding for one of your boys. Do what you want. As long as Ruby is walking down the aisle to me by month's end, I'll be a very happy man."

"Arsehole," Noah grumbled.

"What was that, dear?" Ms. Bancroft countered, her brow furrowed as Noah shook his head.

"Of course, I'll be needing a best man." Nile sat back and crossed his arms over his chest, maybe in challenge, maybe in defense for what Noah might say.

"Was there ever a doubt?" Noah responded gamely. "Who knows, maybe she'll change her mind at the last minute and want to marry me instead. One look at me in my finest and she'll melt into a puddle of goo on the spot."

Opal burst into laughter and smacked the table. I covered my mouth and nose with my napkin so I didn't spew food all over the table as I lost it in a fit of giggles.

Nile grinned. "Dear brother, you realize we have the same face? Ruby is marrying me for my money and sparkling personality, not my physique or handsome good looks."

"Though after today, I now know that you are not lacking

in either of those things! *Hallelujah*! *Amen*! I am one lucky lady."
I chuckled, which made Opal wag her eyebrows.

All three of our remaining dinner party went completely silent. Nile with a naughty purse of his lips, Noah with a suddenly surly expression, and Ms. Bancroft, who looked officially scandalized.

"Well, I never." She gasped and fanned her reddened face as though she couldn't believe I'd share such private information.

"Shit, that was too much information, wasn't it?" I looked away, finding the nearest exit and considering flight.

"Darling, I think it's best if we keep our bedroom play to ourselves, hmm?" Nile picked up my hand and pressed a kiss to the back. He was smiling while he did it, but I still felt like an idiot.

A flush of heat raced up my neck and burned against my cheeks. I grabbed my wine and sucked back several gulps in a row.

"Back to the matter at hand. I'll have everything planned for the last Saturday of the month, which incidentally is also the last day of the month. Will that be sufficient to meet your timeframe?" Ms. Bancroft changed the subject, for which I was very thankful.

"Brilliant," Nile stated and sipped on his wine.

"As far as the wedding dress and maid of honor gown goes, Opal and I can go shopping and find one. I'm a pretty common dress size. Shouldn't be a problem."

Before Ms. Bancroft could knock my plan, Nile spoke. "Sounds like a fun day for you and your sister. Get to know more about where you'll be living and shopping. You can take my driver, and he can assist you with everything you'll need."

"Can we go tomorrow?" I asked, feeling a bit excited about the idea of shopping with my sister and actually having the money to do so. Well, Nile's money, but he had loads of that, so I wasn't about to sweat the small stuff. I had my sister here,

I'd chosen the brother I wanted to marry, and for once, I was excited about it.

Nile nodded.

"Can one of you help me with the setup for school?" Opal asked, thankfully changing the subject off the wedding and my sex life and putting it on to something important.

"I'll help you get situated," Noah offered.

"That's mighty kind of you, Noah. Thank you." I felt my nose tingle at the kind way he was treating all of us. I had expected his anger to continue, but he'd had his outburst and now seemed like he was genuinely okay with my decision. Perhaps he wouldn't hold it against us after all. I hoped Noah and I could foster a healthy relationship. He was going to be my brother-in-law.

"Then it's settled. Tomorrow you'll shop for gowns with your sister while Noah and I meet with some advisors regarding the family business. The day after, Noah will help Opal get set up at Cambridge."

"And what will we be doing while they are doing that?" I asked, my tone low and rather husky.

"I'll be taking my fiancée out on our first date."

Episode 69

Good Enough

SUTTON

She cried all night. Dakota McAllister, now Goodall, the strongest woman I'd ever met in my entire life, was a wreck. The beating she'd taken by her father a few days past was nothing compared to how she was dealing with the news that all the men in her family were total pieces of shit. I'd known growing up by the way Old Man McAllister doted on his great-grandchildren that they were special to him. Everyone in town knew that. But he didn't protect them from their own father's drunken tirades. He also hadn't believed his daughter Amberlynn when she said she'd been assaulted by one of his business partners. Even forced her to marry her rapist when she found out she was pregnant with his child. For that alone, he could rot in Hell for all I cared.

My concern was my wife.

I poured us both coffee, and right as I was about to add the cream and sugar, Dakota shuffled into the kitchen. She had my beat-to-heck, old-ass robe on that my mother had bought me for Christmas years ago.

"Hey, got a cup ready for you," I offered, holding it by the handle.

Dakota slogged over so slowly it was as if her feet were filled with cement. When she got to me, she didn't take the cup; she face-planted against my chest. Her arms came around my waist, and she went still. I could hear the even cadence of her deep breaths.

I set down the mug and wrapped my arms around her, just being there in the moment in any manner that she desired. Holding her like this gave me an intense sense of pride. My woman, *my wife*, came to me for comfort. It was all I'd ever wanted. What I'd hoped for when I decided to enter the auction and bid on my dream girl. And here I was, living it. The circumstances sucked, but I'd show her to the best of my ability that I would always be there for her... If she'd let me.

"Thanks for last night. And for being honest," she murmured against the white T-shirt I'd pulled on with my plaid pajama pants.

I rubbed her back and set my chin to the crown of her pretty hair. "I'm always going to be honest with you, darlin'. There just isn't any other way. We have to communicate and trust that we're going to have each other's best interests at heart. I didn't buy your hand at that auction because I wanted to cause trauma to our families or take over your farm. I did it because I've wanted you since I was fourteen."

She pushed back enough that she could lift her head and look me in the eyes. "Because I wooed you with my horseback riding skills?" There was a teasing lilt to her voice.

I grinned and curled my hand around her nape. "Nah. Because when I saw you up on that horse, I saw true love. Love of the land. Love of the horse. Love of nature. You're a natural land worker. You respect it the way it should be. I knew then that a woman like that was exactly the type of woman for me."

Dakota cocked an eyebrow in question. "Oh yeah?"

I dipped my chin. "Well, maybe the fact that you have an athletic body with nice tits and a handful of tight ass didn't hurt either. And don't even get me started on the strawberry-red color of your hair or your mesmerizing eyes. Shee-it. When you put all of that together... Nuthin' but perfection. And all mine." I grinned, then ran my hands down to her firm buns and squeezed until she started laughing.

"That's better. I like seeing your smiles, not your frowns." I leaned forward and kissed her. "Coffee?" I asked.

"Please. Thank you." She took the steaming mug I'd made for her and moseyed back to the counter and sat on a barstool. Once she'd taken a drink, she pushed her hair out of her face and sighed. "I can't believe all the crap my grandmother went through. She must have felt so alone. Being pushed to give up the love of her life. Forced to marry and have the child of a man who hurt her. Every day must have been torture."

I leaned against the counter and nodded, letting her get out whatever she needed to say. We'd hashed it all out last night. What she'd found in the journals, and what I'd been told over the years. The next step was taking her to see my grandfather. Maybe then she'd have a bit more closure.

"Maybe that's why my father is such a bastard," she lamented.

"I don't know. Alcoholism is definitely a genetic thing that can be passed down. Some of it could be environmental. Monkey see, monkey do. Your grandfather was a drunk. His son is a drunk. You and Savannah have to keep an eye on that trait. But remember, your father was exposed to his dad and his ways. Learned exactly how to react to a woman from the way his father treated your grandmother. The cycle can continue like that for years, but you and Savannah have gotten out. I may enjoy a couple beers at the end of a long workday, but I'm just as happy to go without, too."

"Yeah, same. I never drank much in my teens because I sure as hell didn't want to get caught. Savannah and I were smarter than to court any of our father's abuse. Life itself seemed to do enough of that for all of us."

"Did you find out about the money in your grandmother's journals?" I asked.

She nodded. "Yeah. She'd been saving up for a decade. She even secretly was taking birth control so she wouldn't have any more children. Something that really angered him because he wanted an army of little yes men to run the farm for him and my granddaddy."

"And the naming thing? Why weren't all of you Campbells?" It had always been something that stuck in my craw, an enigma about the McAllister family line that my family had pondered over the decades.

"Apparently my grandfather said he wouldn't leave the farm to anyone not named McAllister. My mother was technically Amberlynn Campbell-McAllister, and my father is Everett Campbell-McAllister. Everett then demanded our mother give us just the McAllister name when we were born so we'd be certain to have claim over the land as the next of kin."

"What was her escape plan?"

She huffed and slumped in the chair, staring at the coffee mug for a minute before she spoke again.

"The night she died was the night she was going to escape. They'd gone to a party. According to her journals, he always drank heavily at the town gatherings. Then he'd come home, she'd help him to bed, and he'd pass out. Drunk as a skunk as usual. Amberlynn planned to take my father and the money she'd saved to the bus station. She was headed to Texas. Since she knew a lot about farm life, she'd hoped to find a job on a farm or a ranch out there. She'd saved a little over $2,500 which would have been equivalent to $25,000 back then."

"Wow, that's incredible. Honestly, I wish she would have taken my father up on his offer to take care of her and her

child. Amberlynn's life would have been drastically different."
I thought about how happy my mother was with my dad, and it gave me pause. I frowned as the truth of that statement rolled through me. "Then again, none of us would be here right now if things had been different."

"True." She nodded. "I'd still like to talk to your grandfather, if that's okay with you."

I smiled. "Of course. He's itching to officially meet you. The entire family wants to have us over for dinner whenever you're ready."

She shrugged. "No time like the present, right?"

I went over to her side and looped my arm around her shoulders. "We've got all the time in the world to build a relationship with my family. I'm more concerned about you, that shit heel we haven't heard hide nor hair from, and the farm situation."

Dakota slumped over the counter. "Everything my father touches turns to trash. The money you and Erik Johansen wired barely got the past due debts closer to caught up. We're still in the red by hundreds of thousands. It's going to take that first million just to get us back to black. Then we'll use Savvy's million to ensure we're paid up on staff and getting things fixed up around the farm. There's a lot of work ahead. I don't know…" Her voice cracked.

I rubbed her neck. "It is going to be a lot of work, but you're not alone. You've got me now. You've got my family and all our ties. We will make the ranch successful again."

She turned to the side, wrapped her arms around my waist, and lifted her chin to look at me. "How are you this nice? My whole life I was told you Goodalls were no-good, dirty, rotten scoundrels, and here you are, offering to help make a competing farm profitable."

I cupped her cheeks. "Dakota, we own well over fifty farms across the nation. I'm sorry to say, your little farm isn't competition for us."

Her mouth dropped open. "Fifty?"

I nodded. "That's why I've been in and out of Montana so much. I'm responsible for buying, selling, trading, and setting up each new location with what's needed based on set Goodall procedures and practices. We have a high quality bar for cattle, breeding, agricultural farming, and the like. Which is also one of the first things we're going to set up on your farm. Growing oats and alfalfa."

She snarled like an angry kitten. "I told my father we needed to do that, but he thinks it's a waste of time and space. He says the money is in the cattle."

I shook my head. "Not when you have to feed thousands of them. Growing your own product ends up saving a lot of costs, and it's relatively inexpensive to get going. Especially since you have a neighbor who owns all their own equipment."

She smiled brightly. "You'd let us borrow your fancy machines?"

"No," I scoffed. "But as your husband, I'll have my guys work the land on our machines and get things in order. I'll be talking to my father later on today. I figure we'll be taking an all-hands-on-deck approach with the situation you got going on over there. I took a walk about yesterday when you were in the house, and there is a lot to be done. It's going to take months as it is to get things in order to be successful. And that's provided your daddy doesn't fuck up all our progress."

Dakota scowled. "What do I need to do to get him to go away?"

Getting Everett McAllister to leave the land he saw as his birthright? That was a tough one to call.

I shrugged. "My guess? Money. Buy him out."

"With what? My good looks? I already told you. Both Savannah and I put our deposits into the business fund. I already put in the first million you sent. Savannah's will be coming by month's end since she'll need to get married in order for the contract to be met."

I nodded and rubbed at the scruff on my jaw. "I'll give you the rest of what I promised now. Another two million. Offer what you think he'll take. Then, together, we'll get the land back to what it was and what you envision it to be."

"I can't ask you to do that." She spoke through a sudden onset of emotion. Her eyes teared up. But I'd seen my wife cry enough over this man and their family history…enough was enough.

"You're not asking, darlin'. I'm telling you; we are *married*. Your problems are now my problems. So we've got a problem. The two of us put our heads together, and we solve it. How's that for a plan?"

"I agree wholeheartedly. In a marriage, if this is to work, we absolutely need to work through our problems together. But this is far bigger than that. This is millions of your hard-earned money, and I…"

"Our money," I interrupted.

She shook her head frantically. "No. No way. And besides, I'm pretty sure we both signed prenups."

"I'll be having that changed. I've told you once, darlin', and I'll tell you again. Me and you. Our marriage. No time limit. You want out right now, I'll give you the money and let you walk away. I'm telling you the God's honest truth. I want to be *your* husband. I want to have a future with you. I want children and marital spats and chasing after you on a horse when you get mad. I want birthdays and anniversaries and just about anything and everything that comes with it."

"Sutton Goodall, you don't know what you're saying," she breathed, a hitch to her statement.

"I'm saying I'm in love with my wife, and I want to keep her forever, dammit! As a matter of fact—" I paused, getting more pissed off by the minute. I stormed into the living room and into the small den. I pulled out a file cabinet drawer and grabbed the one labeled "Marriage Contract." I brought the entire thing into the kitchen.

Dakota's eyes widened as I waved the folder in the air.

"You see this? This is our contract." I took out the papers, made a point of waving them in front of her face, then promptly ripped them straight in half. Then I did it again. And again. And again. Until small, inch-sized pieces littered the counter and floor.

"No more contract. Dakota, you are my wife. I am your husband. That's it. Our story may have just begun, but it doesn't have a determined end. We're just going to live it. You, me, the farms—this is now our legacy to leave our future kids."

"You're in love with me?" Her voice shook, and her hands trembled.

I inhaled a harsh breath, my nostrils flaring as I looked into her eyes. "Woman, I'm tired of telling you and you not believing me! Not only did I fall in love with you when I was a teenager, but I fell in love when you walked out on that stage in your cowboy boots and a dress you absolutely hated. I fell in love when I kissed you at our insta-wedding ceremony and you tried to punch me in the face a second time. And I sure as hell fell in love with you the first time I slid deep inside you. That was a homecoming for me. One I intend on repeating every day for the rest of our lives. So you're either in this with me, baby, or I'm going to have to do more to convince you. What's it going to be?" I stood a couple feet away with my hands firmly planted on my hips, waiting for her tirade.

She shocked the hell out of me by getting up, turning around, and undoing the robe she wore. My wife was blessedly buck-naked underneath. I watched with intense focus as she let the material fall off her shoulders and puddle around her feet.

Dakota was a vision. Prettiest thing I ever did see. And she was all mine.

Mine to kiss.

Mine to fuck.

Mine to love.

It was about time I proved all those things once and for all.

Within half a second, I had her in my arms and my mouth on hers. I lifted her up by the ass, which she helped by hopping up and wrapping her long legs around my waist. She kissed me as though her life depended on it.

Raw. Real. Dakota.

Delicious.

I carried her up the stairs and set her down on our bed. Her chest rose and fell as I stood by the side of the mattress staring down at her beautiful body.

I ripped the T-shirt over my head, and she licked her lips, her gaze taking in my bare chest. I slowly inched down my pajamas bottoms and groaned when my erection sprang free, the air teasing the wet tip. Arousal pooled low and heavy in my groin, making my sac tighten and ache with need.

"Do you have something to tell me?" I asked, wrapping my hand around the base of my length and giving it a hearty stroke. I moaned and tipped my head back at the instant pleasure pouring through my veins while tingles of electric energy spread everywhere, making my heart pound a steady rhythm.

"Are you fishing for compliments about your body?" She got up onto her knees and shifted forward until our bare chests touched.

Her pink nipples grazed my pecs, and I hissed, fisting my hands against the desire to hold and caress them. But I wanted to hear the words she'd been denying me since all this started. I was more than her man. More than a cock that gave her pleasure.

"You know what I want to hear." I placed my hands to her slightly rounded hips and held on.

She looped her arms around my shoulders, bringing us even closer. Her face just inches from mine. Her eyes were alight with lust and desire. Her fingers combed through my hair and teased the longer locks.

"I love your body," she spoke.

"Mm-hmm. Kind of got that memo, wife. What else?" My voice was low and gravely, my emotions all over the place, while my body wanted nothing more than to take hold of my woman and fuck her until she screamed.

"I love your smile…" she whispered and ran the tips of her fingers along my lips.

I kissed them as they passed, eager for the smallest taste of her.

"I love your protective nature…" she continued coyly.

I rolled my eyes. "That's it." I cupped her face and looked her dead in the eye. "Woman, you love me. Now just admit it so I can fuck you until you scream and then make love to you until you sigh."

She scrunched up her nose, continuing the game.

Boldy, I reached down between us and cupped her sex, inserting two fingers knuckle-deep. She gasped and moaned, her head falling back as she thrust against the intrusion.

"Now I'm not going to love you here…" I jacked my fingers a few times until she started to move with the ride, then I promptly pulled them out and covered her heart with my palm. "Until you love me here." I drew an invisible heart on the skin where I could feel the real muscle beating wildly.

"You're an ass," she griped. "And mean!"

I shrugged. "Admit you love me, and you get what you want."

She smirked. "I could take care of myself, you know." Her hands moved away from me, and she cupped her succulent breasts with her hands on a moan, then trailed them down toward her sex.

I was faster.

I had her back against the bed and me poised between her thighs within a single breath. I centered myself right at her entrance, lubing my cock with her arousal until she moaned and thrust her hips against me, trying to force what she wanted most.

"Look into my face right now, Dakota, and tell me you don't love me," I demanded.

Her lips snapped together.

I grinned wide. "Good enough." I slammed home, both of us crying out in pleasure.

Episode 69B

Full Circle (Bonus Scene)

DAKOTA

"Stop twitching and fiddling with your clothing. You look perfect. Jesus!" Sutton cursed as he tucked me to his side, then knocked on his parents' door. He'd just confirmed his love for me, followed it up with a round of impeccable sex, and there we were, standing on the Goodalls' porch, ready for some forced family fun. Ugh.

Why couldn't we have just stayed in bed and left the entire world behind?

I played with the hem of the dress I was wearing, feeling slightly ridiculous. Besides the dress Madam Alana had put me in for the auction, I hadn't worn one in a long time. I ran a ranch with an all-male staff. Dresses were impractical in my line of work, so I didn't own many. I thought they might make me seem less like a ball-busting ranch manager and more like a feminine homemaker. Something I imagined Sutton's parents wanted in their kin.

"I'm the enemy to most of your family!" I hissed under my breath while adjusting my boobs in the pushup bra I'd stupidly chosen.

He shook his head. "Not anymore. Ma and I had a long chat, as you know. She's all about making amends and ensuring you feel welcome."

I huffed. "Decades of disdain for my family doesn't go away in the blink of an eye."

"Just relax." He curled his hand around my bicep, reminding me that I wasn't in this alone. We had each other. And besides, we were already married. There wasn't much they could do to change that, and Sutton claimed to be in love with me. He wanted forever.

I had no idea what I wanted anymore. Everything was so confusing. From the moment he'd won the bid for me, to the harsh reality I'd had to face about my family history. Now to this moment. Standing on the porch in enemy territory.

Mrs. Goodall opened the door and smiled wide. "You could have come right in." She held the door open.

"Thanks, Ma," Sutton said, then sniffed the air. "Hot damn. Is Dad grillin' porkchops?"

She chuckled. "One of your favorites. We figured since this was the first dinner with our new daughter-in-law, we'd pull out all the tricks in our bag to get her to like us."

I jerked my head in shock and put my hand over my chest. "You don't have to get me to like you. I've been learning a lot about the past lately, and, quite frankly, it seems none of you have anything to worry about. I'm the one that needs to work to earn your favor," I admitted woefully.

Linda waved her hand in front of her face. "Nah. We're going to let bygones be bygones, right? A few days ago I said some crummy things out of fear and jealousy that I shouldn't have. You and I have settled things as far as I'm concerned. You've done nothing to earn any scorn from this family, so you leave those worries out on the porch. Ya hear?"

Sutton laughed. "Told ya everything was fine. Come on. Let's get a beer."

"Sounds great." I pushed a lock of my hair behind my ear and ducked my head. I wanted to believe everything would be fine, but I'd let the evening carry on and see what happened.

Sutton led me through an open-plan living room that had an enormous U-shaped sectional in front of a massive fireplace. The entire wall was made of natural rock. A giant beam ran across the hearth, which held a myriad of framed pictures of the Goodall clan. They faced the room so every guest could see how proud the owners of the home were of their family.

We didn't have anything like that at our farmhouse. Not since our mother died anyway.

I stopped and gestured with a chin lift to the fireplace. "Can we add a mantle above our fireplace? One like that?"

"Sure can." Sutton beamed. "My father, brother, and I salvaged that wood from our old barn. We have more we could go through. Pick a piece you like from the same batch."

"Would you like that in our home?" I asked, not knowing his design preferences. We still had a pretty empty house that needed filling.

He turned me to face him and looped his hands around my waist, crossing his wrists at the base of my spine. "I like that my wife is calling the home I built for us *ours*, and I very much like the fact that she wants to add personal touches that make it more special. Especially using pieces restored from the land."

"Maybe I'll engrave it with S + D, so everyone will know how much you love me," I teased.

He pressed me closer to him. I lifted my chin so our faces were only a few inches apart.

"Don't threaten me with a good time, woman." He dipped lower and took my mouth in a series of quick, flirty pecks on the lips.

I couldn't help but giggle at the absurdity between us. Who would have believed I could be this gushy and schmoopy with any man, let alone a Goodall?

"All right, you two. Enough neckin'. Let's get you both a

drink. 'Sides, your granddaddy is eager to meet your bride. Best not to keep him waiting," Linda directed.

I hugged Sutton around the waist and walked with him into another area of the house. It was beyond magnificent. The kitchen boasted an open setting with a butcher-block bar cutting through the space. The entire back wall was half kitchen counter and cooktop, the other half windows.

"Wow," I said. "It's incredible." I gasped as I looked out at the Goodall land. I thought we had a lot of acreage, but ours was nothing compared to the vast and endless horizon I could see looking out their kitchen windows.

Linda grabbed us both beer from the fridge, placed the edge of the bottle on the wooden butcher block, and smacked the metal cap right off. She repeated the process and handed one to me and the other to Sutton.

"Cool! Will you teach me that trick?" I asked, my mouth hanging open in shock.

She grinned slyly. "Sure will. Come on, you two. Everyone is outside enjoying the golden hour."

I sipped my beer as Linda went through a side door that opened to a wooden deck overlooking the land. The back patio was much like the deck we had at our house.

Sutton led me over to his father, who was manning the grill. The most delicious smells wafted through the air and made my mouth water.

"Dad, I want to officially introduce you to my wife, Dakota," Sutton announced with a booming, pride-filled tone.

His father wiped his hands on a towel he had over his shoulder and then stretched his arm out. "Duke Goodall the Second, but you, little lady, can call me Dad or Senior. Most everybody does."

Smiling, I shook it. "It's good to meet you, Mr. Goodall. I mean, Senior." I frowned as the name felt like I had a dozen marbles rolling around in my mouth unnecessarily.

He grinned as he looked at Sutton. "She's a looker, I'll give you that. Seems sweet too."

Sutton laughed out loud. "She's definitely a stunner, but don't let the sweet looks fool you." He put his arm back around me. "My wife is as sassy and unpredictable as a red fox!"

I opened my mouth and glared, about to nail him for calling me out, when Sutton glanced over his shoulder. The sound of shuffling boots scraping along the wooden deck had me turning around.

"Well, I'll be damned. It's like seeing a ghost," an older, handsome gentleman in his early seventies stated. He wore a well-loved, beat-to-hell black Stetson, a plaid button-up, Wranglers, and a pair of boots so old I didn't think they made the brand anymore. At least I'd not seen a pair that old.

"Granddad, I'd like you to meet my wife, Dakota," Sutton said, introducing me.

"You look exactly like her." He inhaled sharply. "Amberlynn." The man removed his hat and put it over his chest. "God rest her soul."

I put my hand out. "Dakota. And you are Duke the First?"

He dipped his head in acquiescence. "It's uncanny." He continued to stare, awe in his clear blue gaze. "How about that. My grandson falling for the spitting image of the one that got away... It's funny how life comes full circle, isn't it?"

"Actually, yeah, it is. Funny. Weird. Uncomfortable." I clenched my teeth when he finally took my hand. It was warm, and he placed his other one over the top.

"You are lovely, my dear. I'm glad to finally meet you. Welcome to the family." He let my hand go and clapped Sutton on the shoulder. "Well done, son. She's a beauty."

"This I know, Granddad," Sutton said, standing tall as could be.

After the semi-awkward introduction to his father and grandfather, Sutton introduced me to Junior, who was Duke Goodall the Third in the lineup. I simply waved to Bonnie since we'd already met.

I sucked back my beer and was just about finished with the first when another appeared on the table in front of me. Bonnie grabbed my empty. "Figured you'd need that second one right about now."

"Thank you!" I chuckled.

"Dinner's ready. Grab a chair and we'll do a quick prayer," Linda hollered.

The family gathered around the large rectangular patio table with room for eight and took their seats. Plates and silverware were already set along with all the other fixings for dinner, including a leafy green salad with fresh tomatoes, corn on the cob, warm rolls, a pasta dish, and a platter of sizzling porkchops with at least two or three dozen servings on it. When the Goodall clan barbecued, they went all out. A definite plus in the pro column that was my new life.

Linda reached out and took my hand and her husband's next to her. I followed along and took Sutton's hand as he held his sister's, and so on until we were a complete circle.

One unit.

A family.

I shivered as the realization hit me.

I was part of something. It wasn't just me and Savannah anymore. I had an extended family. A group of people who so far had been super welcoming and kind—considering I was supposed to be their nemesis.

Linda thanked the Lord for the food and then shocked the heck out of me when she said the next part.

"And thank you, Lord, for bringing Dakota to our family. We haven't seen our Sutton this happy in ages. Our family is growing, and the rest of us couldn't be more grateful. Bless this food and all of our loved ones on this fine day. Amen."

"Amen," I repeated, then glanced at my husband, who literally couldn't have been smiling any bigger. I cupped his cheek. "What?"

"It's just..." He inhaled a slow breath. "I wanted this with you and my family most of my life. Just tryin' to soak it all in and be thankful."

I closed my eyes and hummed, forcing myself to let go of all my preconceived notions about my new life and just enjoy the moment.

"I'm feeling very blessed right about now too," I confided.

His eyes sparkled as he lifted his beer. I clinked mine against the neck of his, and we both drank, sharing a beautiful moment and making a memory together.

I hoped I'd never forget it.

When the food had been eaten, several rounds of a card game called Hearts had been played, and night had fallen, I moseyed out to the front porch for a little breather. Sutton, his father, his mother, brother, and sister were all battling it out in a very rambunctious game of poker inside. I left them to it, my hand curled around a decaf coffee loaded with Emmett's Irish Cream liquor. My belly was warm, and my heart filled with joy and love.

As I exited the house, I found Sutton's grandfather rocking in a double-seater swing.

"Hey." I gestured to the inside. "They're still going at it."

He chuckled and patted the seat next to him. "Sit with me, girl," he offered.

I took the seat, and he settled the movement to a barely-there sway that shifted forward and back.

"I sense you've got some things on your mind about my history with your family."

I sighed and blew out a harsh breath. "It shouldn't matter

what came before all of this between me and Sutton, but it does."

He nodded but didn't speak, content to let me ask what I wanted to know.

"Did you truly love Amberlynn?" I started with what I thought was an easy question.

"Love of my life. Was beyond hurt when she left me. Then I found out why and I wasn't only angry, I was murderous. I would have ended my entire life for Amberlynn just to get her out of that horrible situation."

"Why didn't you?"

He seemed like the kind of man who wouldn't take no for an answer. If the love of his life, as he claimed, had been attacked, impregnated, and told she was going to marry another man... I couldn't even fathom how Sutton would respond in the same circumstance.

"It was a different time, and I was a pimply-faced teenager. Not quite a man. And you may not know this, but your great granddaddy was a big guy. Back then, he was like a boxer. Nothing but muscle and drive. He believed Steven Campbell, the man who would be your grandfather, over Amberlynn. No matter what either of us claimed, he didn't care. He had his eyes set on growing his business. Ultimately, that relationship did in fact help him succeed—in business, that is."

I closed my eyes and let my chin fall toward my chest. "Why didn't you run away together? Disappear in the night?"

"It's the single decision I regret when I look back on my life. Especially after he killed her in that car wreck."

My breath caught at the honesty in his words. Everything my father and great-granddaddy had told me *was* a lie. It wasn't an accident, and she didn't willingly choose Steven Campbell over Duke Goodall. Then later, before she was able to escape, she died at the hands of her jailer. Because he was drunk. Just like my father always was. A mean, horrible drunk.

He reached out and took my free hand. "I'm sorry, darlin'.

I should have tried harder. Pushed more to get Amberlynn out of that situation. But I was so hurt and helpless. I didn't believe there was anything I could do but move on. It was the wrong choice, and I've regretted it my entire life."

I squeezed his hand. "I regret hating the Goodalls. I believed everything my father and great-grandfather told me about your family. Believed it as fact. We all make stupid decisions and believe things we shouldn't because we trust those we love."

He pressed his lips together and stared out at the land, likely facing the ghosts of his past.

"Sutton and I are proof that things can get better. That the past can be turned around and wrongs made right." I made the statement and was surprised to find I truly believed it.

"Is that what you and my grandson are doing? Righting wrongs?" he asked softly.

I pushed off the porch with a toe to get us swaying again. "He would say yes. For me, I feel like I just got lucky that Sutton found me. He's so much better than any man I've ever known. But don't you dare tell him that, or he'll get a big head." I nudged his shoulder with my own.

He laughed heartily at that. "I think you are the perfect woman for a man like my grandson. Smart. Lotta sass. And a whole helluva lot of spirit."

That had me snickering. "I'll be taking that as a compliment."

"It was meant as one. Ranch life is not for the timid. It's hard work. And based on the calluses I feel grating along my palm, you are no stranger to hard work."

"No, sir, I am not."

"Mmm. That bodes well for my boy. A hard worker with an angelic face? He was a goner before you ever laid eyes on him. That's how it was with my Amberlynn. Saw her walking through the field of wildflowers, only thirteen years old to my fifteen. She was the very sun that shined on me. Love at first sight, as they say. Asked her out at school that next Monday."

"I've seen pictures and read..." My eyes widened as I remembered what I had in my possession. Some things that Duke might want back. "Do you have a quad or a horse I can use real quick to run over to my house?"

He lifted his chin to the side of the house. "Round the corner. Keys are in the ignition on all the quads. They sit there for any of us to use as needed."

"Great! I'll be right back. Tell Sutton if he happens to come out." I set my half-empty coffee cup on the porch railing, then beat feet down the steps and around the house. As he claimed, there were five quads all lined up. The keys in the ignitions.

I popped onto the first one, turned it on, and backed out. Then I was rumbling down the main path that would fork off toward my home with Sutton.

Once there, I raced into the house and rifled through the journals and the stack of letters. I'd make copies of the journal pages that involved Duke, but I didn't want him to see the stuff about her attack. That was intensely personal and would likely hurt him deeply. Once I'd gathered what I needed, I left the house, hopped on the quad, and drove back over.

Sutton was leaning against one of the columns drinking my freakin' coffee.

"Hey! That's mine!" I snapped.

"What's yours is mine, baby." Sutton took another swallow.

I stomped up the stairs and snatched back the cup. There were literally two sips left. I drank the rest down and glared at his handsome face.

"Don't call me baby! And you can make yourself useful by refilling my cup. And do not go easy on the Emmett's. Thank you very much." I pushed the mug into his hand helpfully.

Before I could get away, Sutton grabbed my arm, hauled me against his chest, and laid a fat smackeroo on my mouth. He tasted of coffee, Emmett's, and straight-up sex. I instantly wanted to fuck him. Damn it!

He tasted so good and knew exactly how to get me going by twirling his tongue and sucking on my bottom lip. I pressed closer, taking the kiss deeper until a moan left my lungs.

He pulled back abruptly. "To be continued at home." He made a point to lick his lips and glance down my body. I immediately imagined him licking me somewhere else.

I curled my fist around his shirt and was about to tell him exactly where I wanted him to continue when I heard, "Still here, newlyweds," from the side of the porch where his grandfather sat.

"Shit!" My cheeks heated with embarrassment.

Sutton chuckled and moved to the door. "I'll just refill our cup."

"My cup!" I countered.

"Mmm-hmmm," Sutton hummed and then disappeared.

I took a calming breath, then shoved my windswept hair out of my face.

"It used to be like that between me and Amberlynn too. Passionate. Combative." He grinned.

"Speaking of Amberlynn, I found these in the attic back at the farmhouse. I will admit to having read them. I made copies and will be sharing them with my sister, Savannah. I'm sorry if you feel that is an invasion of privacy." I handed him the stack of letters he'd written my grandmother.

His hands shook as he reached for them. He quickly pressed the stack directly over his heart. "She kept them all those years," he whispered, pain and joy mixing together.

"She did. She also wrote about how much she loved you in her journals. But there were some other private things I need to remove before I give you copies. If that's okay."

He lifted a hand to cut me off. "This is more than I could have hoped for. I thought she hated me for the way I let her go. How I moved on with my life. Married a good woman. Had children. Built the Goodall brand to what I'd always wanted it to be. I just wished she'd been by my side while I did it. That doesn't mean I didn't love and adore my wife, Bernadette. May she rest in peace. But to know Amberlynn kept me with her all that time..." He swallowed slowly and shook his head. "It's a gift. Thank you for sharing this with me, Dakota. I'll treasure them."

"You're welcome. Thank you for welcoming me to the family." I patted his knee, and together we sat side by side and stared out over the land, content in the way things had eventually turned out. At least I was starting to be content.

Then Sutton walked out with a fresh steaming cup and a plate with a slice of cherry pie on it and two forks.

"That pie for me, husband?" I teased, reaching out and taking the cup.

"It's for both of us, darlin'. What's mine is yours, and what's yours is mine, remember?" He winked.

I definitely had found contentment.

It was any time I was with my husband, Sutton Goodall.

Episode 70

Taste of Home

ERIK

Right after my fiancée told me she wouldn't run away from me, from us, she did exactly that. I watched her red waves shoot behind her as she dashed through the throngs of museumgoers, weaving in and out like a professional downhill skier.

"Something wrong with Savannah?" my father asked, his palm resting on my shoulder.

I shook my head and sighed. "I don't know. She seemed to become unsettled all of a sudden. Maybe about all of this, about picking out a dress, going back home, the Jarod situation. Honestly, I'm not sure. We're still figuring one another out. I'm constantly worried about the possibility of losing her."

An abrupt shove to the center of my back had me stumbling forward a step. "Well, get to chasing after her, son. I didn't raise a fool. Anyone can see how much that girl means to you. When the woman of your dreams runs in the wrong direction, it's up to you to chase her down and show her exactly what she's running away from, in the hopes she'll choose to stay instead."

"*Helvete!*" *Hell*, I swore, then briskly stormed through the halls of the museum in order to locate Savannah. My heart was in my throat and my chest wound tight as a drum. My father was right. He was always right. There was no way I was going to lose her by letting her slip through my fingers. Communication was key to all of this. But I couldn't change the fact that she'd sworn she wouldn't run and had said that she had chosen *me* of her own free will. Then she did the exact opposite and ran again. Either way, I needed to find out what was going on in that beautiful mind of hers once and for all.

Finally, I reached the outside doors. I shoved them open so hard one hit the exterior of the building with a massive slam as I jetted out and took the stairs two at a time, heading back to the street level.

I stopped on the sidewalk and looked in both directions, actively searching for Savannah's telltale fiery hair. My heart pounded a hefty beat against my ribcage while my hands shook.

"Erik." I heard Savannah's voice come from just behind me. I whirled around and took in every ounce of her features. Her pale skin and intense blue eyes. The rosy hue at her cheeks and on the tip of her nose, likely from the chill in the air. The wild waves of that awesome mane of hair I adored.

I couldn't have been more than ten footsteps away from her, but the relief at seeing her there, just standing outside the door, not having run away was almost enough to have me falling to my knees in gratitude and prayer.

"You're here," I gasped, reaching for her like a dying man lost at sea clamoring for the sudden appearance of land on the horizon.

"Of course, I'm here," she said, coming straight into my arms and hugging me tight. "I just needed a little air. That piece of art brought up so many emotions, I kind of lost it in there a little. It's a powerful painting. I can understand now why it's world-renowned," she offered.

I cupped her cheeks and shook my head while staring into

her face, seeing everything I could ever want standing right before me. It took Herculean effort to admit my fear. My hands still shaking with adrenaline, I moved to cup her cool cheeks. "I thought you ran."

She nodded avidly. "Oh, I did. I thought I was going to have a full-blown panic attack. I think the day just got to be a bit too much for me. Then I took in the painting, how the man was screaming, holding his face as though he was about to lose his mind, and all these random thoughts and emotions slammed into me and I just… Whew." She pushed her hair out of her face. "Had to take a breather. I'm sorry I startled you." Her nose scrunched up and her eyes seemed to take in my features. There was no way I didn't look like a frightened man who believed he was on the cusp of losing everything.

"*Elskede*, you more than startled me." My voice cracked, and I gulped down the sourness building in my throat. "I thought you ran from me." I tapped the center of my chest, my words spilling out raw and ravaged.

Her eyes widened, her brilliant mind working as she took in my haggard appearance. Realization cut across her expression. "No, oh my God. I mean, I can see how it looked, but honestly, I just needed a moment with some fresh air to get my emotions in check." Her features crumbled into one of extreme concern. "I'm so sorry you thought I was leaving *you*. And right after I said I wasn't going to. My goodness, that looks so bad!" Her bottom lip trembled as she took in my face. She lifted her hands and traced the edges of my brows and then my cheekbones and finally my bottom lip. Her touch was a soothing balm to my fractured heart.

"Erik, honey, I told you I'm not going anywhere, and I *mean* that. There may be times where I need some air, or I may choose to be alone to work through a complex issue, but that doesn't change what I feel for you. I want to marry you in two weeks. I want to explore this relationship. Each new day it becomes more and more clear that somehow, someway, I made the right decision. Not only for my family's situation, but maybe even for me."

I swallowed against the sudden onslaught of elation, not trusting the feeling for even a minute. "Really?"

She smiled softly. "Yes, really. I'm looking forward to settling in after the wedding. Just the two of us. I'll get back to my coursework and maybe learn more about the beer business. I was thinking it might be interesting to see some of the farms and processing plants where you brew beer. Would that be an option? I'd like to learn more about something that you're interested in."

The level of relief that filled my veins was all-consuming. Instead of responding, I threaded one hand through her luscious locks and wrapped an arm around her waist, hauling her entire body against mine. Then I took her mouth in a deep and meaningful kiss. Her tongue flicked against the seam of my lips, and I opened gladly. She curled her little tongue around mine, seeking a deeper taste. In turn, I held her close, tipped my head to the side, and drank deep from the well that was her mouth.

I was starved for her taste.

Savannah seemed to return that feeling, kissing me as though she left her entire essence in every press of her lips to mine and every sweet swipe of her tongue. With every nibble of her teeth to my bottom and top lips, she gave all of herself. I hoped she could feel me returning that gift.

She moaned, that sound going straight to my dick, hardening it behind my jeans. I had to pull away, not only so we could both breathe, but in order to get a better handle on my physical response to this woman.

Her gaze and expression were dreamy, no longer filled with anything other than happiness. It's a look I wanted to remember forever. The moment I realized I was definitely falling in love with my fiancée. Savannah was everything I wanted, standing by my side, supporting me through life, as I did the same for her and her dreams. I just needed to trust the process. Put the work in to show her what our life could be like if she'd fully give herself to me.

I wanted her hand in marriage.

I wanted her body in my bed.

More than all of that, I wanted her heart.

I learned early in life that if you wanted something—anything—all you had to do was work hard, be smart, and make good choices. It might not have been the smartest choice to bid on a bride at an auction, but the connection between us was undeniable.

"You guys ready to go?" My mother's voice came from the top of the stairs, while my father made his way down.

I curled an arm around Savannah's shoulders. She planted her curvy body next to my side, looping her arm around my waist.

"I'm thinking Savannah and I could use a stiff drink." I looked down as her face lifted up. I pressed a small peck to those kiss-swollen lips. "Fiancée's choice. What kind of food and drink would make you feel good after such a whirlwind of a day?"

She pursed her lips. "You won't like my idea." Her voice seemed small. "Let's go wherever *you* want."

I shook my head. "No, *elskede*. I want to know what place entered your mind."

She shook her head. "It's stupid. When you have all of what Oslo has to offer…"

I turned her toward me and held her pressed to my chest, exactly where I wanted her to be as often as possible. "Tell me." I pushed a lock of hair behind her ear and then stared into her eyes, waiting patiently.

Savannah rolled them and her lips twitched into a coy smile. "Fine. Your mother and I walked past a Hard Rock Café earlier."

That was quite possibly the last place on Earth I'd have

guessed, but really, it shouldn't have been. It offered American food, music, and scenery. Ever since the auction, she'd been moving through life on my terms and my turf. This could be the exact thing she needed to find a bit of her footing. Having something familiar had definitely helped me since we arrived. Being with my family, sparring with Jack, checking in on the business—all of those things put me at peace and gave me a sense of belonging I didn't feel in the States. Savannah hadn't had anything remotely normal for her since she'd stepped out on that stage.

"I think it's an awesome idea. And I haven't had an American burger in ages. *Mor, Pappa,* we're headed to Hard Rock Café," I announced firmly, making it clear there was no negotiation to be had. Savannah wanted a taste of home, and I was going to give it to her.

"Love the place," my father answered immediately. "They have some interesting rock memorabilia I'd like a second look at. Not to mention their steak nachos are fantastic. Reminds me of visits to the States."

"Then it's settled. We'll walk there; it's not far. Savannah and I passed it on our way here," my mother said, then hooked her arm with my father's and moved ahead of us.

I nudged Savannah but kept my arm around her shoulders as we walked to the restaurant.

Once we got there, we were seated at a table for four with a view of the street.

Savannah immediately started dancing in her seat as she picked up the menu.

"My girl is happy, I see."

She bit into her bottom lip half-smiling, her eyes big and bright. "They have ranch here!" She bounced up and down the way a small child might when offered their favorite ice cream.

I frowned, not knowing what she was talking about. "Ranch?"

"Ranch dressing. It's literally the best condiment or salad

dressing on the planet. It's amazing when you dip your fries into it."

"Can't say that I've had it, but I'll try anything just to see that smile on your face." I lowered my head and kissed that smile. She hummed as I did so.

"Okay, you two. You're acting like you're already newlyweds. We need to get you married off first!" my mother teased. "And now that we have the dress, we're moving in the right direction. Savannah, is there a particular color you'd like me to wear for the event?" she asked.

She shrugged. "I'm planning to have Dakota wear peach, so you could wear something you like in that color vicinity. Though I still need to touch base with Dakota about everything. I guess I shouldn't have said we'd have the wedding at my family's ranch when I haven't cleared anything with her or our pa."

My parents both went silent suddenly.

"You haven't told your father you're getting married to Erik?" my dad asked.

Savannah's entire body slumped. She locked her hands together between her thighs and rolled her shoulders inward, making herself seem smaller. "Um, my family is a bit complicated."

I clenched my teeth as I put my arm across the back of her seat and shoulders for support, then I waved the waiter over to interrupt what I knew was about to be a very unhappy conversation. We were finally at a good place in our moods, and I was desperate to keep it that way. My fiancée needed a break from the heavy. She'd had a lot thrown at her in a short amount of time. Now was when we would build memories and share good experiences. "We'll talk about it more later. We need drinks."

The waiter approached, and after several rounds of Savannah getting more excited about recommending American dishes, we finally settled on a mixed appetizer plate of all the fried foods she demanded we order so we could dip them into this magic sauce called ranch. Not to mention the two of us ordered different dishes so we could share. Her idea, not mine. Though I liked the idea of sharing anything with Savannah. It was an intimate gesture partners did with one another so they could experience more together.

The food was delivered, and we each received our own small saucer of creamy white salad dressing. Savannah had requested two for herself, which I teased her about endlessly. Though I did make a mental note to have whatever this ranch dressing stuff was put into a container we could take home tonight. That way, she'd have something she clearly loved available to her whenever she wanted.

"Okay, now the first thing we should dip into the ranch is a mozzarella cheese stick," she instructed all of us. It was hilarious how seriously she approached this delicacy from her country.

My mother pointed to the red sauce that had come with the sticks. "What about the marinara? That sounds like it makes sense. Breaded mozzarella in marinara is very Italian." She looked at the white dressing suspiciously.

"Trust me," Savannah said. "Dunk it in your ranch. And don't be shy about it. This is serious business. You want to coat the entire bite."

My father did so with gusto as my mother barely touched the edge. Me, I watched Savannah and copied her, appreciating the way her cheeks pinked up and her eyes became soft when she looked at me with approval.

"Now eat it!" She beamed, then eagerly shoved half a piece of fried cheese covered in white dipping sauce into her mouth. The guttural moan that followed had me adjusting my seated position, imagining her groaning for another reason entirely.

I bit off the first half and was shocked to find how well the dressing paired with the breaded cheese. I hummed at her deep groan, her eyes closed in bliss.

"This is delicious," my father said, submerging the rest of his stick into his saucer.

"I wouldn't have believed it, but this is something else," my mother agreed, going for a full plunge of the rest of hers into the dip.

Savannah was already done with hers and had picked up a french fry. "Now try the fry. It's pure Heaven. You will not be sorry," she instructed, her expression one of pure delight. It made my heart tighten to see her joy in sharing a bit of her culture with me and my parents. These were the times that would bring us closer as a growing family.

We followed along with Savannah's suggestions, and no truer words had been said. The fries were magnificent with the dipping sauce. Something about it just paired well with each item.

For the rest of the meal, we dipped everything into the ranch, laughing and cackling like hyenas as we shared food and made bets on what would taste best. It was the most fun I'd had with my parents in years, especially since the accident. More proof that Savannah was the exact right woman for me.

When we were done, my father demanded we check out all the memorabilia, which was really interesting. Savannah was just as eager as my father to inspect the collection, discussing which musician was famous for what. We each shared memories we'd made listening to music that matched a specific item. They had a guitar signed by David Bowie that my father went on and on about, which moved into a discussion about rock music over drinks in the bar.

After we hit up the gift shop and every last one of us was filled with good food, good times, and lots of drinks, we walked out of the Oslo Hard Rock Café wearing none other than matching sweatshirts.

As we drunkenly pushed into a rideshare car, I held Savannah close and whispered in her ear, "Hard Rock Café is now our place. We're going to eat there and collect memorabilia for years to come." I twirled a finger around her soft hair, loving how it would naturally go back to a loose corkscrew curl every time I let it go.

She cuddled against my side and nodded. "We're going to have an amazing life." She sighed, closed her eyes, and promptly fell into a drunken, happy snooze against my shoulder.

I kissed the crown of her soft hair. "I'll make certain of it."

Episode 71

Fight or Flight

FAITH

I crossed my legs and stared into the endless expanse of blue sky through the airplane window. Joel sat across from me scowling intensely. It was the only look I'd received since I demanded we charter his fancy jet and get our asses back to Las Vegas. There was no way on God's green Earth that I was going to sit in the lap of luxury in Greece while my father had been kidnapped and was likely being tortured by my ex.

God, please let my father make it through this unscathed. I'll do anything, I prayed silently. *Even if it means turning myself over to Aiden and letting my father raise Eden alone. It would be better than losing him.*

Joel cleared his throat loudly enough to garner my attention. I stared into his beautiful face, and my heart sank. Giving up this incredible man would be the second hardest decision of my life. Again, I'd make any sacrifice so all the people I loved, including Joel, were safe and protected from evil incarnate.

This had to end.

None of us could move on with our lives until Aiden's reign of terror stopped. I was prepared at this point to do whatever it took to keep those I loved safe. If I had to walk into a den of vipers and offer myself up as a sacrifice, I wouldn't even look back. I'd lift my head and walk straight into the mouth of Hell.

"Mimi, Mimi!" Two little voices screeched as first Penny, then Eden slammed into my legs. Olympia entered from the back bedroom, where the girls had been taking their afternoon nap.

Both children had messy bedheads and smiling faces.

"We dare yet?" Eden mispronounced the word "there" and patted my knee while Penny spoke in rapid-fire Greek to her father.

He shook his head. "No, we're not *there* yet, girls." He enunciated the word for Eden's benefit. "Soon. How about you get some snacks and watch a movie while I talk to Mimi?" Joel pointed to the large flat-screen TV at the front of the plane. Already his flight attendant was setting places for the girls, complete with sippy cups and pre-chosen meals that would fit Eden's dietary requirements.

"Did you check her sugar levels?" I asked Olympia.

"Of course, I did. I have paid attention and studied up on her diabetes so that my new grandchild has all her needs met. She is perfect but needs to eat. As do the two of you. Don't pretend like I didn't notice you skipped breakfast earlier. You must get something in your system in order to stay focused on the matter at hand, no?" She stood with her hands clasped, waiting for a response.

I nodded solemnly. "I'm really not hungry, but I'll try in a bit. Thank you for your concern and for taking such good care of Eden."

Olympia lifted to her full height, a proud expression settling across her features. "Who better?" she offered.

"There is no one," I said. But that thought also had me

once again worrying about my father. He'd spent almost every day of Eden's life catering to her every need, almost more so than I had. He didn't deserve any of this. Losing his restaurant. Being beaten up and having his home trashed. And now…God, I could only imagine what Aiden and his twisted disciples were doing to my father while I was stuck hovering somewhere over the Atlantic, desperate to get to him.

Joel's phone rang, and he immediately answered it, stood, and moved toward the bedroom at a fast clip.

I scrambled to unbuckle my seatbelt and follow. "You've got the girls?" I asked Olympia.

She cocked a haughty brow.

I waved a hand. "Never mind. *Of course,* you do." I reiterated her words.

She nodded and fluttered her fingers, suggesting I go after her son.

"Thank you," I muttered, heading to the back of the plane toward the bedroom and office space.

I found Joel pacing the floor in the small office. I entered and shut the door behind me, pressing my back and hands to the door as I waited to hear any news about my father.

"You have him?" Joel asked, then closed his eyes, relief spreading through his curt response. "How bad is he?"

Instantly, tears sprang to my eyes as visions of my father being abused ran through my mind in a sickening reel of broken images. He'd just barely survived the last attack when Aiden had taken Eden. My father was strong as an ox, at least that's the way I viewed him, but he wasn't a spring chicken anymore either.

"Explain," Joel grunted and took a seat on the small couch on the opposite side of the room. He slumped forward, his elbows coming to his knees, one hand pressing the phone to his ear, the other covering his eyes.

I pushed away from the door and perched on the edge of the seat next to him, holding my breath as Joel listened intently.

Eventually his head lifted, and his gaze met mine. It was tortured, but still a flame of brilliant anger could be seen.

"Where is he now?" He spoke evenly, his tone direct and focused. He nodded at me and reached a hand out, curling it around my nape. "You got to Marino before any real damage had been done?" He asked the question as though he were confirming information he already knew. He nodded to me, and I finally let the tears fall. "This is good news layered on top of the bad."

I gasped for air and put both of my hands to Joel's thigh, holding on for dear life.

"And Diego's people?" he asked, listening intently before he let out a long, weighted sigh and closed his eyes. "Fuck. I'm not sure the favors he owed me can even begin to compare to this level of carnage."

Carnage.

"Joel," I pleaded on a whisper, needing to know what was happening.

Joel removed his hand from my neck and held up a finger in a gesture that told me to wait a minute. I felt like I'd waited an entire year to hear news about my father's well-being. I was splitting at the seams with fear, my concern making nausea swirl in my gut.

"The cops? You're kidding. How did they get involved?" Joel once again stood and paced the small space like a rat in a tiny cage.

He rubbed the back of his neck and nodded. "Whatever you have to do, Bruno, do it. I want him found. I want him hung up from his toes and gifted to Diego as payment for the lives lost. We'll be touching down in…" He lifted his arm and checked his shiny Rolex. "About four more hours. I'm going to schedule a meeting with Diego. I'll set it up in one of the meeting rooms at The Alexandra. If medical attention is needed for his men, make it happen. I'll be in touch soon," he grated and then ended the call.

"Is my f-father o-kay?" I croaked, tears falling down my cheeks.

He nodded and opened his arms. I folded against his chest so deeply he had to sit back in order to keep us upright. I burst into body-heaving sobs, the fear catching up to me in a wave of emotions.

Elation.

Relief.

Anguish.

All of it wracked my frame in convulsions that I couldn't control. Joel held me through it all. As I broke, he kept me together, protecting me, being the solid foundation I needed to cling to during such a tumultuous experience.

"W-what h-happened?" I stuttered.

He rubbed my back and arms while hugging me close.

"I'm not going to go into detail with you, Faith. Just know that a lot of my team was lost, many of Diego's men, and all of Aiden's—with a single exception."

"What are you talking about? This sounds like there was some type of battle." I frowned. The skin around my eyes felt stretched tight and throbbed. My entire body ached like one large, festering, painful wound.

He nodded. "My men surrounded the location where they were keeping your father. Diego's people went in and captured the target."

"Aiden?"

He shook his head. "No, darling. They captured your father. My cousin Bruno specifically led him out of the fray, taking two bullets as he did so."

I clutched at the lapels of his suit jacket. "Your cousin was hurt?"

"Faith, a lot of men were hurt. Far worse than we ever anticipated. Aiden's men went nuts, using machine guns and explosives. And there were more of them than we'd ex-pected."

I put my hand up to my mouth to cover the gagging noise

that was a precursor to me being sick.

Nope. Too late.

The sour tang of saliva hit my tastebuds, and I ripped myself away, just barely making it to my knees by the side of the desk where I hurled into a garbage can until my stomach was emptied of last night's dinner.

Joel knelt next to me, holding my hair as I continued to heave. Tears mixed with vomit in the metal can as I sobbed and retched.

When it seemed as though the worst of it had passed, Joel handed me a clean white handkerchief. I wiped my mouth and blew my nose, and then tossed it on the side of the can so it could be laundered or tossed.

I moved the trash aside and sat on my bum, crossing my legs. Joel mimicked my pose and took both of my hands.

"Bruno is being treated alongside your father by my personal physician at The Alexandra. We will go straight there when we arrive. Two of my guards will take Mother and the children to the penthouse. My team is setting up a private suite of rooms in the conference center to triage the more minor injuries."

"This sounds unreal. A triage in a hotel? I mean, that kind of thing only happens in a natural disaster or a warzone. Not because of some jilted, psycho ex-boyfriend. It's insane. It's fucking insane!" My voice rose to an unnatural timbre. That's when the growing weight of what he'd said covered me like a bucket of acid. "Oh my God. There are men who are dead because of *me*." My eyes bulged as though someone had wrapped their hands around my neck and squeezed, cutting off all the air. "It's my fault." I choked and clawed at my throat, trying to remove the invisible hands squeezing my airway. The sensation of being choked spread and bloomed across my chest, constricting my ability to breathe with each new startling revelation.

If I'd just given Aiden what he wanted, none of this would

have happened.

My heart beat so fast I gasped for air. My entire body heated to what felt like the temperature of the sun, and sweat misted my skin. Black spots sprinkled across my eyes, making my vision fade in and out.

The last thing I saw was Joel's fear-stricken face as I blacked out.

I came to on the couch in the office, the sound of the plane still roaring in my ears. The first few buttons of my blouse had been opened down the front, and a cool cloth rested on my forehead. There was another one on my neck, and Joel was alternating placing wet cloths on each wrist.

"Faith, darling, you're okay," Joel soothed as I blinked and took stock of my body. There was a heaviness to my chest, but nothing overtly hurt.

"What happened?"

"I think you had a panic attack or hyperventilated. We'll have you checked the second we touch down in Las Vegas, which is still too far away for my liking," he complained. "Faith, my love, you scared me. You stopped breathing, went completely pale, got sweaty, opened and closed your mouth, and then passed out. I barely caught you before your head hit the desk. How are you feeling now?"

I eased up to a seated position, removing the cloth at my neck and holding on to the one at my forehead, but then I pulled it off. "Better. I'm no longer in pain, and I can breathe easier."

He eased a lock of hair behind my ear. "Watching the light

go out of your eyes, Faith… I don't ever want to relive that. Okay?" His voice was low and raspy, as though the admission took more out of him than he wanted to admit.

I placed my hands over his. "I'm sorry. I think I just freaked out. Knowing that people died trying to save my dad from a madman who's obsessed with me… It's a lot to take in."

"It is." He nodded. "Though none of it is your fault. It's his. When a vile being hurts another person, it's not the victim's fault. It's the attacker's. When Aiden assaulted you, it wasn't because you're pretty or wore inappropriate clothing or simply existed. It's because there are monsters who live among us. Aiden is a monster. You wanting nothing to do with him is not the problem. He is the twisted waste of space in this scenario. Not you. Don't ever blame yourself for any of this."

My bottom lip trembled as I did my best to let his words sink in. "But if I hadn't left, he'd never have done any of this."

"And what of you? How is your life less meaningful or less valuable than anyone else's? You don't deserve to be terrorized by him any more than your father or those men tonight. At least with them, they went into battle knowing what was at stake and who the enemy was and were prepared to fight. Just because many of them lost doesn't take away the honor of their service or the righteousness of why they put their lives on the line."

I cuddled against Joel's chest. "I hate this. There's no winning for anyone."

"Well, there will be no getting too far away for Aiden either. While you were scaring the hell out of me, Diego called." Joel reached out to the side table, grabbed a remote, and turned on the television.

Video footage from a news helicopter was playing on the screen, the camera angle hovering over a dirty-looking industrial section of warehouses.

A newscaster commented, "We're coming to you live tonight from the scene of what sources say was a gang war gone wrong. In a rough section of Las Vegas, in an abandoned industrial warehouse, gunshots were heard by neighboring communities. According to our sources, the casualties in tonight's tragedy have risen as high as eighteen individuals. Members of the Latin Mafia are suspected of being involved. Also, surprisingly, men associated with hotelier Aiden Bradford were among the fatalities. Information has been leaked that Mr. Bradford himself was suspected of having been on site but fled the scene. All of this comes to us on top of a major IRS investigation that started last week at the young business owner's primary location, El Diablo Casino and Resort. The authorities do not know if the two are connected, but a BOLO has been issued to all law enforcement agencies as Aiden Bradford has been deemed a person of interest in what the local community is calling the Warehouse War."

An official *Be on the Lookout* had been issued for Aiden? As what? An armed and dangerous fugitive? A suspect in a...*war*?

"My God...eighteen men?" I gulped, tears making my vision blurry as I stared at the screen.

Joel shut off the TV. "We'll know more when we get there."

"And he's still missing. How?"

Joel looked as though he wanted to crumble into a million tiny pieces, which was exactly how I felt. "I don't know. From what Bruno and Diego shared, he's gifted at disappearing when things go south. Instead of leading his men into battle, he tucked himself into a dark corner while everyone else risked their lives doing his dirty work. Then he slipped out of sight when things went bad."

"That makes sense. He was always spineless and able to weasel out of anything. So what do we do now?"

Joel leaned us both back to relax against the couch. "We rest. We refuel. We get ready."

"And what are we getting ready for?" I tipped my head and stared into his beautiful eyes.

"For the exact moment he's weakest. Then we strike

without mercy," he growled low in his throat.

"And how do we do that?" I whispered, focused on the life preserver Joel's tone was offering.

Joel's eyes closed, and his lips tipped up into a wicked smile. "I have a plan."

Episode 72

An Alternate Option

NOAH

"Why are you pouting?" Opal asked as I drove toward Cambridge from our estate home in Oxshott.

I frowned. "I'm not pouting."

She huffed. "You totally are. Is it because you don't actually want to take me to check out Cambridge? Because I would have been fine accepting the car and driver Nile offered."

Opal sure was a pistol.

The more information that I learned about the woman, the more I actually enjoyed her company. She had a no-bullshit way about her that I preferred far more than Ruby's reticence to share. That woman was hard to figure out. She didn't reveal her feelings or work through a situation out loud as I'd found Opal did. It was comforting, in an odd way.

"Nonsense. I offered to assist you in getting set up for university, and I am committed to doing so," I explained.

"Because it will make you look good in my sister's eyes?" she asked rather accurately. Again, honesty being the prevailing method of communication for this woman.

"Not exactly."

"You realize that when my sister makes a decision, she sticks with it? There's not going to be much you can do to change her mind. Especially as it pertains to marrying Nile. Not to mention the fact that she chose right," she added, much to my irritation.

"Is that so?" I was instantly curious why she thought my brother—my twin—was better suited to Ruby.

She shrugged. "If the shoe fits, wear that sucker until it falls apart or you can afford better."

"Are you saying that Nile is better than me and that's why she chose him?" A fetid taste coated my tongue as I spoke.

"What do you think?" Opal turned the question on me.

"I think she chose what she believed was the *safest* option, not the best option." I truly believed that. Nile was a buttoned-up, broody snob who would absolutely treat Ruby well. He would wine, dine, and dress her up like the perfect Pennington wife. He would not cheat or be unfaithful, but the odds of him falling in love with her or of them having a passionate, exciting marriage was slim to none, in my opinion.

"Copout." She snorted and focused her gaze out the window, taking in the dreary, rainy landscape.

Opal had a regal, elegant appearance while her sister Ruby had a wild edge that attracted male attention wherever she went. Opal was pretty, beautiful even, but her beauty was understated. It didn't smack you in the face when she walked in the room. It was the kind that grew on you the more you took in her features. There was a commonality between her facial structure and her sister's in the soft rounded face, slim nose, and perfectly arched brows. But where Ruby was light, Opal was dark. Opal was a just-poured, fresh-brewed cup of English tea sans cream, whereas Ruby was a lushly poured cup with cream and two sugars, befitting a sweeter palate.

"Why would you say that?" I asked, genuinely interested.

"You can't handle the fact that you lost the prize. Admit it.

It kills you that your brother won her hand over yours. You lost the battle." Her words were as dry and brittle as a day-old biscuit.

She may have been right in her assumption, but I could still win the war. A battle was but one of many in any good war. I gritted my teeth and gripped the wheel tighter, making sure to keep the speed steady as I let her comment roll around in my mind.

I *was* upset that Ruby had chosen Nile. Absolutely. Our sibling rivalry was well-known and not likely to change over the course of our lives. It's the curse of being successful identical twins. We were born to achieve, and that was what Nile and I had done since we'd become adults. Our grandfather adding the twist of having to be married in order to earn the governing interest in our family's business holdings only exacerbated an already ticking time bomb of sibling competitiveness.

"More than anything, I'm disappointed in Ruby's choice," I offered honestly. "I felt a connection with her that went beyond the boundaries of The Marriage Auction agreement. Had she chosen me, I would have been devoted to her and her alone."

"And Nile won't?" Her expression took on one of concern. "Is he going to be mean to her? Does he have any sick and twisted sexual interests or a bunch of women on the side?" She asked all three questions in one breath as though she needed to get all her fears out at once. "Tell me! I need to warn her if that's the case," she snapped.

I shook my head and rubbed at my temples. "No. Not even close. Nile is hyper-focused on doing the right thing at all times. She'll live a charmed life the next three years. It just won't be *her* life she's living; it will be his. Nile's an incredibly busy man. His work ethic is unmatched. When she's not hosting an event on his behalf, attending one with him, or tending to his sexual needs, she'll have nothing. That's not a life I would want for her. Had she chosen me, we could have created something beautiful together. I'd help her find herself. Show her the world.

Whatever it was she wanted, I would have bent over backward to give it to her."

"Honestly, none of that matters in the grand scheme of things." Opal sighed. "To Ruby, this is a three-year commitment and nothing more. She needs and wants his money. She made it clear last night at dinner that they were compatible in the bedroom, so there isn't any concern there. And believe me, I'd have heard if there was. Ruby has...um...some hang-ups when it comes to sexual things, mostly because of our upbringing, but I'm not going to go into that. Her past is hers to share if she chooses to do so. And standing at her husband's side at events or hosting them doesn't seem like hard work. Believe me when I say Ruby has worked harder than anyone I've ever met. And she's done so with an incredible amount of grace and grit. She could not only use an easy lifestyle for the next three years, she's earned it."

There was far more information to unpack and discuss about what she shared; I didn't even know where to start. Instead, I let the quiet of the countryside steal over us for a few minutes while I thought about all she'd said. The smartest entrepreneurs tended to listen first, think about things, then react. Knee-jerk emotional reactions often ended the possibility for great business deals.

For one thing, if Ruby had sexual issues in her past, I was doubly stupid for taking her to Eyes Wide Open. Every day that passed since I'd made such a ridiculously bad choice, it seemed to come back and haunt me. Other women I'd dated loved going there. Seeing the taboo nature of the club in person and getting to see something only the filthy rich could have a chance to set foot into...I'd believed she'd be impressed.

"And what about you?" I asked, wanting to change the subject from my thoughts regarding my error in judgment.

"What about me?" Her nose crinkled as if she were smelling something foul.

"Are you okay with her entering into a marriage of

convenience that lacks passion and love?" I had hoped Ruby and I could be a love match, but the more I learned about Ruby's true intentions, the more I realized there was a lot I didn't know about her.

"Um, you think I'd be here sitting in a car with a person I've known a few days after having my entire life turned upside down if I wasn't?" she scoffed.

"And you're okay with her soon-to-be husband pulling strings to get you in and paying for your schooling, all because he wants to win the upper hand in our family's inheritance?"

Her head turned to me, and her chocolate-brown eyes melted into a fiery glare. "Are you judging me? You of all people? The man who was in a war with his twin to marry my sister and is still butt-hurt about losing? That is so rich!" she cackled.

I scowled at her. "I don't know. You seem self-sufficient and not the type to accept charity, especially knowing it's going to affect your sister's life for the next few years."

Opal covered her mouth, practically laughing herself silly before she got hold of her breathing and relaxed against the leather seat while shaking her head. "You have no clue about the real world, do you?" she fired off snidely. "Everything I do is for *Ruby*. Everything Ruby does is for *me*. That's true love. That's loving another person, your *sibling*, more than yourself. Putting them above anyone else. You wouldn't know what that looks like. You'd have to take the silver spoon out of your mouth long enough to evaluate reality."

"Oh, please. You're going to ride her coattails monetarily until you earn your degree. And then what?" I challenged.

"Then it's my turn to take care of Ruby." Her chin lifted. "Whatever she wants and needs, I will be the one providing. Monetarily, physically, emotionally. Whatever it is, I will give it to her. She has spent her entire life protecting me from the darkest, dankest depths of actual Hell on Earth. I owe everything I am and everything I will ever be to Ruby. Money is a means to an end for us. It's what we never had growing up in a podunk, ass-backwards town. But Ruby went to work the second she could get a permit and made sure I was taken care of, fed, clothed, and safe from the shit she suffered every damn day. I am indebted to her. And here she is, shackling herself to a man she doesn't love so I can get the education I need to make a good living for the both of us. I will not let her sacrifices go in vain."

"You mean to tell me the entire reason Ruby entered The Marriage Auction is so that she could give you a better life?" I huffed, disbelieving anyone could be so selfless.

"Give the man a trophy!" Opal said dryly while slow-clapping.

I clenched my teeth, and my nostrils flared as I let out a long-heated breath through my nose to calm my arse down. The competitive fire-breathing dragon within me wanting to burn this conversation to ashes.

"And once I'm done with school, which incidentally should be around the time she'll be divorcing Nile," she continued, nonplussed, "we'll move somewhere we both want to be and start our real lives. Together."

"Your real lives," I repeated, shaking my head.

"Yep. That's the plan, Stan." She clucked her tongue.

The wheels in my mind started to turn a million miles an hour coming up with a new, far better idea which could potentially solve both our problems. "What if there was another option?" I dropped the bait.

"Than my sister marrying your brother and scoring loads of cash? I doubt there's a better option available to two broke-ass girls born and bred in a trailer park in Mississippi."

I grinned widely, the pieces of my new plan locking together in perfect harmony.

"Let me ask you something. No lies. No side-talk. No bullshit."

She tilted her head. "I'm listening." The snark and

brashness were high with this woman.

Sod all, she was fun. Not only was she smart, she was also a clever little minx. Never making promises but putting most of their rubbish on the table for me to wade through like the cunning scavenger I was. I hadn't made my millions sitting back and living off my family's money or my trust. I'd waded through the muck and stink of situations and figured out the easiest, most plausible fixes and made those happen.

It's why I owned so many entertainment businesses. They were easy to take over, refurbish, and make successful using tools and tricks of the trade I'd already gleaned from other experiences. Most businesses had good bones, they were just lacking a bit of excitement, good management, and marketing. I was an expert at all of those things. I could see a problem and fix it better than most, and in a quarter of the time.

Looking at Ruby and Opal's situation, combining their wants and desires with my own and finding the best solution would be key.

"I get that you're incredibly intelligent. You wouldn't have been accepted into so many universities and have the stellar GPA you have if you weren't."

"Flattery will get you nowhere, pal. If this is where you're headed, trying to win me over to get to my sister, you're out of your mind. I don't make decisions for Ruby."

Ah, the exact response I wanted.

"But you'll let Ruby make all the decisions for both of you and just follow along with her plans like the good little sister, instead of making them yourself or using your superior intellect...?"

"That is not true!" Her ire came to play, which was exactly what I'd hoped for.

"Seems to me like Ruby makes the decisions, and you do what she says." She moved to open her mouth and interrupt me, but I held up a finger to stop her. "Let me finish." She clamped her mouth shut and glared. "What if I presented you with another option? Something that would make you the one to fall on the sword, instead of your sister. Giving *her* the freedom to choose what she wants in life instead of doing everything to ensure you get what *you* want."

Opal frowned. "I'm not sure I'm following. Get to the point because you're angering me, and I'm hell on wheels when I'm mad."

No doubt no truer statement had ever been made.

"What if I offered you the ability to marry me for the same amount of money, six million dollars, and for the same time commitment, three years, with the ability to continue your schooling as you've already been promised?"

"You're insane. Why the hell would I marry you?" Her entire face scrunched up into a sour expression.

"So your sister doesn't have to enter into a loveless marriage. She won't have to be on some stuffy rich man's arm for the next three years, and you'll have plenty of money to offer her so she can set up a life wherever you're going to school."

Opal was quiet for what felt like a long time. Eventually she made a sucking noise, nibbling on her plump bottom lip. It only made her more attractive. I wouldn't have minded flicking that bottom lip with my tongue. My trousers suddenly felt a bit tighter as the image presented itself.

"And what would you get out of this?" she asked.

I smiled, knowing like I always did when I'd gained the upper hand. Ruby and Opal were each other's kryptonite. A bond like that was unparalleled. Unbreakable.

"Governing interest in my family's holdings."

She squinted. "It means that much to you to beat your brother at something?"

"My brother believes I'm incapable of running it. I'd like to prove him wrong, amongst other things." I admitted these flaws because I'd learned over the course of the last few days that Opal responded positively when I was being honest.

"This is crazy." She shook her head and crossed her arms over her chest.

I seized the opportunity before it was lost and took the next exit and pulled over. I stopped the car and turned toward her so I could plead my case.

"You admitted that your sister has been doing all the giving since you were children, correct?"

She nodded but didn't say anything. Internally, I cheered.

"You also admitted that you are both in this together. She has her plans, and you have yours. Isn't it about time Ruby gets to do what she wants for a change? Live her life by her own desires?"

"I mean, yeah. That would be great, but..." Opal twisted her fingers together and frowned deeply.

"No buts. If you marry me, I get what I want—the extra interest in my family's businesses—and you get six million dollars and the ability to save your sister from a life she doesn't want. All while earning your degree from a prestigious university."

I waited with my heart in my throat for her to answer.

"It seems too easy..." She chewed on that bottom lip again.

"Do you want your sister to be happy and have her own life based on her own choices, or do you want her giving up everything for the two of you like she always has?" I turned the scenario around once again.

"What's the catch?" She stared into my eyes, hers unflinching, a true competitor if there ever was one.

"No catch. It's very simple. You just need to answer one question." My spine tingled as my groin tightened and my dick stirred to attention.

She licked her lips, and, all of a sudden, I was desperate to cover those candy-coated pink bits of flesh with my own and taste her answer...the answer I knew I was about to get. Celebrate the win I was about to have.

"What's the question?" She gulped, and I watched the long, swanlike expanse of her throat move as the temperature and weightiness of the humidity in the car heated up right alongside the tension oozing between us.

"Opal Dawson, will you marry me?"

Episode 73

My Knight in Pajama Pants and Cowboy Boots

DAKOTA

"Dakota!"

I could barely hear my name being called through the cobwebs of sleep.

I ignored it, preferring to rub my face against my personal heater, aka my husband's firm, heavenly scented chest. There was this perfect little divot I'd claimed as mine that settled just above his right pectoral and shoulder. I felt like Goldilocks, having tried every spot on his body and finally finding the one that fit my cheek and cushioned my neck just right for sleep.

"Sutton!"

I definitely heard my husband's name screamed by a familiar female tone I couldn't quite place in my foggy, sleep-deprived state.

The man himself jolted awake, his hand gripping my bare ass tightly, his other arm wrapping around me protectively as we both were startled by the sudden banging on our front door and the endless screeching of our names.

"Dakota! Sutton! The barn is on fire!"

We both heard that at the same time.

I lifted my head and looked at him, and he looked at me until the same cry ripped from the silence of our bedroom.

"The. Barn. Is. On. Fire!"

The words came with more pounding on our door.

We shoved off the covers and rolled to opposite sides of our bed. Sutton tugged on his pajama pants, and I tossed on his T-shirt and the pair of ratty denim shorts I'd thrown in the hamper yesterday.

Half-dressed, we scrambled down the stairs. Sutton flung open the door so hard it banged against the opposite wall. His mother came into view, her hair a mess of tangled curls, her body clad in a housecoat, and her feet in boots.

"The McAllister barn is on fire," she shouted and pointed across the field to my family's land. We could easily see large plumes of black smoke drifting into the early morning, barely lit sky. A haze of golden red curved around the tops of the tree line we couldn't see past.

"Fuck!" Sutton said, pushing bare feet into his cowboy boots. We always left our mucky shoes at the entry to the house after coming in.

I did the same, and the two of us set off at a dead run across our patch of land, jumping over the fence, cutting between our two properties, and hightailing it down the dirt road. He was faster than I was, but not by much. Everything I had worked for my entire life was on the line, and I needed to get there as quickly as possible.

I pushed myself to run as though the hounds of Hell were nipping at my heels.

When we arrived, one side of the barn was completely lit up, flames spreading out wildly. The horses were whining, their noises turning to actual nightmarish screams as Jarod held a lone water hose against the side of the barn, attempting to put out the fire. It was like pouring a bottle of water over a forest fire, making no change in the outcome.

The sound of wood cracking and splitting roared through the quiet of the morning as the fire took over the entire roof, giant pieces breaking away and crashing to the ground before our feet.

Sutton pulled me back just before a few broken pieces landed, the sparks of embers prickling and burning my bare shins.

"Oh my God." I pushed my hair out of my face, taking in the terrifying display before me. "The horses!"

Right as I said that, the rest of the bunkhouse ranch hands came with buckets of water and more hoses, dousing what they could get to.

"It's a lost cause!" Sutton yelled over the blazing inferno as he motioned for help and ran straight into the burning barn. I followed him, holding his shirt up to my nose, the black smoke making it hard to see. I opened the first horse stall, and Blackie galloped out through the front, almost trampling Sutton's father and brother, who appeared out of nowhere, their own handkerchiefs held to their mouths as they entered the fray.

"Get out of here," Duke Senior hollered to me.

I shook my head and went to the next stall and opened the door. Both horses were at the back of the stall cowering, their big brown eyes filled with fear. I went over to them and smacked one and then the next hard on their hinds. "Yaw!" I howled, and the two jetted out the opening, disappearing into the smoke but heading in the right direction.

The heat from the ceiling and burning sides of the barn was becoming unbearable. Sweat trailed down the center of my spine and along my hairline as my skin misted with sweat. My lungs tightened with every inhalation as the smoke thickened, making it hard to breathe.

One of the horses across the way screeched and pounded against the door as a groaning sound pierced through the air.

"The roof is going to cave in! We have to get out of here,"

I heard Sutton's brother, Junior, roar through the madness.

I tried to make it to the pinned horse right as an enormous piece of the upper loft crashed into his stall in a ball of fiery doom.

The horse abruptly stopped screaming as the entire stall became engulfed in flames.

He was gone. One of our best breeder stallions.

As I moved blindly to the next stall, freed horses were escaping two at a time, one knocking me into the tall wooden sides, pinning me to one of the doors.

Which was when I heard it: the cry of the one horse I loved more than any other.

Marigold.

My mother's stubborn horse was at the very end of the barn. Her cries clear as day.

"Marigold!" I screeched at the top of my lungs, pushing through the mayhem, determined to get my baby out of this mess, but I was barely at the midway point, and the smoke was thicker than molasses. Red flames mixed with darkened silhouettes as I used my hand to fumble along the stalls one at a time, opening the ones I could.

I bumped into a tall, strong male body I recognized by touch, the skin of his bare back slick with sweat and pocked with small burns from the embers floating down from above. I was wearing Sutton's shirt, and there he stood bare-chested, putting everything, including his safety on the line for me and my family. There were blackened, bloody streaks at various points on his back that I could just barely make out. I slid my hand along his sleek skin.

"Baby, you're hurt," I croaked as my tongue swelled in my mouth and I sucked in a cloud of blistering hot smoke. I bent over and coughed, trying to keep the shirt fabric over my mouth and nose as I did so.

"Dakota, what the fuck? Get out of here, now!" Sutton barked as he twirled around.

"Marigold," I sobbed. "I have to save her," I cried, my tears drying the second they fell as another round of body-wracking coughs took over. Pain lanced my chest, making it feel as though I was being squeezed around my entire ribcage in a vise grip.

Before I could say another word, my husband bent in half and tossed me up and over his shoulders, turning in the opposite direction from where I wanted to go.

Within a minute, my vision went from murky black to bright white light as my lungs filled with crisp, clean air. I sucked in as much of the life-giving stuff as I could manage through the soot covering my face and mouth. I spit and hacked against the ground while Sutton patted my back.

"I'm okay, I'm okay," I choked out and stood up to my full height and took in the scene in its entirety.

The barn was completely overtaken by red, orange, and yellow flames that lifted high into the sky, the smoke floating in enormous plumes.

This was when I heard sirens as the fire truck barreled down the dirt road. Thank God.

And still, I could hear the remaining horses scream as they were burned alive. Men from neighboring farms, mixed with the Goodall clan and their workers, alongside all of our ranch hands were hard at work, trying to keep the fire from spreading past the barn. The rescued horses stood at a safe distance, unbound, watching their brethren and their home burn.

"Marigold," I whispered, searching among the horses dotting the fields and not finding her. I started to shake, my body going into full shock as I realized the severity of what was happening. Not only was I losing one of the biggest parts of our land as the barn burned, our work horses and breeding horses were dying in the most vile way possible. And Marigold, the last remaining piece of my mother, the one good thing that was mine, was going to die right along with it.

I inhaled a full breath and ripped out of Sutton's arms.

"I'm going back in for her," I stated, moving toward the front of the barn.

"The hell you are!" Sutton grabbed my wrist and tugged me back, locking me against his heaving chest. "It's too dangerous, Dakota," he bit out.

I shook my head, my mind on one thing and one thing alone. "I have to save her. She's a piece of my heart. The only remaining thing I have of my mother that's worth anything to me," I croaked, clutching at the filthy shirt I wore while the heart I spoke of pounded so hard I felt as though it would burst straight through my ribcage.

Sutton stood breathing, holding me by the biceps, his face dirty with soot, grime, and sweat. His nostrils flared as he glanced at the inferno and then at me. "Stay here," he growled.

"No." I clutched on to his neck like a clingy octopus. "You are not risking your life for me. For my horse."

"I love you, Dakota. Remember that, no matter what," he said in a tone that sounded like goodbye.

I shook my head and dug my fingers into the skin of his neck. "No, no, no, no. You can't. I won't let you do this."

He physically yanked my hands away and held them in front of us. Then he kissed me hard and fast. The tastes of wood and ash covered my lips as he pulled away. He went at a full run, his form braving the broken entrance like a knight in shining pajama pants and cowboy boots. Sutton willingly entered the fiery mouth the dragon in order to save my horse.

What the fuck was I thinking?

He's going to die.

"Sutton! NO!" I screamed like a banshee when the realization truly hit that he very likely would not make it out of that barn alive. It was already falling apart at the seams.

As the thought entered my mind, the entire entrance crumbled in on itself in a loud, high-pitched guttural sound that would haunt my dreams for years to come.

"Sutton's inside!" I hollered at no one and everyone.

The front and side of the barn collapsed before my eyes, and my heart stopped. All I could hear was an ear-piercing internal dial tone like a drawn-out, endless beep as I stared in utter shock and horror.

My husband was still inside.

I didn't tell him I loved him.

Tears filled my eyes, blocking my ability to see anything other than the burst of blurry colors through my watery gaze. The firefighters surrounded the remaining half of the barn with their full battalion of men and water hoses.

I cried out, screaming uselessly as I fell to the earth, my bare knees digging into rocks and splintered wood, cutting into my kneecaps. But I couldn't feel pain. I couldn't feel anything.

He was gone.

My vision started to waver in and out as I stared at the destruction. Horses screamed. Men hollered. Firefighters called out tasks, but all I could do was rock back and forth, hugging myself as my entire world crumbled around me.

I fell onto my palms, my head dipping forward as I convulsed. People called my name, someone feminine and friendly rubbed my back. I could barely hear the phrase, "It's going to be okay," repeated over and over.

None of it mattered. Not if I'd just lost the person who could very well have been the love of my life as he tried to save my fucking horse.

I breathed through the snot pouring out of my nose and the nausea swimming in my stomach as a sour taste stole across my salivary glands. I was going to puke.

Gritting my teeth, I wiped my nose with the back of my hand and rubbed it on my shorts before I heard the tell-tale sound of a galloping horse. I knew that gallop. That gait.

I peered through the haze of my grief and saw the most beautiful sight imaginable.

The smoke cleared in the distance, and there he was,

galloping on my baby from the land at the back of the barn, headed straight for me. He looked like a war hero from centuries ago, a natural-born rider who'd saved my horse and ridden her bareback out of the mouth of Hell. My body swayed as I watched him slow down, lift a leg, and swing it over the side of Marigold, sliding down my horse until his booted feet hit dry earth. Then he was running toward me.

Alive.

Beautiful.

All mine.

When he got to me, he pulled me up by the armpits and hauled me into his arms. I burst into tears, clinging to his heated skin as I let it all out.

"I love you, I love you, I love you. I'm so sorry I didn't tell you. I love you," I continued. He gripped my ass and hiked me higher until I'd wrapped my legs around his waist and clung to him like I'd never have the chance to again. The simple truth was I might not have had the chance to hold him had things turned out differently.

"Kota, baby, it's okay. It's okay, darlin'. I got you. We got out just in time. We're fine. We. Are. Fine," he repeated.

At the *just in time* comment, the outpouring of tears doubled within me, and I shuddered against him, holding on for dear life.

Eventually he brought me over to a bale of hay where he sat down. I didn't move from his arms, and he didn't attempt it either. For a long while I stayed there, breathing in his smoky, earthy scent with my head tucked against his neck and shoulder, clinging to my husband.

"I thought I lost you," I whispered, a shiver wracking my frame at the mere thought.

"You didn't lose me, and you're never going to," he promised.

I lifted my head. "But I thought I did. I thought you went in there to get my horse and I'd lost you both. Why would you do that? Why would you go into a burning barn when you could have died!" I croaked, my bottom lip trembling as I admitted my fears to him.

He cupped my cheek, and his green eyes filled with compassion. "I was saving a piece of your heart. If I'm going to have all of you, I couldn't let a piece die right before my eyes. Not on my watch." He covered my heart with his soot-covered hand. "This is mine to have and hold, to love and protect. I did what I had to do in order to keep this from breaking in half at the loss of something you love. The woman I love has had enough loss. It's up to me to protect her from that."

Tears fell down my cheeks, and I let them as I stared into his handsome, dirty face. "You're going to regret making me fall in love with you," I whispered.

He grinned huge. "Not in a million years, sassy pants."

I frowned and scrunched up my nose. "I'm not sassy."

"Baby, you are. Now shut up and kiss me so I can help everyone get the horses we saved into our stalls with food and water."

I sighed as I placed my hands on his shoulders. "Thank you for saving Marigold. Thank you for protecting my heart."

He smiled. "You're welcome. Thank you for admitting you love me. Not that I didn't know your stubborn self was eventually going to say it anyway."

"Oh my God! Can you just be cool and not throw something in my face for one day in your entire life!" I groaned.

He grinned, cupping my cheeks. "Kiss your husband, lady, so I can get to work."

"Fine!" I spat, then took his face and kissed the daylights out of him.

Needless to say, it was a good five minutes before we came up for air to help settle the animals and figure out what happened.

Episode 74

This Is Our Family Now

SAVANNAH

"The barn caught fire? How in the world did that happen?" My voice rose as I listened to my sister tell me one bad thing after another.

"We don't know officially, but you know exactly who I think did it. It's pretty obvious, Savvy." My sister's tone was scathing and deeper than normal.

Our father.

"Did anyone get hurt? How about the animals? Oh my God...Marigold." I covered my chest where my heart beat a frantic rhythm as I waited for Dakota to give me possibly the worst news ever. My mother had loved that damn horse. Sometimes I believed maybe even more than us. Later, I realized it was the one thing my father hadn't tainted in her life. Still, it wasn't enough to keep her alive.

"No humans were hurt. And Marigold's fine. Sutton went into the burning inferno and risked his life to save her. I'm still mad as hell about that. But secretly, I'm beyond relieved he saved her. I swear to God, Savvy, if I'd lost her too, I'd have found Great-Granddaddy's shotgun and taken our father out myself."

"Kota, no. Just because he resorts to violence doesn't mean we have to," I said but then realized who I was talking to. Dakota had attempted to punch her own husband after he kissed her at their wedding ceremony. She did sucker punch him at the signing of the contract. My sister definitely had some unresolved issues from our shared past. She'd also received the brunt of Pa's fists after Mama died. And she was the lone female working a cattle ranch. She had to be more than tough to get the job done on a daily basis, not to mention to earn the respect of the men working under her. However, I believed violence was never the best option.

"We lost six horses, Savvy. *Six* we didn't have to lose. Most of our best breeding stallions. As if whoever set the fire knew exactly where to start it."

"Oh my God." I gasped and stopped pacing the bedroom to sit on the bed. Erik was leaning against the headboard, bare-chested, his hair a wild mess from sleep, his eyes tired and currently looking at me with immense concern.

I eased back, still wearing the Hard Rock Café sweatshirt we'd bought last night and my panties. When we'd made it home after fried food and copious drinks, both Erik and I crashed. I think I fell asleep before my head even hit the pillow. Only to be awakened by Dakota.

"It's bad, Savannah. Seriously bad. The entire barn is gone. Only things left are dangerous pieces of snapped wood and some parts of the stalls that didn't fully burn to the ground. I'll send you pictures. Hold on," she murmured.

While she did that, I pushed closer to Erik, who promptly curved his arm around my shoulders and resituated me against his chest. I sighed as I rested against his strong frame, appreciating the instant support he provided when he cuddled me close.

The messages on my phone dinged, and I pulled up the

images.

"*Kristus!*" *Christ!* Erik cursed as we looked at the charred images of what had once been a beautiful barn. There was a lot that needed to be worked on back home on the farm, but the barn had not been one of those things. Our great-granddaddy had made sure it was always in tip-top shape, and Dakota had kept it that way since his passing.

There literally wasn't much left.

"I'm...I'm... I don't know what to say." I had trouble believing what I was seeing.

"We have all of our current horses in the empty pasture for now, but Sutton is having space, food, and everything they need set up in some of their empty stalls. We're going to have to pair them up, but at least it's something for the time being."

"The Goodalls are housing our horses for us? Feeding them?"

"Yeah. I told you, they are not who we've been raised to believe they are. All of their family, as well as their workers were here helping save the animals and prevent the fire from spreading to the house and the fields. We lost a lot, but we could have lost everything had everyone not chipped in."

"I can't believe this. We just barely caught up on the liens against the property and finally had a little money to catch up with some of the necessary maintenance..." My voice cracked at the severity of it all. "We're back to square one. Now we need a fucking barn." I sniffed, pushing back tears. I'd cried so much lately, and I was finally getting to a point where I was looking forward to the future and all the good it might bring. It seemed every time I did, we were hit with something else life-changing.

Just when I started to think things couldn't get any worse, I was reminded that they always could and would.

When would it settle down?

All I wanted was a few damn months of peace and serenity. Was that so much to ask for?

"I needed to talk to you anyway. Sutton is giving me all the money from the auction now. He's also going to take a step back from Goodall business and help me get this ranch back into the black."

My eyes widened, and I held my breath.

"Why would he do that? They're technically our competition," I reminded her gently about what we'd believed about the Goodalls since the time we could crawl.

There was quite a long pause before Dakota sighed. "They're actually not. Did you know that the Goodalls have over fifty farms across the nation? They are major players in the industry. The farm next door is their home, and they keep it relatively small compared to the others they buy, refurbish, and fold into their much larger company."

"No way," I said, truly shocked. This was news to me.

"Yeah. They're multi-millionaires to celebrity levels, but far more understated. Sutton wants to help us get our ranch back to its glory days, and I'm going to let him. Do you have a problem with that?"

I blinked numbly, the wild information my sister was imparting finally adding up to two plus two equaling four. I shook my head, then realized she couldn't see me. "Uh, no. Whatever you think is best. I trust you and your judgment. After I marry Erik, you'll have another two million. Which is what I was going to call and talk to you about today."

"Oh?"

"Yeah, I had wanted to come home and have the wedding on the ranch in the wildflower field. Set up a simple wooden stage, arbor, and rent some chairs and all that. But as you know, time is running out, and now with the barn...maybe we should look elsewhere."

"You're coming home!" Dakota screamed, sounding elated. "Oh, thank God. This makes me so happy, Savvy. There's so much more I need to tell you about that I'm finding in the journals that Mama and Grandmama left behind. And then of course the fact that I've fallen in love with a big, hunky cowboy who drives me crazy in both good and bad ways and..."

I sat up, pushing off Erik to do so. "Wait a minute! Did you just say you've fallen in love with your husband? Sutton? The no-good, pushy, demanding, in-your-face neighbor who you swore you hated?" I smiled and turned to look at Erik, grinning like a loon.

He chuckled in return rather knowingly, because I too was starting to have serious feelings for my soon-to-be husband. This would mean that both my sister and I had somehow fallen into The Marriage Auction for all the wrong reasons, those being money and desperation to save our family's land, but may have come out of it with our intended mates. Perhaps entering The Marriage Auction had actually been part of God's plan.

"I didn't mean to fall in love. The stupid, sexy jerk just won me over time and time again. There's also the fact that he fucks like a stallion. And you can forget about the whole marriage only lasting for three years business. He's made that very clear. Sutton has us having kids and grandkids in the future as though it was meant to be and there is no other possible alternative." She laughed heartily, and considering the circumstances, that was a boon.

My heart filled to bursting with love and happiness for Dakota. She deserved a man who loved her that way. She deserved everything.

"Kota," I whispered. "You're in love with your husband. I'm so happy for you."

"Shocked the shit out of me too, but I knew for sure I was in love with him when I was frightened to my core at the belief that he wasn't going to make it out of the burning barn. It's crazy, isn't it?" Dakota asked. "I honestly never thought I'd find someone I could love and want to spend the rest of my life with, but here we are."

"No crazier than me catching feelings for the giant Viking who dotes on me daily." My cheeks heated as Erik cupped my jaw, dipped forward, and softly, quietly, kissed me on the lips.

"*Min kjære,*" he whispered in Norwegian.

I hadn't heard that one before, so I'd have to ask him later what it meant, but I knew by the tone and the way in which he delicately said the phrase that it was sweet. I watched as he slid out of bed, his form clad only in a pair of dark-red boxer briefs. His golden body packed with honed muscle was on display, and it reminded me how we hadn't taken that last profound step.

Enjoying the view of all the beauty before me, I licked my lips, imagining him sliding deeply inside me, our bodies touching from chest to knees in the most intimate of dances.

"That's awesome," Dakota answered, breaking me out of my lust haze. "So when are you coming home?"

"Erik and his parents are ready to fly out and start planning now. His parents are amazing. You're going to love them. And they are super eager to be involved in everything because they haven't spent much time with their son the last couple years."

"Why?"

I thought back to our discussion about the helicopter accident, him losing a best friend, the PTSD he still dealt with, and the many, many scars and surgeries he had to go through to even get to this point in his physical and mental healing, and I found I wasn't ready to share such private information about my man.

"It's a long story, but it's all good now. They are very excited and have been treating me like a part of their little family already."

"I love hearing that. This whole Marriage Auction thing could have gone so much worse. At first when I found out you entered, I was so angry with you. Now I realize I was stupid, and you were right. The money I made isn't going to be enough. Sutton is recommending we buy out our pa completely. Get him off the deed and move on from there. He plans to sink his own money into our farm too now that we lost the barn. He says whatever it takes, because he knows how much our legacy means to me."

I shook my head and got up to pace. "Not happening. I'm part of this too. The two of you can't make unilateral decisions about the farm's best interests and future without me. I have just as much skin in the game as you do..." And I did. Whether I truly wanted the responsibility or not, I was still part of it.

"I understand that, Savvy, I really do, but you're not here. We have to move now. It's only a matter of time before our father does something else to ruin all we've accomplished. We just barely paid the liens, and now we have no barn. Where are we going to store our horses, the feed, and everything in between? We lost all of our saddles, bridles, horse maintenance equipment... The primary breeding horses are dead, Savannah. DEAD." She sighed heavily. "We have nothing but the cattle and a bunch of horses that have no home, no food, and no fucking saddles to ride them. What do you expect me to do? Not take my husband's assistance because of what? Pride?" She scoffed loudly. "We no longer have that option."

I ground down on my teeth. "Just don't do anything major until I've talked to Erik and we've made our way back. We'll make a plan together. All four of us. I'm sure if I tell him we need to go home as soon as possible, we will," I stated rather confidently, even though I hadn't yet asked.

"I'll schedule the jet and tell my parents to pack, and we'll be off. Family first, *elskede*," Erik announced from where he stood leaning casually against the bathroom doorframe with his arms crossed over his bare chest, a toothbrush dangling from one hand.

"See? Erik says we'll leave today. I'll send you the flight info and let you know when we're on our way. With the time difference and travel, we'll probably be there tomorrow. Do you think it would be okay to stay in the main house? Pa isn't going to be there, is he? Then we can be in my room, and his parents can stay in your old room or vice versa."

"Yeah, as far as I know, no one has seen our father. Sutton has some people keeping an eye out in town, especially at the bars. They'll give us a call when he's found. The Sheriff definitely wants to interrogate him on this newest possible offense. God, I can't believe this happened. It's so…"

"Devastating," I muttered, feeling my chest tighten as I imagined all those sweet horses losing their lives. And how all of this loss would affect the ranch's bottom line. More and more I was starting to feel like we were working our asses off to save a sinking ship.

The real question was, for what?

We hadn't been particularly happy growing up there. Our mother took her own life on that land. My father beat the hell out of her and Dakota there. Pa took a different abusive approach with me but still just as damaging. I hadn't spent regular time on the farm in years since I'd been away at school, and even then, I hadn't missed my life there, just the animals and my sister. And then of course, there was Jarod. The man I'd believed once upon a time was the love of my life. The man I left behind.

I most certainly was not looking forward to coming face-to-face with that part of my recent past so soon, especially after his phone chat with Erik. Regardless, I'd put my big girl panties on and do what needed to be done.

"We'll be there as soon as we can. I love you."

"I love you too. I'm glad you're coming home. I need you here," Dakota declared. It was the first time she'd admitted needing me. The sensation of pride that flowed through my veins lifted me up to stand at my full height, straightening my spine, and raising my chin.

"I'll be there soon, and we'll fix everything together. Me, you, Erik, and Sutton. This is our family now," I said with as much gusto as I could manage under the circumstances.

"You know, you're right. This is our family now. We have men in our lives who want to not only love us, but they also want to support us and the things we value. It will take some getting used to, letting others into our circle."

I smiled. "It won't hurt too much," I teased.

"Trust is hard for me. You know that," she confided.

"I do. With good reason. But now you're in love and married to a man who loves you in return. Let's not look that gift horse in the mouth. Let's embrace this new side to our lives. Our family is growing, and it's going to be beautiful. Once we get a handle on everything."

"Yeah, you're right. This too shall pass, and we'll get back to the good stuff."

"See you soon, Kota."

"Love you, Savvy."

Erik came up behind me and enveloped me into his arms. "This is our family?" he reiterated against the skin of my neck. "I like the sound of that."

I leaned back against his solid frame, knowing he'd hold me up no matter what. "Me too, honey. Me too. Let's talk to your parents and get to packing. I'm needed back home."

Episode 75

Trouble in the Countryside

MADAM ALANA

"They are not answering their phones. Not my texts, emails, or voicemails. Something is wrong. I know it in my soul, *cheri*."

My loving husband looked at me with a sparkle in his eye. His ever-present optimism shining through.

"*Mi amore*, they are adults very likely living their lives. Don't assume anything is wrong when you have no confirmation of such things." Christophe eased back against the cushy leather seat of our jet and glanced back down at his book. He was reading an autobiography about an American rock star he favored.

"I'm genuinely scared, Christo. What are the odds that I would be unable to reach three different women in three separate locations over the last two days?" My voice warbled, proving my fears.

Christophe marked his place with a bookmark, shut it, and set it on the seat next to him. "Come here, *mi amore*." He wiggled his fingers in a come-hither move.

I unbuckled my belt and stood, taking the few steps

between us from where I sat across from him on the plane.

Christophe gripped my hips the moment they were within reach, tugging me straight onto his lap. I cuddled against his powerful frame and sighed as his warmth soaked through my skin and calmed the jitters plaguing me. It had been over forty-eight hours since I'd had any form of communication from Faith, Savannah, and Dakota. Ruby, however, had kept in constant contact. I was becoming close with her as she progressed through the process. She'd notified me just the other day that she'd chosen Nile, and they were moving forward with wedding plans for the last day of the month. She seemed excited, eager even, to start this new chapter of her life.

I had a soft spot for Ms. Dawson. She reminded me of myself when I was her age. Eager to please, willing to work hard for the things she desired. Her desires being security and stability. I think Ruby would ultimately be happy if she ended up falling in love with her husband, but only time would tell with Nile Pennington. He often seemed cold and assessing, though perfectly polite and rather tender toward Ruby. Who knew? Maybe they would one day be a love match like Christophe and me. Either way, my concerns were no longer for Ruby.

My sights were set on Montana. Dakota had been the least communicative of the bunch, but I'd expected nothing less from the ballsy and focused McAllister. The surprise, though, was Savannah. She'd been meticulous in responding to my texts with, *I'm having a good time. Settling in. Erik and his family are treating me well.*

I was so concerned, I'd planned to pop in on each one of them to assess their situations.

Having lived this life myself thirty years ago, I knew all the pitfalls and possible dangerous scenarios that could occur when no one was keeping an eye on things. I'd never let any of my candidates experience what Celine did. It's why I went into this business in the first place.

"We're touching down in Montana shortly," my husband reminded me. "You'll have answers very soon. Try to relax and not get yourself too worked up. I'm sure everything will be okay."

Everything was not okay.

Christophe and I walked around the charred, taped-off remains of what must have been a massive barn that had recently burned down. The yellow police crime scene tape and signs posted around the destruction warned against trespassing.

"What in the world happened here?" I stared at the devastation, trying not to get my high heels stuck in the muck. I'd forgotten to unpack my boots on the plane in my rush to get to the McAllister farm as quickly as possible.

"Looks like a recent fire. I hope the animals made it out okay," Christophe said.

"Who the hell are you?" a male voice demanded from somewhere behind us.

Both Christophe and I turned around, my husband immediately coming to my side and wrapping his arm around my waist, especially when we noted the rifle pointed in our direction.

The older man was scrawny in stature and rather unsteady on his feet, as though it took extreme effort to stay standing. He stared at us both down the barrel of his gun, healing bruises a rainbow of colors over his ruddy-looking cheeks. Christophe pushed me behind his much larger frame, protecting me from this madman. A shiver raced down my spine, and my mouth went dry as I clenched the back of Christophe's shirt and peeked around his shoulder.

"We're looking for Dakota McAllister-Goodall. I understand this is her farm," I called out, a bit afraid that the wild-looking man might shoot first and ask questions later if we weren't forthcoming about our reason for being there.

"This is my fucking farm. Always has been, always will be." He narrowed his eyes over the gun. "My daughter thinks she can steal my birthright from right underneath my nose, but she's dead wrong! I'll never leave, and I'm going to prove it to everyone!" he sneered.

"I'm sorry, Mr. …"

"I'm Everett McAllister, and you're on my property. I want you city folk to get on up outta here before I shoot. Somethin' I'd be well within my rights to do." He slurred and stumbled forward a couple steps. His gun wavered, and I ducked behind my husband, a small whimper slipping from my lips.

"Let's go." I tugged on Christophe's shirt. "He seems unsettled. I don't want to anger him any more than he already is."

"Mr. McAllister," I called out, my voice sounding weak and scared, because I was frightened out of my mind. "Dakota Goodall is a friend of mine. I haven't heard from her, and I got worried. Thought I'd pay her a visit. I see now that was a bad idea…" I tried to defuse the situation while stepping backward, yanking Christophe along with me.

Mr. McAllister didn't say anything for a bit before he tilted his head and slung the rifle over one shoulder, pointing it in the opposite direction, thankfully. "Never seen you around here before. Not sure I'm in the position to be believing some stranger who shows up wearing fancy clothes claiming to know my daughter. I think you're lying. You're from the bank, aren't you?" His gaze turned steely. "You're coming to take my land right out from under me! I can see it in your eyes!" he roared, lifted the gun up into the air, and shot heavenward.

That was our cue to run. We hoofed it back to the car and jumped inside. Our driver already had it in gear, and once our doors closed, he spun the tires and jetted off, hopefully toward safety. Once we hit the end of the long gravel road, I could finally breathe. We took our time coming back from what felt very much like a near-death experience, when I noticed a man on a horse trotting in our direction off in the distance.

"Everyone okay?" our limo driver asked.

Both of us sat for a moment assessing the situation, shocked by what had just occurred. "Yes. Thank you for getting us out of there so quickly," I offered. "Though now we're back to square one. Can you simply park here at the side of the road, and I'll check my contacts to locate an address for Sutton Goodall?"

The driver nodded but rolled down his window as the man on the horse was about to pass us.

"Excuse me, sir. You wouldn't happen to know where Sutton Goodall lives, do you?" the driver asked the cowboy.

"You're there already." He gestured to another driveway right next to the one we'd come from. "Head down that dirt road, and when you come to the fork, take a right. Will lead you to a two-story home. That's where he lives."

"Much obliged," the driver said, and the gentleman on the horse tipped his hat and carried on his way.

"Smart thinking," Christophe stated. "I forget how nice and neighborly small towns can be."

Our driver put the car back into drive and drove the vehicle down the road our horse-riding friend had instructed us to take. We rolled up to a beautiful two-story house with an incredible view of the farmland it sat on. It was charming and reminded me a lot of the French countryside.

Christophe got out and opened the door for me. Together we approached the home and took the stairs. I knocked heartily on the door and waited.

I did so a second time.

A third.

"Maybe they're not home?" Christophe noted.

Which was also when I heard the sound of feet barreling down the stairs.

"Hold your frickin' horses," a female voice stated, and then the door flung open to a wild-haired Dakota, dressed only in a man's T-shirt. Dakota's eyes widened, and her mouth dropped open.

"Hello, darling, so good to see you. May we come in?" I smiled.

"Madam Alana, fella I don't know..." Dakota said and then popped her head out and looked left to right as though she were checking to see if anyone had seen us before she grabbed my wrist and tugged me inside.

Christophe followed behind, never letting me too far out of reach. When I visited clients, he preferred to go with me in most cases. Wanting to ensure I was safe at all times. Rich people could get into some questionable activities, just as anyone could. Only they had the money and, more often than not, the connections needed to push things under the rug and avoid punishment. I wouldn't allow my candidates to be at risk. The business of creating intimate, long-standing relationships could be dangerous if you didn't know what to look for.

"What in the world are you doing here?" Dakota asked as she shoved a hand through her messy hair, pushing it back and out of her face.

She looked exhausted with dark circles under her eyes and a series of light greenish yellow bruises that were close to being fully healed around her neck. She kept holding her side as though she were cradling her ribs.

Fury unlike anything I'd ever experienced since losing Celine rose to the surface, enflaming me with deadly anger.

"Did Sutton Goodall lay his hands on you?" I hissed.

The man himself came barreling down the staircase barefooted and bare-chested, wearing nothing but pajama bottoms.

"Of course, I laid my hands on my wife. All over her. Repeatedly." He waggled his brows as he reached our small group where we stood in the entryway. He put his hand to the back of Dakota's neck, leaned over, and kissed her temple. "I'm not sure if I say it's nice to see you, Madam Alana, because of the reason I'm assuming you're here out of the blue. Probably heard about the assault and the fire, I'd imagine. Before we get into it, I should probably start some coffee."

"Thanks, honey," Dakota preened.

Preened.

Dakota.

Just when I thought the experience couldn't get any stranger, it did. Dakota Goodall, who I'd once chastised for using her fist against her husband, had a dopey, woman-in-love expression plastered across her pretty face.

"What is going on here? Assault? Your barn burning down?" I asked, feeling like a top that had been spun around and around, especially after our harrowing adventure not fifteen minutes ago.

Dakota nodded. "Um, I think we have a few things to update you on. Let me run upstairs and put on some jeans and then we'll chat over coffee and breakfast." She pointed to the direction Sutton went. "Kitchen's in there." Then she reached out a hand toward my husband. "Hi, I'm Dakota Goodall."

"Christophe Toussaint." He shook her hand. "Alana's husband."

"Cool. Good to meet you," she said, then pulled me into an unexpected, swift hug. "Happy to see you both. I'll be right back," she finished, then raced up the stairs.

"I am finding all of this hard to believe." I pushed away the remains of the startlingly large egg, pancake, and bacon breakfast Sutton had made for the four of us.

Christophe picked the remaining pieces of bacon off my plate and put them onto his. My husband was in heaven. An American-style breakfast on a farm in Montana was high on the list of things he wanted to experience.

"We're still waiting to hear from the arson investigator. It's a huge loss for my farm. The barn, six horses, all the equipment. And there really isn't any natural way for a fire like that to start. It seemed intentional. Specifically started where our breeding stallions were, alongside Marigold's stall."

"Marigold?" I asked.

"She was my mother's horse. Mine now. I'm the only person she'll let ride her. My father wanted to sell her off right after Mom's passing, but I pitched a huge fit. Eventually he relented, but he's always hated her. My guess? He's retaliating for me pressing charges on the assault. And according to the Sherriff, he's been out of jail since not long after he attacked me. I'm sure he's pissing mad at me and the big guy here." Dakota hooked a thumb behind her back where Sutton was hovering, his hands on her shoulders supportively. "He beat the tar out of my pa when he found my father hurting me."

"And I'll do it again if he so much as shows his smarmy face 'round here, which is why we haven't been able to land eyes on the man since it occurred. But somehow he must have weaseled his way onto the land to set fire to the barn. Likely trying to hurt his own daughter and bankrupt the ranch for good," Sutton hissed.

Dakota reached back and took his hand, bringing it to her mouth and kissing the center of his palm. He hummed sweetly in response while a cold sweat formed on my brow.

The two seemed so natural with one another already. As though they'd been together for years, not weeks. It warmed my heart but also ramped up the concern that they were being targeted maliciously by her father. A man I believed I'd just met.

"You are looking for your father?" I asked instantly.

Dakota's brow furrowed. "What's the matter? You just turned pale as a ghost. Are you okay?" She stood up as I reached for Christophe's hand.

"*Cheri*, I hate to tell you this, but we just left your farm not an hour ago. The man we met claimed he was your father and the landowner. He held us at gunpoint for trespassing."

Sutton went completely still. "I heard that gunshot. That was you? And you're sure it was her father?"

"He claimed he was Everett McAllister."

"Son of a bitch!" Sutton barked. He dropped the frying pan he was about to clean back onto the stove and pounded up the stairs.

"Oh my God." Dakota walked back and forth, suddenly frantic. "I have to do something…"

"I didn't know you were looking for him. I'm sorry, *cheri*!" I exclaimed.

Dakota waved her hand in the air in a *don't worry* gesture, but a pit formed in my stomach that I knew I wasn't going to be able to get rid of any time soon.

"And what of Savannah and Erik? Have you heard from them?" I asked.

"Um, yeah. They're on their way here to help, and uh…" A knock on the door sounded right as Sutton came down the stairs, taking two steps at a time.

"No, no, no." Dakota ran to catch up to her husband. "Don't go out there alone. He has a gun, and he'll use it.

Especially on you! We need to call the Sheriff!" Dakota cried, pulling at Sutton's arm.

Both Christophe and I followed the two to the front door when a knock sounded again.

Sutton ripped open the door, and there stood five people: Mr. Johansen and Savannah, an older couple, and a dark-haired man who looked about Erik's age.

Savannah's innocent, blue-eyed gaze met mine, and her eyes bulged. "Madam Alana?"

"*Bonjour, cheri.*" I offered a small wave.

"Holy hell." Savannah stared at me, shock the prevailing response. "Who's in trouble?"

"Right this moment, your father. Now move aside," Sutton grumbled low in his throat.

"Sutton, no! Erik, don't let him leave!" Dakota screeched.

Mr. Johansen bodily stopped Sutton with a hand to his chest. The dark-haired male moved Savannah out of the way and took her place to assist Erik.

"That bastard is out there right now, taking stock of his handiwork. He needs to be taken down. Now!" Sutton snarled.

"I'm calling the Sheriff. Please, baby. Do this the right way," Dakota pleaded.

"I will do the right thing. By wiping him off the face of the earth, once and for all." Sutton's words were a promise and a threat rolled into one.

"Oh, *cheri*," I whispered to Christophe. "I believe we came to town at the exact right time."

Episode 76

Blood Brothers

JOEL

The second we landed in Las Vegas, I gathered my family and rushed them into a waiting limo. Our driver knew exactly where to take us and was all business, something I appreciated greatly. The girls bounced around happily, looking out the windows while Faith and I both seemed to be lost inside our own heads. My thoughts ranged from murderous anger to bone-shaking fear as we approached The Alexandra.

I'd already received word from Bruno that he and Faith's father were being seen privately in the resort's medical office while the others were in one of the larger conference rooms. My on-site doctor had recruited several of his peers, each of whom were promised handsome payment for their discretion.

The entire situation had gotten entirely out of hand. Lives had been lost, and for what? A man-child who wanted his favorite toy back? There had to be another way. One thing I'd learned over the years was that there was always an ace in the hole. You just had to find it. I'd never encountered a problem that couldn't be solved by throwing money at it. With the IRS on his tail, freezing his resources, it was likely I could make this problem go away with money. Something I was prepared to do.

There was also the fact that the police were looking for Aiden, not only as a person of interest in the tragedy that had occurred at the warehouse, but because Bruno had dutifully and anonymously leaked the video surveillance he'd found of Aiden and his bodyguard committing a murder and then kidnapping Mr. Marino.

Simple fact was the man was fucked. If he didn't want to face the police and the charges against him, he'd need money and a lot of it to get out of the country. Unfortunately, none of Bruno's team had laid eyes on the man since they'd escaped the warehouse prior to the authorities arriving on scene, which meant I'd have to contact him through an alternate source.

When we pulled up to The Alexandra, a team of six guards surrounded our vehicle, all dressed in black suits and wearing surly expressions. I got out first, my eyes scanning the area around us to ensure there weren't any of Aiden's men hiding in the shadows, even though I trusted my men had already done the same. Faith came out next, passing me Eden. The child clung to my jacket, her mouth twisted in a sour expression.

I cupped her face and pushed a lock of hair behind her ear. "What's the matter, little one?" I cooed as Faith helped Penny out of the car. She bent over and lifted my daughter into her arms.

"I not wanna go home," Eden pouted. "I wike ocean home." She planted her chin against my neck. My heart soared with the knowledge that this innocent, incredible little human loved her new home with me, my daughter, and my mother. It quickly cemented my desire to handle this matter as urgently as possible and get back to what was important. Building our lives together.

I pressed my lips together, trying to hold back any emotion so I could set the best fatherly example for the child. "Eden…" I rubbed her back soothingly, holding her tighter to my chest as

I put my chin to rest against the crown of her head. "We're not staying in Las Vegas forever. We'll go back to our ocean home in Greece soon. Okay?"

She lifted her head. "Really?" Her eyes lit with joy.

"Yes, sweetheart. We're only staying here to check on your papa and see if we can move him to our ocean home. Would you like that?"

She grinned huge, nodding wildly. "I miss my papa!"

"I thought so." I smiled as one of my men helped my mother out of the vehicle.

Together we walked through the throngs of patrons straight to the private elevators that led to the penthouse. Once we settled the girls and my mother in the luxurious suite, I gave the team instructions not to let anyone in except me and Faith. My guards were armed to the teeth, something I hated with every fiber of my being but also knew was a necessity after what had occurred between Aiden's men, Diego's gang, and my security teams.

"I'm so scared," Faith admitted, clinging to my hand as we took the elevator to the conference floors.

"I am unsettled as well, my love, but we know your father is alive, and that is what is most important. We'll handle everything else one step at a time. Okay?"

She nodded and leaned against my side.

Her belief and trust in my ability to keep her and her father safe was an honor I wasn't willing to lose. I needed to get to Aiden and rid her of his terrible rot in her life once and for all.

When we reached the medical office, we found Bruno lying on a bed, hissing around a brown leather belt he had clenched between his teeth. Dr. Marbury had just dug a bullet out of the muscle in Bruno's thigh, dropping it into a metal container that clinked ominously as we approached.

"This is highly unusual, Mr. Castellanos. The injuries many of these men sustained are almost impossible to treat in this setting. Had I known the severity of the situation, I wouldn't have agreed to bring other medical professionals in. GSWs, second degree burns..." He shook his head, clearly upset.

Faith covered her mouth as she gasped, squeezing my hand in a vise-like grip.

"Whatever it is you need to do the best job possible, I will have it brought here. Ask and you shall receive," I assured the young doctor.

"Do you happen to have a hospital ready to go? A surgical unit? This is unethical," he grated and went back to work on stitching the nasty bullet hole in my cousin's thigh.

"I assure you, Dr. Marbury, that you will be rewarded for your commitment and discretion as promised. I have just arrived and need to evaluate the situation. Then we shall discuss how to come to an appropriate and respectable payment for such extenuating circumstances." I switched my attention to my cousin. "Bruno, you okay?"

"Mostly flesh wounds. Doc says I'll be fine. I've had worse." He grinned and then winced as the doctor applied another stitch.

"Do you need more pain medication?" I asked, frustrated that Bruno was in such obvious distress.

"We ran out after the first several patients," Dr. Marbury announced, his focus once again on Bruno. "When we set up this medical office, I didn't plan for a massive influx of seriously wounded patients. I've given him oral medication, but I ran out of everything else." He scowled.

"I understand your concerns and appreciate all you are doing to help." I pursed my lips as tension pressed against my chest. The weight of the situation becoming too heavy to carry as the minutes passed by.

"I don't think you understand, Mr. Castellanos. It's a shit show out there." He pointed a gloved hand in the direction of one of the biggest conference rooms.

"Where's Mr. Marino?" I asked. Faith made a small whimpering noise, her body trembling as I held her hand.

"We pulled him in to assist the wounded. What we really need is a hospital with nurses," he complained.

"We'll leave you to it. Come, Faith. Let's go find your father." I led her out of the room and down the hall toward where I heard the most noise. It actually sounded as though a convention was currently in progress.

When I opened one of the double doors, I was not prepared for what we saw.

There were men *everywhere*. Each in various stages of disarray. Either they were lying on the floor, bleeding onto the carpeting, or they were assisting a fellow wounded peer. A handful of gentlemen in white coats were tending to what seemed to be the worst patients. There were at least thirty men, far more than I could have imagined.

It was madness.

Complete and utter madness. I had not expected what most closely resembled an emergency setup the likes of which you might see in the aftermath of a war or a natural disaster.

"Dad!" Faith called out.

Robert Marino handed a wounded man a bottle of water and then lifted his head. A horrified expression stole across his face at the sight of his daughter.

"No, no, no." He shook his head, fury turning his olive skin tone a bright red.

Faith slammed into him, and he wrapped his arms around her, holding her close.

"Jesus, Mary and Joseph, Faith. Why are you here?" He cupped the back of her head and closed his eyes. "You're supposed to be far away from all of this." His voice shook as he held on. Robert's gaze met mine. "You promised you'd keep my girls safe." He glared. "I counted on you to be a man of your word."

"I'm sorry, Mr. Marino. There was nothing I could do to prevent her from coming to your aid. And I suspect you understand how persuasive your daughter can be." I leveled him with a knowing look.

Faith pulled back and cuddled against her father's side. "Don't be upset. Joel's right. I was coming to get you no matter what. Nothing could keep me away." She cupped her father's cheeks and looked him over. "Are you okay? Did he hurt you?"

"No, *cara mia*, I am fine. Joel's men got to me in time," he stated calmly.

"What happened?" she asked.

"It was my worst nightmare come alive. One moment I was evaluating my burned-out restaurant, trying to decide what my next steps would be after spending most of my life as a restauranteur. At my age, a man doesn't want to start all over alone. And then there's you and Eden with your new life in Greece..." He shook his head. "When Aiden approached, I lost my mind. All I could see was everything he'd done to you. To us. And I...I attacked him. I had him pinned down, but I didn't see the second man. He came out of nowhere and knocked me out cold. I woke tied to a metal chair in a warehouse."

"Dad, I'm so sorry. That had to be frightening," Faith croaked.

"At first, Aiden was playing the gentleman card. Saying that he loved you and didn't want any harm to come to you, he just wanted you back. Swore he'd do anything to get in your good graces," he snarled. "Then he started demanding to know where you were. What I knew about Joel. When you were coming back." He shook his head. "I didn't tell him anything. Not a thing. One of his goons was about to smash my hand with a hammer to get me to talk when gunshots rang out."

"Oh my God!" Faith snuggled closer to her father.

"I leaned to the side until I fell to the ground hoping I wouldn't get hit by gunfire. Then a member of the Latin mafia untied me, but once he stood up, he took a bullet to the head. May he rest in peace." Robert shivered, deep lines creasing at the corner of his eyes as though retelling the story was reminding him of his horrifying experience. He sniffed and cleared his throat. "Out of nowhere, a man that looked an awful lot like Joel rescued me, getting shot in the process. He's being seen now by the head doctor."

"Bruno, my cousin and the head of my security. We checked on him when we arrived. He seems to be faring well comparatively," I noted, taking in the chaos that surrounded us.

I watched as Faith's gaze flitted around the room of groaning men in various stages of pain and suffering. "I can't believe all of this is because of me." She swallowed and pressed her lips together. I knew that expression was a precursor to tears, but I was proud to see that she straightened her spine and stood taller instead. My Faith was brave, even after everything Aiden had put her through the last few years.

I shook my head. "Do not take this on yourself, Faith. There is one man responsible. Only one. I think intellectually you understand that, but your heart is so big that you take it all onto your own shoulders. You are not the cause of this disaster. Aiden Bradford will one day burn in Hell for all he has caused. I will make sure of it."

Anger rose within my gut as I clenched my teeth, ready to put my plan into effect, when a large hand locked around my shoulder.

"Count me in, *hermano*." Diego Salazar's voice was guttural and filled with ire as he stepped closer to our small huddle. "I lost several men today. I seek revenge." His maniacal half-smile was cold, his facial expression much like a snake's right before it strikes with its poisonous venom.

"You have lost too much already, Diego." I sighed. "What you consider your debt has long been paid. I think it's best and safer if I deal with Mr. Bradford myself."

"Then you'd be thinking wrong, *ese*." His eyes were steely black pits that shined pure hate through their murky depths. "I will get my revenge by removing his eyes and feeding them to him, right after I've gutted him like a fish and showed him his insides."

"In the name of the Father, the Son, and the Holy Spirit." Robert made the sign of the cross, touching his head, shoulders, and chest as he held Faith close.

"We'll discuss it further privately," I assured Diego, wanting to move away from Faith and her father.

Faith clapped her hands suddenly. "All right. What can I do? I need to help somehow. Whatever is needed."

"Actually, darling, that sounds like a great idea. I'd like to chat with Diego for a bit. Why don't you and your father go check in with one of the doctors and have them put you to work."

Faith nodded and came over to me. She wrapped her arms around my neck, got up onto her toes, and kissed me hard and fast. "I love you," she whispered against my lips.

"And I love you." I smiled softly while staring into her stunning eyes. Ones that reminded me of the pristine waters of my homeland. "You are a gift to this world, Faith. Not a burden. Never forget that." I dipped my head and took her mouth once more, then reluctantly pulled away. "I'm going to discuss things with Bruno and Diego. I'll check in with you in a bit," I lied. "Here, I'll take your purse and store it in the medical office."

"Oh yeah, that makes sense." She removed the small satchel that she had hanging across her body and handed it to me. "Thanks, baby." She smiled tentatively, took a big breath, and nodded. "I'm ready to help. Point me in the right direction, Dad."

Faith and her father headed over to one of the white coats tending to a man that looked like he'd been run over by a truck.

I said a silent prayer for him and all the men who were wounded and had lost their lives, then I faced Diego. "Let's discuss things outside." I jerked my head toward the doors.

Diego followed me out, and I led him down a hallway that fed to smaller conference rooms. I opened one and made sure no one was inside.

I set Faith's purse on the conference table and pulled out her phone, typing in Eden's name as her four-letter passcode. The phone came to life as expected. She'd given me the code to take a photo of them back in Greece, and now more than ever before, I was grateful that she'd trusted me. Even though I knew she'd likely feel betrayed by what I was about to do.

"What do you have in mind, Castellanos?" Diego crossed his arms over his chest. "Whatever it is, I'm in. No marker needed. He killed my men in cold blood. He must pay. No one messes with the Latin Mafia and lives to tell about it," he sneered, his face contorting into one of malevolence and pure rage.

"And what of the police?" I cocked my head to gauge his response. "We have an entire conference room full of wounded individuals that directly lead back to you and me. I'm not even sure I can pay off the doctors to keep quiet about this."

"You figure out how to keep the docs quiet, and I'll handle the police. I have many, many, connections." He smirked. "Where do we start?"

I took a deep breath, closed my eyes, and held up Faith's phone. I went to recent calls and scrolled to the only contact that my lovely bride-to-be would label "The Devil."

"I'm going to make Aiden Bradford an offer he simply can't refuse."

Diego frowned. "Money?" He scoffed. "And what of my revenge? I will not stop until my men's deaths are avenged."

"I understand completely. Here's what I have in mind," I stated and then went into meticulous detail about how I believed my plan would play out.

Once I'd gone over the finer details of my plan, Diego's nostrils flared, his black eyes lighting with a gleaming, wild fire as he rubbed his hands together.

"I didn't think you had it in you, Castellanos. Mad respect, *hermano*." He clapped me on the back. "After this, you and me, we are *hermanos de sangre* for life."

Hermanos de sangre.

Blood brothers.

That was not something I was prepared to wrap my mind around at that moment. Instead, I lifted the phone and pressed the button to call "The Devil" himself.

Aiden answered on the first ring. "Faith? Is that you?" The bastard was so damn predictable when it came to my woman.

"It's Castellanos. I want to meet."

Episode 77

Will You Marry Me?

OPAL

"Opal Dawson, will you marry me?" Noah asked point blank, surprising the dickens out of me.

I blinked wordlessly for several seconds, the humidity so thick in the car, moisture was beading and fogging up the windows.

"I can't believe I'm even considering this," I huffed, clenching my teeth together as everything he shared swirled around in a loop within my mind.

If I married Noah Pennington, I'd get six million dollars. He said I could continue my education and let my sister off the hook. The marriage would only have to be for three years, and it wasn't like I had anyone waiting for me back home. He'd give me the same deposit my sister had received and the first two million after the wedding. Meaning I could immediately use that money to set Ruby up in a place near the school. She could go back to sculpting, take college courses, work a regular normal job…anything she wanted. And it would be *me*, her baby sister providing it. Not Ruby taking the hit like she always did.

Finally, I would be able to pay her back for all the sacrifices she'd made throughout the years to ensure my safety and success. My skin rose with gooseflesh as I weighed the pros.

More importantly, what would be the cons?

Marrying a man who was essentially a stranger. Being tied to said stranger for a period of three years. Living with a man I could hardly manage to talk to for ten minutes at a time without getting into an argument. Sharing a bed with said man like a normal wife would be expected to.

What if he didn't like what he saw once he unwrapped the package? I'd not been with a man before. I had zero sexual experience. Ruby had made sure of that since we were children. And after seeing what my sister went through, being passed around to all of our fake "daddies" by my whore of a mother, I never wanted to have sex. I planned to live my life one hundred percent celibate.

Before I could finish going through my concerns internally, Noah broke my concentration by rolling down the window. Instantly, a burst of cool air entered the car, making it far easier to catch my breath.

"Thank you. It was getting pretty stuffy," I noted.

"The more I think about this idea, Opal, the more I like it." He tapped his long fingers on the steering wheel. "You're young, smart, and just starting out your life." He frowned suddenly. "Actually, how old are you?"

That had me chuckling out loud. He didn't even know my age. Boy, was he going to regret his offer when he found out. "Nineteen."

"Bloody hell. You look twenty-five." He shoved a hand through the longer dark layers on top of his head.

"I'll be twenty in a week. You're what? Twenty-six?"

He nodded.

"Not that far apart in the grand scheme of things. Besides, I'm of legal age and probably a lot further along in maturity than most of the gold-digging bimbos you usually date."

"You're barely legal," he grunted. "And I do not date gold diggers because I don't actually take women out more than once. Women tend to get ideas in their heads about marriage and children if I ask them out a second time."

I rolled my eyes. He was such a prick. "If you're changing your mind, feel free to start the car and take my happy ass to Cambridge. No skin off my teeth one way or the other."

He shook his head. "Exactly why you're the perfect person to marry." He beamed. "You're honest. You don't pretend you want me for any reason other than my money. A very specific amount of my money." A deep laugh left his lungs as he rested his back against the seat, turning only his head to face me. "In this scenario, I'm the one paying for you, so that I can score the additional interest in my family's holdings, which will doubtless make me far richer than the six million I'll be spending."

"You have a weird thought process," I stated dryly, not holding anything back. If this man wanted me as his wife, he was going to get the real me. And the real me held no punches. I struck first and apologized later.

"Be that as it may, I still think this is a great idea. Nile will never see it coming. It's genius, I tell you. I can almost see the anger on his pretty boy face when he finds out that I scored one over on him. And with something this huge?" He chuckled. "Brilliant. Bloody brilliant. You must marry me, Opal." Noah shifted to the side and gave a boyish smile, all big eyes and white teeth.

"For the record, you have the exact same 'pretty boy' face as your brother. Think on that before you use it next time as a barb. Doesn't really hold the same weight when you share a face."

He chuckled. "Duly noted, love."

"I just, I don't know. Usually I run these things by Ruby. Maybe that's the best plan…"

He shook his head. "Absolutely not. If you tell her, she'll tell Nile, and we'll be done for. He'll whisk Ruby off to the chapel without a moment's notice. I think you're seriously underestimating the importance of my brother being the top of the heap in our family's holdings. It's a pride thing."

"And how is it any different for you? You're willing to marry the sister of the woman you had planned on marrying just to one-up your brother. It's unbelievably childish."

He waggled his eyebrows. "And yet, you're considering the offer. I can see the wheels turning behind those gorgeous eyes of yours."

"What did I say about flattery?" I cocked a brow. "You are barking up the wrong tree there, buddy. You do not have to woo me into this. Not that I'd believe you were interested in me for anything other than a finger to put a ring on to get what you want."

"But..." He grinned in that charming way that made my cheeks feel hot, once more waiting for me to continue.

"If, and I mean *if*, I agree to marry you, we're going to have to work out some serious parameters," I noted.

"Such as?" he asked gamely.

I chewed on the side of my cheek. "Such as where are we going to live? I can't stay in that house with my sister and your brother or that grouchy Ms. Bancroft for much longer."

He shrugged. "We'll move out. Easy."

"And what about school?"

"I told you that I wouldn't take that away. I'm a man of my word, Opal. You'll find that out soon enough as my wife. Whatever I commit to, I complete."

"What I mean to say is, if I go to Cambridge, isn't that going to be far from where your business is?"

He paused and tapped his lips. "This is true. Cambridge is an hour and a half from London. I wouldn't want you driving all the way there and back each day. Would you be open to attending university in London?"

"London would be better for Ruby too, I imagine." I frowned, the goal of Cambridge slipping away from me by the moment. Mentally I slapped myself, ashamed of my selfishness. Ruby had given up everything she'd ever wanted, needed, and hoped for in order to give me a good life. I owed her far more than I could ever repay.

Bits and pieces of our disgusting childhood flashed before my eyes. The parade of men our mother would allow to come to our trailer. The times where she'd offer one of her daughters up for "play time" in order to make rent that month. Ruby had protected me then too. Allowing herself to be abused over and over so that I wouldn't be.

I'd do anything for her.

Anything.

Sweat pricked at my hairline, and a sour taste entered my mouth as the memories started to swirl and coalesce into other times where I'd come home from school to find my mother with one or two of her johns. One man would be pounding away at her from behind, the other going at her mouth, right in the middle of the living room. I was seven, Ruby was nine.

Even then, Ruby was smart enough to sneak us out of the trailer, her hand clenching mine. I'd dutifully follow her. She'd find a shady spot under an old tree near our trailer park, and together we'd sit and do our homework. That was when she'd tell me that it was up to me to get good grades and keep my head down so that no one paid me any attention.

"Opal-Loo, you're going to be the best of us both. Already you're better at my homework than I am. That means you're super smart." She tapped my forehead lightly. "Use your brain to learn all that you can, and one day, all of this will be gone, and we can live together in a big skyscraper house in the sky. Like in the movies. You want that, don't you?" she asked. "To get away from here, from Momma and those scary men?"

I nodded with big eyes, my sister's words my entire world.

"Okay then. Keep your head down and don't bother no one. Don't make eye contact if you don't have to. Be respectful always to your teachers. Do your homework and pay close attention in school. Read all the books you can get your hands on, and you'll be the smartest girl in the whole

school in no time at all. I believe in you, Opal."

"But Momma always rips up my books."

"Then we'll hide 'em. We'll dig a hole and put all of our treasures right here, in a box for safe keepin' under this tree, where no one could find 'em. What do you think about that? It will be our secret. Me and you."

I could feel a tear slip down my heated cheek as the memory started to fade.

"Hey, hey… What's the matter?" Noah's soft hand cupped my cheek, and he wiped the tears away with his thumb. His eyebrows were knitted with worry.

I shook my head. "Just thinking about, ya know…everything you've said," I lied.

"And it made you cry?" He cocked his head to one side, his hand still holding my face. "You know, if you married me, it wouldn't just be you and Ruby anymore. You'd have me to confide in too."

I scoffed. "Is that right?"

He frowned. "That's right. Why don't you tell me right now who hurt you? I'll destroy them."

I burst into an uncomfortable forced laughter, the sound echoing off the small space seeming much louder in the car. My past was not a path I was willing to go down with him right now. Probably not ever. Marriage aside. What happened between me and my sister and how we were raised wasn't up for discussion. Most of the time it was buried in Pandora's box under that same tree Ruby and I used to dream under. Once in a while, something would jog the old wounds and bring them to the surface, but now was not the time to let those demons run free. Nothing good would come of it.

"What are you, my therapist now? I thought you wanted to be my husband?" I wiped at my eyes and pushed farther into my seat, needing a little distance from the man.

He stiffened in his seat and rubbed his hands over his face. "Okay, we've discussed school and where we'll live. London being the primary location for both. I can make those things happen quickly. What other issues are you concerned about?"

"What will I be expected to do as your wife?" The question came out sounding rather vulnerable, and I hated it. Showing my fears wasn't something I liked doing in front of anyone.

He opened his mouth and then closed it before repeating it again, very much looking like a fish out of water. "Honestly, I don't know. I've never been married or in a long-term committed relationship before."

"Come on, you have to have some idea. Ruby said she'd be going to business events, traveling with Nile, attending charity events, things like that."

He scrunched up his nose. "I don't normally spend a lot of time attending such events the way my brother does."

"Figures. You want to be the head of your family's company, but you don't want to do any of the responsibilities that are normally required of a person in that position?"

"I didn't say I didn't want to. I just never have. Maybe I could use someone like you, or my *wife*"—he put emphasis on the word *wife*—"in order to help me navigate some of the more community-related things. Would that be something you'd like to do?"

"I mean, charity functions sound worthy of your time. And I love art and museums. Fancy events tend to happen in those types of places, so I wouldn't be opposed to hanging on your arm for that type of thing."

He nodded and smiled. "Okay, now we're getting somewhere."

"You are so eager," I accused.

"You have no idea," he deadpanned.

A little thrill of excitement skated down my back and settled at the base of my spine as he stared at me, a hint of interest in his dark gaze.

"Are you flirting with me?" I asked boldly.

"Is it working?" He grinned wickedly, blatantly turning on the charm.

I didn't want to admit it, but it was in fact working. My temperature was starting to rise, and arousal skittered through my nerve endings, making me feel twitchy. Which was also when I remembered there was a big fat elephant in the car that I hadn't taken into consideration through all of this.

I closed my eyes and took a deep breath. "Um, there's another problem we haven't exactly discussed. It's not usually something I share..." I swallowed down the embarrassment coating my throat.

"I'll solve any problem. Tackle any situation that gets in my way of achieving what it is I want. Just tell me what it is, and I'll handle it."

"I don't have much experience when it comes to relationships." I tried to start telling him the rest, but he interrupted me. Something I knew was going to be an ongoing issue between us if I agreed to marry him. The man was the most eager beaver I'd ever met. Like a brand-new puppy meeting his or her owner for the first time. All wagging tail and flapping lips.

Noah shrugged. "A non-issue. We'll work through anything day by day. Figure out how to be a married couple on the fly. No one really knows how a marriage is going to go even when they've been together for years. Really, it will be fine."

"You don't understand." I groaned, my cheeks becoming two hot burners of cherry-red skin, proving my complete and utter humiliation at what I hadn't yet shared with him.

He reached over and took my hand, covering it with both of his. "Trust me, poppet. Whatever reservations you have about a relationship with me, I can handle them. Most people think I'm easy to talk to because I don't judge others and am considered very open-minded, unlike my twin."

I shook my head. He had no idea.

"Tell me. Trust me. Whatever secret that's holding you back from agreeing to be my wife, I can handle it."

"I'm celibate," I blurted, the admission feeling like sour

lemons on my tongue.

He stared at me for what felt like a full thirty seconds but was probably only a few. That fish out of water mouth thing happened again before he finally said, "Ooookayyyy. Well, obviously that will have to change once we're married."

I ground down on my teeth and breathed through my nose. "Noah, I don't have much experience with men because I've never been with one. I'm not only celibate, I'm a virgin."

Episode 78

An Easy Out

SUTTON

"Get out of my way," I growled at Erik, the large Norwegian who stood a good two inches taller than my own six-foot size. The man with him was no slouch either.

"What's going on?" Erik asked.

An older couple stood a few feet away, the male holding the woman close.

"Sutton, think about this! You kill my father and I'll be visiting your ass in a penitentiary, not sitting on our porch talkin' 'bout our future," Dakota hollered.

Savannah wedged herself between the door and the two men. "Hey, big guy." She patted my chest right over where my heart was beating a mile a minute. "It's good to see you. Think we could go inside so you can update us on what's happening?" Savannah had an angelic appearance with her bright red hair and sky-blue eyes, but she had a softness to her that my Dakota didn't have. My wife was sexy angles, abrasive, and had a raw sensuality I couldn't get enough of. However, when I looked into Savannah's placating expression, I saw what she didn't want to show, her fear. A fear that a rotten, alcoholic, abusive bastard had imprinted not only in her, but in my wife.

I wouldn't have it any longer. Old man Everett's trail of abuse would end by my hand.

I ground my teeth so hard I thought I heard a molar crack in protest. My nostrils flared, and I shook my head, not ready to let go of the fact that I wanted to wrap my hands around Everett McAllister's neck the same way he did to my wife. The man had done abhorrent things to Dakota, and I was done. D-O-N-E. Trying to kill her horse. Burning down the barn. Nuh-uh. No way was I going to let any of that slide any longer. As her husband, it was my job to protect her.

"I'll say this one more time." I turned my head and sneered right into the Viking's rugged face. "Get. Out. Of. My. Way."

"Yes, Sherriff? This is Dakota Goodall. There has been a sighting of my father on the McAllister farm. Please hurry. Sutton is ready to tear his head off. Mmm hmm. Yeah, we'll see if we can. But Everett has a rifle and has already threatened the lives of two people." I heard my wife's voice in the background.

Good. She was calling in the cavalry. Didn't change the fact that I was going to put my fist through the man's face.

"Johansen, you're either with me or against me. McAllister already has a head start. This man beat up my wife. Spent years terrorizing both our women. You okay with that knowledge?"

Erik frowned, his gaze turning hard as I watched his lips twist into a snarl. As I suspected, he didn't like that thought one bit.

"I'm in," he said gruffly, and I smiled. Two large, imposing men were better than one. Especially with a pipsqueak of a drunk like McAllister.

"Me too. Any man that lays his hand on a woman deserves whatever he gets," said the dark-haired fella.

"No!" Dakota yelled. "You're supposed to be preventing this, not helping him!" she screeched, clearly distraught.

Which was when the older man eased his wife behind him

and stepped forward. "Henrik Johansen," he introduced himself. "If some man has been hurting Savannah and her sister, I want to help. I can keep watch here while you and my son check things out," he offered.

"Well, all right. Let's go." I nodded at Erik and his friend.

"*Attendez une minute*," came a loud, deep booming voice from behind me, speaking in French. Christophe, Madam Alana's husband, spoke. "*Monsieur* has a gun," he reminded us of that fact that her pa was armed.

I grinned maniacally. "Do either of you know how to shoot?" I asked the guys.

"Of course," Erik said. "Our home butts up against a natural forest. Wild animals can approach or attack at any time. We are all trained to shoot."

"Jack, by the way." The dark-haired man held out his hand, and I shook it. "Do you have any additional weapons? Not that we intend to use them, but I'd rather go into an uncertain situation protected."

"Fuck my life," Dakota groaned. "Savvy, speak some sense into them."

The voluptuous redhead shrugged. "I mean, it's three men against one little old man. And if it means at the very least catching and detaining him for the Sheriff…"

"He is a drunk who has a gun. He could shoot first and ask questions later," Dakota argued.

"Clock is ticking. Let me get some fire power," I grunted and then pushed my way back inside the house.

I headed to the office where I kept my gun safe. Dakota was right on my heels.

"Baby, don't put yourself in harm's way. Let the Sheriff deal with my pa. He's unhinged. Lord knows what he might do if he sees you and two additional strangers coming up the drive." She wrapped her arms around my waist from behind as I entered the code to my safe. "It's unwise," she complained.

The safe clicked open, and I pulled out my trusty shotgun

and two pistols. Dakota still clung to me, only this time she pressed her entire body to my back, her nose poking between my shoulder blades. "We just got to a good spot between us. I don't want to lose you now."

Hearing the quivering sound in her voice stopped me in my tracks. I set the guns on the desk. Then I turned around and cupped her cheeks.

Her eyes were wild and worried, her skin pale as snow.

"Darlin', I'm not going to do anything crazy. What I am going to do is remind him why he's in trouble with the law, and I'll keep him talking until the Sheriff arrives. I swear."

"But what if he shoots you?" she whispered, her voice cracking with the effort.

"He may be an asshole, but he's not that stupid. He's not going to go against me with two other men at my back. Stop worrying. I've stared down the face of worse and come out unscathed. I'm doing this whether you want me to or not." I dipped my head forward and took her sweet mouth in a hard and fast kiss. She tasted of coffee and syrup from this morning's pancakes. For a brief moment, I thought about spending a bit more time taking that tasty mouth for a longer ride but needed to get this over and done with. "I got this. Your father is a drain on society. It's time he gets the message firsthand that he is not welcome on McAllister land. Not now. Not ever again."

She clutched at my biceps, her nails digging in. "Technically he still has ownership. There's no way he will go easy."

I rubbed my thumb over her bottom pouty lip. Mmm, the things I wanted to do with that lip. I sighed and shook my head. "No, he won't. But it's my job to protect you, and this is me protecting my wife."

She closed her eyes. "I don't want you to get hurt. You're still healing from the barn burns…"

"Those were nothing. I got more intense rug burns on my knees when I rode your fine ass from behind the moment we got back last night."

"Jesus Christ!" She whacked my arm playfully. "Tell the whole world, why don't you?" Her feisty side came bursting forth. I loved taming my wife's attitude when she got riled. Most of the time with my fingers, tongue, and cock, but playtime was gonna have to wait.

I chuckled. "There's my sassy pants."

"I am not a sassy pants. Ugggh. You're infuriating!" she grouched.

"Yeah, yeah, but you love me." I kissed her quiet once more. "Push aside, baby. I need to deal with this."

"Fine. But if you get shot, don't be expecting *me*"—she pointed to her chest—"to be the one to take care of your ass. I warned you," she continued ranting.

God, I loved this woman. The fight in her did it for me in every way possible. I could feel my dick hardening behind my jeans already with the desire to bend her over my desk and pound her into kingdom come. Maybe then she'd quit her bitching.

With precise movements, I stuffed my pockets full of extra ammo and then shut the safe. I carried the weapons to the waiting men and passed them out. Which is when we heard the sickening sound of gunfire in the distance.

"Shit! We're too late. Let's go!"

Erik, Jack, and I piled into my truck. I sped up the drive that led to the McAllister house and was horrified at the sight that greeted us. Without thinking twice, I screeched to a stop and flung my body out of the truck, shotgun in hand pointed directly at McAllister himself.

"You got a death wish, boy!" McAllister yelled from where he stood holding not only a shotgun in one hand, but a pistol in the other. Before him were two of Dakota's farmhands on their knees, hands behind their heads. A third man was curled on his side, his arms wrapped around his gut that was bleeding all over the ground, staining the dirt a reddish-brown sludge.

McAllister had a pistol pointed right at Jarod's forehead, a rifle clutched to his side. "Admit what you did, or I'll shoot!" he demanded of the man.

The man who had been shot was one of mine. Brody Hardin. A good guy that I'd lent to Dakota to help in the aftermath of the damage from the fire. He had a wife and two kids back home.

Anger the same as when I'd found him beating on my wife oozed over my skin like a balmy coating of white-hot fire. I saw red. Without even thinking twice, I ran up on old man McAllister as though I were a linebacker in high school again.

"Watch out!" I hollered at Jarod.

McAllister turned to look at me right as I plowed into him. The gun went off, but I was pretty sure the young man shifted at the last minute.

"Get up, get up, get up!" someone yelled at the men as I trampled McAllister.

"I've got him," another accented voice cried, which I hoped meant Erik and Jack were helping Brody and Jarod.

I tussled with Everett, the wily old coot. The gun went off again, but it shot behind us at ground level, not getting anywhere near my body. With all my might, I rolled us until I was on top. I no longer had my gun but was fighting with him to gain a hold of the pistol. He'd dropped his rifle when I slammed into him but kept a tight grip on the handgun.

Pretty soon, everything was a blur.

I acted on instinct alone as I clung to the wrist that held the pistol and pounded my fist into Everett's gut. He twisted his wrist just enough that the gun waved in the air as I held on. He shot it rapid-fire over his head until the barrel was empty and all I could hear was the *click, click, click*.

With the gun empty, I finally got my chance to destroy this motherfucker once and for all. I had him pinned exactly where I wanted him, with my hands to his shoulders, my weight holding him in place.

Everett McAllister looked at me with such hatred I'd remember that look for the rest of my life. Knowing beyond a shadow of doubt that it was the same way he stared at my wife and her sister. Disgust and disdain. The same reason his own wife committed suicide to rid herself of the demon she couldn't escape.

"You're pure evil," I fumed, staring the demon right in the eyes.

He didn't scare me. The only thing that scared me anymore was the thought of losing Dakota and the future we were building. This man was the only thing stopping us from having the life we'd earned.

"You deserve to die," I snarled, wanting to end his miserable life right there and then.

He grinned around bloody, broken teeth. "And if you kill me, you think Dakota will forgive you? You kill me, you lose her," he sneered.

"Wrong. I kill you, she breathes easy for the rest of her life. A life she'll spend with *me*. Happy. Loved. Cherished. Having my babies. Growing old sitting on the porch of a house I built just for us."

"Do it, I dare you," he taunted, lifting his chin, his eyes gleaming with revolting excitement at the mere idea that if I took his life, I'd be ruined.

It would be too easy.

For a long time, I held him down and stared at the miserable old man. He had nothing. No one to love him. No one to care about. He was alone. Death would be too good for him. An easy out.

That's when I smiled wide. "Not today, asshole. I think prison will teach you all about consequences and retribution." Then I pulled my fist back and punched him so hard in the face, blood flew out his mouth as his jaw went to the side with the power of my hit.

He was out like a light.

I stood up and then kicked the piece of shit in the ribs for good measure, hoping I broke a couple in the process. "That's for Dakota, you miserable piece of shit."

As I turned around, I saw the Sheriff's lights flashing as his truck came barreling down the drive. Behind him was an ambulance, thank the good Lord.

Jarod was lying on the ground, Jack pressing a wadded sweater he must have been wearing to the side of the man's head.

Brody had been moved, a huge pool of blood marking where he'd been when we arrived. I spun around to see that Erik was tending to Brody, pressing what looked like his own shirt to Brody's bleeding stomach. Already I could tell it was bad. Thankfully they'd got him out of the way of the flying bullets and set him up in the bed of my truck, which had bright red blood pooling around his body, getting bigger by the second.

The paramedics raced out of their vehicle and went straight to Brody. The female medical professional headed over to Jarod. Jack pulled back the cloth, and the paramedic assessed the wound, then asked him to keep holding it to his head.

"It's a graze," she called out. "Focus goes to the gunshot wound," she clarified and then made her way back to Brody.

As they were getting Brody on a stretcher, Dakota and my mother and father drove up in his truck. They'd likely heard the commotion and saw the Sheriff's car and the ambulance, deciding to come check on things.

Dakota jumped out of the vehicle and raced over to me. She plowed against my body, hers trembling like a leaf in the middle of a storm.

"I heard all those gunshots, and I just knew it was bad. Were you hit?" She gulped, her eyes tracking down my body.

I gripped her by the shoulders. "I'm fine. Brody is hurt bad. Gunshot to the abdomen. Jarod too. Gunshot graze to the head."

"Oh my God." She gasped, her hand going over her mouth, eyes bulging as she took in the scene. "What happened?"

"Your father had the men lined up execution style. We intervened. I don't think he'll be bothering you for a very long time after today."

I watched as Jack helped Jarod up and supported him at the waist, the younger man's arms wrapped around his shoulders as he led him to the ambulance. There was some conversation about needing another ambulance, but in such a small, rural town, it would be faster if he shared it, which apparently was what they decided as I saw Jarod enter the back. Once he was in with Brody, the ambulance peeled out, lights flashing, horn blaring.

"Is Brody going to make it?" Dakota's voice sounded small and vulnerable.

I pulled her against my chest and held her close, watching as the Sheriff handcuffed her father then used some type of smelling salts to wake him up.

He sputtered to life, blood dribbling down his chin as he immediately started running his mouth. "He tried to kill me!" he claimed, head pointed in my direction. "Arrest him. Sutton and the other one attacked me," he wailed like a banshee.

No one was listening. The Sheriff had been updated as the men tended to Brody. He saw the blood on the ground, the damage McAllister had done. The information given by Jarod and Matthew, the other farmhand who had been held at gunpoint. There was no way he'd believe McAllister over me and several witnesses.

Everett McAllister was done.

Just as I was about to lift my woman's chin up so I could kiss her, she yanked out of my arms, fell to her knees, and vomited in the brush.

I came to her side, pulling back her hair. "It's okay. Get it all out."

She heaved a second time, relieving her stomach as I caressed up and down her spine.

"Blech. Ever since the fire, I've been feeling a little under the weather. It's like I can't get the taste of ash off my tongue." She closed her eyes.

"You've dealt with a lot. After today, it's all over, baby. Your father is going to jail for attempted murder, and that's hoping Brody survives. I need to call his wife and get to the hospital. I want to be there for him."

"Me too. But…"

"You have to get your family settled. You do that, and we'll talk more when I get home. Just pray he makes it."

"I will," she said softly, tears filling her eyes. "I'm sorry, Sutton. I'm so sorry I brought this to your life. You should have never bought me in The Marriage Auction. Your life would be so much easier if you hadn't," she choked out.

I rubbed at the back of her neck. "Dakota, don't you start that talk. The day I bought you was the best day of my life." I admitted the God's honest truth.

"Bought you?" My mother's voice rang out from ten paces away. "You bought Dakota in an auction? A marriage auction. What does that even mean?"

Episode 79

For Dear Life

SAVANNAH

I paced back and forth across Dakota and Sutton's front porch. My heart beat as fast as a hummingbird's wings in flight. We'd waited helplessly as we heard more gunshots crackling in the air. Had Erik been shot? My stomach sank, and my eyes filled with tears as I stared at the tree line, hoping for a glimpse of something, *anything*.

"My boy is smart. He won't put himself into the line of danger...not after he's found you. His safe space." Henrik, Erik's father, put his hand to my shoulder and squeezed. I could feel the support and his own uncertainty thick in the air surrounding us as we waited for news.

Was I Erik's safe space?

I wanted to be. I wanted to be everything to the kind, compassionate, gentle giant.

There had always been something special between us. Since the moment our gazes caught across a dark room during the most terrifying moment of my life, I could feel it. It was him that I clung to. Those kind eyes. Now that I knew him better and had experienced a taste of what we could have in the future, I was ravenous and eager to start our life together. It was why we'd come back. For me, the McAllister ranch was where it all started.

My beginning.

I wanted to take that next step, getting married, where I'd become the woman I was today. So that when I left, I'd officially start becoming the woman I was meant to be.

Sirens split the eerie minutes of silence after the last set of gunshots. I dropped my head, the relief at seeing the Sheriff's truck giving me a renewed sense of hope. Until I saw an ambulance following closely behind. A foreboding feeling slithered through my veins. An ambulance meant that someone had been hurt.

"Please, God," I prayed as the front door flew open and my sister shot out of the house.

"Fuck this. I'm not waiting any longer," she griped, and then took the stairs down the porch two at a time. Which was the same moment that another vehicle stopped on the dirt road coming from the main Goodall ranch. "I'll be right back," Dakota yelled as she ran full tilt to the Goodalls' truck.

"Wait for me!" I cried out and moved to chase after her, but both Henrik and Christophe stopped me, hands up and heads shaking.

"I promised my son we'd keep you safe, and I'm a man of my word." Henrik seemed crestfallen but prepared to follow through on his vow to Erik.

I glared. "What are you going to do? Restrain me?" I growled, anger fueling my response.

"If I have to, *datter*. Yes, I will." Not only did he call me daughter, which never ceased to make my insides feel squishy, he also said it with a hint of grit in his tone. He would absolutely follow through on restraining me if he had to.

I slumped where I stood, putting my hands on the white fence surrounding the porch to hold myself up. My long red hair fell in a blanket around my jawline, hiding my tears as they ran down my face.

Irene wrapped an arm around me and led me to one of the chairs, getting me settled. I swiped at my cheeks, irritated that I couldn't hold back the waterworks.

"What if he's been shot?" I gulped, my chest reverberating with the effort to hold off the sobs that were clawing up my throat, desperate to get out.

Irene held my hand. "We don't know what's happened. We must have faith that Erik, Jack, and your sister's husband are well." She patted the top of our clenched hands. "I would know if my son was hurt."

I swallowed down more tears. "Did you know when he got in the helicopter accident?" I whispered.

She nodded once, almost curtly. "I knew that something was wrong. My heart ached." She moved her hand to her chest and rubbed. "There was a pain that wouldn't go away for hours and hours. Then we got the call he'd been in an accident."

I clung to that bit of superstition. "And you don't feel it now?"

She shook her head. "I do not."

And so, we waited.

Another thirty minutes came and went, along with the ambulance. I watched with dread as it rolled right down the street adjacent to our land. A few additional patrol cars drove onto my family's property, and it took everything I had to not jump over the fence and race across the land. If my feet had been capable of holding me up, I would have. The worry was so intense that I felt glued to the chair, staring at those damn trees, waiting for news of any kind.

Eventually, my dream came true.

One truck slowly made its way up the drive. I counted the bodies in the front and back, my entire system flooded with relief seeing the same number that had left return, sans Sutton's truck.

Erik swung a long, muscular leg over the truck bed and jumped out the back. The second his hiking boots hit the ground, I sprinted into action.

I nearly pushed his parents aside like they were pins being struck by a bowling ball. Apparently, I knocked into Christophe so hard he almost fell over the porch railing. I took the stairs so quickly I ended up leaping at the end.

I only remembered the second Erik's gaze hit mine.

Beauty. Relief. Peace.

My entire form felt like butterfly wings were skating across the surface of my skin. Dirt circled in the air as I bolted across the drive. When I was close enough, he opened his arms, and I sailed through the air, my body crashing into him. He lifted me off the ground, and I wrapped my legs around his waist, my arms to his neck. Then I kissed him. Harder than I had before. Our tongues tangled, and our breath intermingled while we devoured one another. I never wanted this feeling to end.

He tasted like a salt-soaked day at the beach. Smelled of sweat, hay, and dirt. His hands clung to my body as though he'd never let me go.

There was only one word that could describe the experience...divine.

"Jesus, Savvy, get off your man. We need to talk." My sister's voice entered our reunion, and for a moment I wanted to ignore it, happy to just be in Erik's arms and tasting his kiss. He was alive and whole. Unharmed. For the last hour and a half, a part of me had believed that he'd been hurt, and I could have lost all that I'd gained this month. All of this meant I wasn't eager to let go of my Viking. Few would argue with me if they had this hunky male specimen as devoted to them as Erik was to me.

I gave Erik one last peck and let my legs fall from around his waist.

"I'm glad you are happy to see me, *elskede*. I very much enjoyed this homecoming." He grinned wickedly, his hand squeezing my ample bottom with both hands.

I needed to fuck this man. Truly become one with him. As soon as possible.

"Come, we have much to discuss. Not all of it good, I'm afraid," he shared.

He led me back up the porch and into the house where everyone was congregating. For the next twenty minutes, Dakota and Sutton updated us on what had happened. It seemed that my father had shot Brody, then held two additional men at gunpoint. When the guys rolled up on the scene, he had them kneeling execution style, which was when Sutton intervened.

"I don't understand," I complained. "Our pa is a lot of things—an abuser, a gambler, a drunk, and an all-around bad human—but he's never shot anyone before. Not to my knowledge. And he was shooting with a pistol? Where did he get it?" I asked, genuinely surprised at that information.

We owned a couple rifles and shotguns that we kept in a gun safe back at the ranch, but never any pistols.

"Who knows?" Sutton sighed deeply. "All I do know is I have to get to the hospital and make some calls to Brody's kin."

This was the moment that Dakota came over to Erik and me on the love seat. She kneeled next to me on the floor and took both of my hands. "Savvy, honey, there's more. And this is the part that's going to be really hard to hear. Okay?" she warned.

I frowned, and Erik tightened his hold around my back.

Dakota swallowed, her eyes going to Sutton and then Erik

and back to me as though she was stalling.

"What is it? You're scaring me." My voice shook as I held her hands, gripping as though my life depended on it.

"The, um, the other man that pa held at gunpoint and shot, honey…" She licked her lips. "It was Jarod."

Jarod.

My high school sweetheart. The boy I lost my virginity to. The person I'd thought I'd marry. The man I'd left behind not long ago to enter The Marriage Auction. The one I'd believed was the love of my life.

It took a moment for those words to sink in and my brain to assemble them into something that I could understand.

"My Jarod!" I hissed and felt the arm around me loosen and fall away.

I stood abruptly, Dakota falling to her bum in response.

"I need to go to the hospital. Right now," I demanded.

Dakota stood and tried to take my hands again.

I lifted mine up, keeping a two-foot distance between us. "No. I don't want to hear it. I want to see Jarod. Right now," I insisted like a petulant child.

My father, the man who had given me life, tried to kill a man I'd loved at point blank range. I couldn't even comprehend or explain the level of devastation and bone-crushing guilt that came over me.

"I'll take you," Erik spoke, his handsome, rugged face showing concern and empathy.

I closed my eyes, not able to look into his. Just hearing the beautiful lilt in his Norwegian accent made my chest tighten and my heart feel as though it was breaking wide open. He was such a good man.

"You don't have to do that. I know with our history, it seems weird…" I shook my head and swallowed down the vile sludge that coated my throat, not sure how to best explain what I was feeling.

"Whatever you need, it is for me to provide. Let us go." He

held his hand out, palm up. I placed mine within it and held on for dear life.

Sutton drove his parents' truck as his was apparently considered evidence, for reasons I didn't ask to clarify. Mostly I stayed silent as he drove, parked, and led the three of us through the doors of the small hospital.

The moment we entered the lobby, I heard my name called in a high-pitched wail I'd have known anywhere.

"Savannah!" Jarod's mother left a group she'd been hugging—Jarod's father, brother, and sister. "Oh my word, Savannah, dearie." Mrs. Talley plowed into me.

I hugged the round woman, finding comfort in her caramel scent. Jarod's mother baked incessantly, which accounted for her fuller figure and the smell of sweets that clung to her skin. She'd always treated me as part of the family and did her best to host me and my sister for many dinners once Jarod and I became an item in high school. The entire town knew my father was a bad man, but oftentimes in small towns, you simply looked the other way and did what you could to help in whatever capacity you were able. Feeding me and my sister and bringing us endless treats had been hers.

"You must be beside yourself," she gushed as she pulled back and patted the side of her dark hair, now infused with a few more gray streaks than the last time I'd seen her.

It was nice to know she didn't carry any ill will toward me. I'd worried on the car ride over that Jarod's family might not take too kindly to me after I'd broken off my engagement to their son. They'd waited years for us to tie the knot and had made it very clear how excited they were when we became officially engaged.

"I'm definitely concerned. Have you heard anything?" I asked.

"Oh, yes. The doctor updated us a few minutes before you got here. Not to worry, dearie, our Jarod is going to be just fine. He's going to have a nasty scar from the bullet graze, but once he's stitched up, the doctor told me he'll be right as rain in no time." She put her hand over her heart. "Thank the good Lord about that. We'll have to make sure he's all healed up and looking mighty fine again for the wedding."

She expected to be invited to my wedding? I found that incredibly odd, and far beyond any kindness I'd ever expected from her.

A lightness entered my chest, the severity of the situation lifting a bit at hearing Jarod would be okay.

"It's excellent news that Jarod's going to be okay." I let out a happy little sigh as I felt Erik's body hovering just behind me, a silent but fierce support if there ever was one.

Yes. I definitely needed to fuck the holy hell out of this man.

I leaned back, and Erik's hand curled around my hip. "Do you need anything, *elskede*?" he murmured close to my ear from where he stood behind me.

Mrs. Talley frowned, looking at the hand Erik had on my hip and the closeness of our bodies, not to mention the way Erik invaded my personal space.

"I'm sorry, Savannah, dear. You haven't introduced me to your *friend*." She batted her eyes and then smiled stiffly. "Clarice Talley, Jarod's momma," she introduced herself.

Erik eased me to his side and reached out a hand. "Erik Johansen, Savannah's fiancé," he offered politely.

Mrs. Talley stepped back, her eyes widening. She looked at his hand as though it were a live rattlesnake ready to strike. "Your fi-fi…" She shook her head several times, clearly gobsmacked. "Your fiancé!" She put her hands to her hips, and her expression twisted into one of disgust. "What in the world are you talkin' about?"

"I'm sorry, ma'am. I'm not sure I understand what the problem is." Erik let his hand drop back to his side.

"Savannah, you need to quit playin'. This here is no time for games. We are in a hospital, dear. Please set this man straight, right here, right now, before I lose all the good sense the good Lord gave me." She continued prattling on, volume rising with each huff of her breath.

"Mrs. Talley, what joke or game do you think I'm playing?" I wrapped my arm around Erik's large frame at the waist and tucked myself to his side, needing his support and comfort.

Her hand pointed left and right accusingly between Erik and me, her eyes wild, her cheeks turning bright red. Then suddenly she reached for my wrist and yanked me out of Erik's arms and over to stand next to her.

"This here is my son Jarod's *fiancée*, not yours. And he will not take too kindly to his future wife being held like this out in public for all to see. Sweet baby Jesus! What in the world are you thinking, Savannah?"

She thought Jarod and I were still together.

My heart split right in half.

Episode 80

Keep You Safe

FAITH

"*Gracias.*" Hector, one of Diego's men, thanked me as I finished cleaning and bandaging a nasty cut on his cheekbone.

"You're welcome." I smiled wanly and glanced at the clock across the room. It had been over three hours since Joel had left with Diego. Since then, I'd pitched in where I could, but my lower back was screaming from bending over to help wounded men, and my stomach was growling. We'd forgone breakfast on the plane because I'd been in no shape to eat. Then we'd come down here to see my father and skipped lunch. It was nearing late afternoon, and my belly was protesting.

I patted Hector on the shoulder and scanned the room. Most of the men we'd tended to had already left. There were only a few remaining that seemed to need most, if not all, of the attending doctors' attention. At some point, Dr. Marbury had come to relieve his peers. Even I could see he needed rest after what had likely been a shocking and intense morning.

"Dad, I'm going to go find Joel and see about getting food for the rest of us."

My father put his hand over his rounded stomach. "Great idea, *cara mia*. Let me know when you're ready to leave, and I'll go with you."

I left the conference room and started my search by checking the medical office first. Bruno was there, sleeping soundly. Silently, I glanced around the open surfaces of the room, looking for my purse, which Joel had said he would place here for safe keeping. I didn't see it anywhere, but I wasn't about to go snooping through cabinets and drawers and possibly wake Bruno. He needed his rest after being wounded while saving my father's life. I chose not to disturb him and left quietly.

Where was Joel? If I'd had my purse and phone, I would have given him a call, but I didn't know where either were. The only thing I could do now was go back to the penthouse and see if he was there. Checking on the girls was also high on my list, so I headed down a hallway, following a sign that led to the elevators. Before I found the elevators, I heard the unmistakable tone of Diego's raised voice.

I slowly approached the door, which was open about two inches. I saw Joel standing hunched over a conference table pointing down at something that looked like a map.

"We go in here." He pointed at the paper, then shook his head. "Aiden chose well for our meeting. There are only two entrances and exits. I propose that I go in first. Get the man to see reason. Offer him the money and travel information to get out of the country."

"And what of my revenge? You expect me to let him slither away like a *vibora*?"

I tried to remember what that word meant from high school Spanish. I believed it meant snake.

"I expect you to work with me, not against me, Diego. I am meeting this cretin in just over forty-eight hours. I'm going to give him money and a way out of the country in order to get this demon out of my fiancée's life for good. Whatever you do with him after he leaves is up to you. That's the deal. I want no part of your revenge."

Diego squinted, and his face turned hard. "You are on a fool's mission, *hermano*. Bradford will not let you leave the meeting. He will take your money and shoot you between the eyes where you stand," Diego spat, his upper lip raised in a snarl.

I pressed my back against the wall close to the door, my heart beating wildly as sweat misted my hairline and my armpits dampened. My entire body started to tremble with the knowledge that Joel was going to meet with Aiden and offer him a way out of Las Vegas, the country, and most important, my life. I closed my eyes and tried to calm the terror flooding my veins. Aiden didn't let go of something he wanted. Not only was he the most reckless man I'd ever known, he had no moral compass. And nothing scared him.

Aiden would consider Joel the reason all of this was happening. The man standing between him and his prize. The only way to save Joel was to give Aiden what he wanted more than anything. More than his freedom.

Me.

Tears filled my eyes as I continued to listen.

"I'm not ignorant, Diego. This is why we're going through every detail of the mission. My team is beyond skilled. They will be in position with their rifles should the need arise. I've thought of nothing but this plan..." Joel's tone was direct and confident.

It wouldn't be enough. No man was more conniving and malicious than Aiden. He'd kill Joel the second he had a chance.

I wouldn't let it happen. Not while I lived and breathed.

He had forty-eight hours until he met with Aiden. That meant I had less than that to save the man I loved and to protect Eden.

Nothing mattered more than keeping them safe.

Not even my freedom.

I formed my own plan. I knew exactly what I had to do.

I pushed through the door. "There you are!" I smiled warmly, pretending I hadn't heard anything they'd discussed.

Joel eased in front of the papers he had spread on the table, then reached for my bag. My phone was suspiciously not inside the purse but lying on the table. He grabbed both and handed them to me. "How are you, darling?" Joel asked.

"Famished. The doctors have a handle on the remaining injured men. I'd like to go check on the girls and see about an early dinner."

Joel folded up the papers on the table and tucked them under one arm. "Of course. It has been ages since we've had a meal. Diego, we will discuss this further tomorrow. Yes?"

Diego grunted and nodded before heading to the door. He stopped next to me and put a hand on the ball of my shoulder. "One way or another, we will make you safe." He gifted me a small, flat smile. "*Mañana,*" he said with a flick of his hand in the air as he exited.

"What's tomorrow?" I asked, knowing that Joel was about to lie to me.

He shook his head, curled his arm around my waist, and kissed my cheek. "It matters not. Let us go eat."

After an early dinner, the jet lag hit hard, and everyone went to bed early, but I knew I had to initiate the beginning of my own plan.

When Joel exited the bathroom, only a towel wrapped around his waist, my mouth went dry. I stood across the room in nothing but a short, form-fitting, pale-pink negligee. The satin so fine and thin you could see the outline of my areolas through the fabric.

Joel's gaze took me in as I stood backlit by the floor-to-ceiling window that looked out over the entire city of Las Vegas.

"You are a vision, Faith. My every dream come true." His tone was guttural, as though he could barely form the words through the jagged edges of unshed emotion.

I crooked a finger, gesturing for him to come to me.

He was a dog with a bone, eager to comply. I enjoyed the view as his beautiful, bare olive chest was on display. Muscles shifting and flexing delectably as he got closer.

When he stood in front of me, I pressed my hands to his pecs, glorying in the warmth of his body. I was always cold, never able to get warm. Joel was the opposite. A natural hot spring. Providing heat at all times.

Joel curled a finger around my chin and lifted my face up so that he could look into my eyes.

"You are unhappy," he rightfully surmised.

I nodded.

"Today was a hard day." The statement was gentle and knowing.

Once again, I nodded.

"How can I make it better?" His question was filled with compassion and the desire to ease my hurts, whatever they may have been.

I shrugged one shoulder.

He ran his thumb along my bottom lip so tenderly it brought tears to my eyes.

"What would make you happiest, my love? Make you feel most secure? Ask, and I shall give it freely."

This man was the best thing that had ever happened to me outside of Eden. I would remember this moment later, among all the memories he'd already given me in our short time together. I would live through them when I was being defiled by the devil. Something I knew would happen, assuming Aiden didn't kill me first.

"I'm afraid." I admitted the truth. Fear was driving my every move. Spearheading the plan I'd settled on outside of that conference room door while I listened to Joel, the man I loved, expect to walk right into the lion's den and come out unscathed. Diego was right. He'd never let Joel leave alive. I wouldn't let it happen. Still, I needed one more thing from Joel in order for everything to work out as I intended.

"Of Aiden?" he murmured, caressing my cheekbone instead of my lip.

"Yes, but more than that." I looked down and away momentarily, summoning the courage to do what needed to be done.

He frowned. "What is it that you need in order to feel safe?"

I swallowed and bit down on my bottom lip. "I want to get married. Tomorrow."

Joel cocked his head to the side. "I'm sorry?"

"If we get married tomorrow, no matter what happens to me, Eden will be protected. My father won't contest your involvement and co-guardianship. I'll make sure he understands that if anything happens to me, I want you to raise Eden alongside Penny."

He shook his head. "Darling, nothing is going to happen to you. I vow it on my own life." Joel tugged me to his chest, and I rested my head against his warmth. His heart was beating a welcoming rhythm I loved falling asleep to. This was my safe space. With my face pressed against his chest. Add in our bed back in Greece and our girls cuddling around us on a sleepy Sunday, and I was certain I could get no closer to Heaven on Earth.

"I want to be your wife. I want to know that Eden will always be with you. Will be raised with your love and protection her whole life long." I pressed my lips over his heart.

Joel wove his hands through my hair until he cupped my nape, using his thumbs to ease my jaw upward.

"You wish to be my wife. Here and now. In Las Vegas? The place that has brought you so much tragedy and hardship?"

I swallowed down the sting of truth in his words. "I need this, Joel."

"Tomorrow?" he clarified.

I smiled widely. "Tomorrow. We can go to a little drive-through chapel or one of the million chapels on the strip."

He scoffed and clenched his fists into my hair, forcing me to pay close attention to the fierceness in his gaze and the love so clearly pouring from his heart. He dipped his head, his lips hovering over mine. "We will wed tomorrow. Here at The Alexandra. We will be the first to use the rooftop arbor for such an event. I will ensure it is a memorable affair you won't soon forget."

"I love you, Joel. Thank you." I flicked my tongue against his bottom lip teasingly.

His hands left my hair and slid down the skin of my back until his fingers found the hem of the nightie. He scrunched the fabric in his hands and lifted it up and over my head, tossing it to the floor.

"Tomorrow I will make you my wife," he hummed, heat in his gaze as I stood before him, naked as the day I was born while he looked his fill.

My nipples tightened, and gooseflesh rose over my skin.

He slid his hands up my hips and ribcage and over the sides of my full, aching breasts to my shoulders, where he pushed with the smallest effort.

I stepped back until my shoulder blades and bum hit the cool glass of the window behind me. I pressed my palms flat against the surface, feeling a chill race through my entire body, arousal flooding my system.

Joel tugged at the knot holding the towel around his hips until it too fell to the floor. His cock was erect. Long, thick, and glossy at the tip with his desire.

I mewled at the sight, wanting to fall to my knees, take him in my mouth, and taste his need for me.

Like a puma ready to pounce, Joel stepped close, pressing his body against mine from chest to knees. The heat of his front warmed my chilled form the longer we stayed this way.

Then his hand shifted between us, and I spread my legs, eager for his touch. He teased my clit, swirling around the tiny bundle of nerves until I gasped, jerking my hips forward, wanting more.

"Baby," I whispered with pure want.

He slipped his fingers between my thighs and groaned, his face dipping to my neck. "You're so soft and wet for me. I haven't even kissed you, and you're ready to take my cock." He eased two fingers deep, and I lifted up onto my toes so I could force him deeper. I sighed at the blissful, erotic intrusion.

"Joel, I need you."

"I know," he rumbled against my skin. His lips and teeth trailed along my neck, where he licked and sucked, teasing me, making the glide of his fingers even easier.

I could hear the slick sounds his hand made as he fingered me slowly. I was dizzy with lust, with the yearning for release. I doubled my efforts, moving my hips frantically in a counter rhythm to his.

Right when I could feel the tension building to a crescendo, Joel abruptly removed his hand.

I didn't even have the time to complain about being close when he bent forward, wrapped his hands around my thighs, and lifted me up and against the window. I wrapped my legs around his waist, my hands looping his shoulders as he maneuvered me onto the wide head of his cock. With a powerful surge, he thrust deep.

I cried out, my orgasm flaring to life as he rocked his hips, pounding into me. I swore I could feel him in my abdomen as his length filled me over and over, taking me higher with each plunge.

"You are mine, Faith." He gripped my ass between my cheeks possessively, his fingers teasing the forbidden rosette that had never been breached until he slid just the tip of one finger inside.

I held on to his shoulders, digging my nails into his muscular flesh as this new sensation of double penetration sent me skyrocketing to release.

I cried out in delight as he fucked me against the window. He covered my mouth with his own, his free hand curled around my nape. I was pinned by his cock, his finger in my ass, and his mouth and tongue. Joel Castellanos was devouring me whole.

I was his to fuck. His to pleasure. His to love.

And he was mine.

I let go of everything invading my mind and spirit, giving up my body and soul to the only man I had ever truly loved.

He worshiped me right there, pinned to the glass like a rare piece of art crafted from pure love and devotion.

Joel was tireless in his lovemaking, making me come a second time before he roared his release, clinging to my body, his head pressed against my chest as the aftershocks overtook us both.

For long minutes, I clung to him, our bodies still connected as he came back to the present. He slipped from between my thighs but kept me aloft, bringing me to bed and laying me down with incredible care and gentleness, contrary to the way he'd ravaged me against the window.

He went to the bathroom and came back with a warm washcloth with which he cleaned between my thighs before discarding the cloth and tucking us both into bed.

I curled around him, resting my face against the perfect spot on his chest and flinging a leg over his thighs. One of his hands tunneled into my hair as it did every night, the other curving around my bare ass possessively.

"I will keep you safe. On my life, Faith. I will protect you," he vowed, his body easing tiredly into sleep.

I waited until his breathing was heavy and consistent and then murmured, "It is I who will keep you safe, Joel."

Step one of my plan was complete.

Tomorrow, we would get married.

Episode 81

A Dream Come True

NILE

"If you cross and recross your legs one more time, love, I can't be held responsible for us being late to our dinner reservation." I tilted my head, taking in the mile-long expanse of tanned, toned legs. I imagined them wrapped around my waist while I drove deep within my delectable fiancée. Alas, that particular activity would have to wait until after our night out.

Soon, I promised myself. Soon I'd have Ruby Dawson in a variety of ways.

Ruby's gaze flashed, and her lips twitched seductively as she nonchalantly gripped the hem of her short skirt, attempting to tug the fabric further down her shapely legs. It was an exercise in futility as the moment she let the shiny material go, it hiked right back up her thighs.

I took her hand, and she held on tight. As though she was concerned I might let go.

She needn't have worried. I wasn't ever planning on letting go of this woman. If things between us worked out as beautifully as I believed they could long term, perhaps I'd keep her. If she'd have me. Really, in the grand scheme of things, anything was possible. I'd learned very recently to expect the unexpected more often than not.

The mere existence of a woman such as Ruby Dawson, sitting at my side, ready to wed me in less than two weeks' time was proof enough that the unexpected could be a wonderful surprise. Unlike when my grandfather created the rather shocking rule that whichever Pennington brother married first would earn the additional percentage needed for a governing interest in our family's holdings.

My feathers were still a bit ruffled in that regard, but ultimately, I'd gain the interest and run the company as my grandfather and my parents had prior to their deaths.

Ruby leaned against my shoulder and sighed. "I'm really excited about tonight."

"I can see that. You've been fidgeting since we got in the limo. Is it excitement or nerves?"

She pursed her lips. "Maybe a little of both. It's our first *real* date. What if I embarrass you?"

"Not possible."

"Oh, it's possible and likely. I'm not exactly the most graceful woman. What if I accidentally spill an entire glass of red wine on you and ruin your suit?"

"Then I shall retire the suit. I have plenty of others at the ready. I even have an extra one in my overnight bag in the boot as we speak."

"The boot?" She frowned.

"Americans call it a trunk."

Her eyes widened. "Oh, right. I've heard that before."

I nodded. "What else has that beautiful mind of yours in a tizzy?"

She shrugged one shoulder. "Besides the fact that Opal and Noah were acting weird when they came home from checking out Cambridge? Her suddenly saying that she's not sure that it's the right university for her... I mean, what is that? She's always wanted to go to an elite university, and here you are, handing it to her on a silver platter, and she's reconsidering? I don't get it."

In all honesty, I had noticed something different about Noah. Opal's sudden desire to consider a college in London instead of Cambridge, particularly after the strings I'd pulled, did seem rather curious.

"Do you think Noah said something to her?" she asked.

"I couldn't say one way or the other, though I'm not sure it makes sense for him to be involved in a decision such as where your sister chooses to go to school. Why would she change her mind based on what a mere acquaintance might say to her?"

Ruby made an adorable huffing sound and snuggled closer to my side. "I guess you're right. But didn't you see how they seemed to be whispering to one another, conspiring about something?"

I chuckled and patted the top of our clasped hands. "Perhaps they've become friendly after the trip here from America, on top of the long ride to and from Cambridge. I guess one could consider that a lot of time to get to know someone. And right now, with Noah having lost your hand, he may be seeking a friend. Not to mention the harrowing situation your sister survived at the hands of your mother. Maybe she just wants to be closer to you. Cambridge is quite the jaunt. A full hour and a half away."

She moved her head from side to side as though weighing the relevancy of what I shared and possibly releasing any built-up tension in her neck.

"True. I guess I'm just a Nervous Nellie. It's been an incredibly long and stressful week. Let's forget about them and focus on us." She turned her body a bit in the leather seat in order to better see me face-to-face. "Starting with you telling me where we are going." Ruby used her hand to finger-walk across my chest, a sexy, teasing gesture that had my trousers fitting a bit tighter as the desire to kiss her thoroughly fueled my body's reaction.

I too shifted in my seat, pressing her chest to mine, our faces now only a couple of inches apart. She wore a complex perfume this evening that came with notes of honeysuckle and vanilla. It was so enticing I wanted to plant my nose against the tender spot where her shoulder and neck met and stay awhile, simply breathing her in. "And what do I get if I ruin the surprise?"

She grinned then licked her pouty lips. "Will a kiss do?" Her response held a breathy eagerness that spoke directly to the carnal, rather primal side of me. A side I specifically kept under wraps at all times. Grandfather had drilled into us the importance of being a man who was poised and in complete control at all times. Especially when a woman was involved. Respect and chivalry being the prevalent response in any situation.

I'd lived by this edict my entire life. Until I laid eyes on Ruby Dawson and everything changed.

The most rash thing I'd ever done was bid on a woman's hand in marriage. Our grandfather would roll over in his grave if he knew what his marriage stipulation had spearheaded between Noah and myself. And yet, sitting here with Ruby, her chest pressed to mine, her gorgeous face staring at me as though I were the handsomest man alive…I couldn't be anything but bloody chuffed at my position. I'd taken a huge risk, and it was paying off in more ways than one.

Could it be that Ruby was the one woman who could take my mind off work? Who I could find more enthralling than the art of building a musical score for a major motion picture? At the moment, with her scent filling my lungs and her blue eyes sparkling with lust, I realized everything about my future wife was an adventure.

I also really enjoyed watching her becoming more comfortable in my presence, almost bold in her actions. After she'd made her choice, one I was eternally grateful for, it was as if a switch had been flicked and the real Ruby was turned on. In more ways than one, if her rubbing her hands up and down my chest and abdomen was anything to go by.

For a moment, I stared at her flawless face, her beauty unmatched by any other woman I'd taken out or even remotely considered having a relationship with.

"A kiss is a good place to start," I teased.

Ruby smiled and then eased forward, her lips just barely touching mine in a featherlight caress.

"Oh, love, you're going to have to do far better than a scant peck in order to get the truth out of me," I admonished.

A saucy smirk adorned her lips. "Just making sure you were paying attention," she responded playfully.

"To you, always," I whispered before curling my hand around her nape and pressing my lips to hers. She opened immediately. A whimper escaped her as I ran my tongue along hers. Arousal tore through my body and settled hotly between my thighs. She gripped me behind the neck and rubbed her tits against my chest. I slid one hand up her side and boldly cupped one of them with my free hand, the other holding her in place as we devoured one another's mouths.

She moaned low in her throat and doubled her efforts.

We kissed as though we might be pulled apart at any moment. We clung to one another as though the magic swirling in the air between us might fade.

It didn't.

The heat and fervor only grew between us the longer we kissed. By the time she pulled back, we were both panting. My cock was hard as steel, tenting the fabric of my trousers in a graphic display of my virility.

Brazenly, Ruby cupped me over the material, and I groaned, tipping my head back against the leather seat. It felt so bloody good, I wished it would never end.

Her lips came to my neck, where she sucked and nibbled, spiraling my lust for her higher and higher, her hand a tool of extreme pleasure as she stroked me. I thrust my hips against her greedy hand several times before I could feel the need pouring through my nerve endings like a live wire ready to electrocute anyone who touched it. With extreme effort, I stilled her hand before we got too carried away.

"I want this," she murmured, cupping me with intent, her lips hovering just over my ear. "I want to unbutton your pants, shift my panties to the side, and ride this monster right here and now until we both come." Then she nipped at my earlobe, and I had to physically put my hands to her biceps in order to give us some space to cool down or I'd lose all decorum and let her do exactly as she desired.

I sighed deeply. "I want that more than just about anything, my love, but this is our first official date. We have all night and a very large bed awaiting us back at the estate. I'd rather take my time ravishing you properly when we make that final step in our joining."

"Ugh, why do you always have to make sense?" she grumbled. "At least tell me where we're going."

I took a deep breath and let it out slowly, continuing my efforts to calm my raging libido. I didn't want to get out of the car in my current state, and we were nearing our destination.

"We're going to Restaurant Gordon Ramsay," I announced. Instead of having the governess make our arrangements, I'd booked the restaurant myself. I'd done business with the chef many times over the years and knew I could secure a prime location that would surely please my fiancée, who I'd hoped had heard of the celebrity.

Ruby's eyes widened. "Are. You. Freakin'. Serious!" Her voice was suddenly high-pitched. Her body language went from shocked to dancing around in her seat with child-like joy. The innocence made her all the more beautiful.

"Gordon Ramsay is ah-maze-ing! He was the star of *Master Chef.* I've watched all nineteen seasons! Oh my God." She looked from left to right outside of the limo. "We're in London." She spoke something we both already knew but somehow had become very real to her in that moment. "Oh my God. Oh my God," she repeated with glee. "We're going to his first restaurant, aren't we?" She wildly started waving at her face, fanning herself.

The woman was coming undone right before my eyes.

"Calm down. My goodness, Ruby." I ran my hand along her arm. "He's only a man," I chuckled, figuring she must be enamored with Mr. Ramsay's extreme success and rugged appeal. "A much older man. Much too old for you," I added for reasons that couldn't be anything other than jealousy.

"He's not just a man. He's the best chef in the world! He's been awarded sixteen Michelin stars over his career. Now he currently holds seven of them," she gushed, clearly a knowledgeable fan.

"Hardly. He's a genius, I'll give you that, but I've eaten all over the world and have had plenty of incredible meals that were not crafted by Mr. Ramsay. Though I will agree to the man being talented."

She made a strangled sound in her throat as the car came to a stop in front of our destination. Frustrated that the light in Ruby's eyes that was moments ago for *me* was now lost, focused on another man, I exited the car without waiting for my driver to assist. Ruby eagerly popped out, taking my hand. Before I could move us forward, she gripped me by the wrist and cupped my jaw with her other hand, stopping me in my tracks. Which was when she kissed me hard and fast, but with exuberance.

"Thank you, Nile. This is already the best day of my life. Never in a million years did I ever think I'd eat in a Michelin-starred restaurant, but to do so at my favorite chef's flagship location, and with my handsome fiancé…" She shook her head and sniffed, then touched the corner of each eye that had become glassy. "It's a dream come true. An experience I'll never forget. In case I forget to tell you. Thank you for being the best thing that ever happened to me."

Pride filled my veins, and I lifted my chest, standing at my full height. Giving her something that meant so much to her made me feel seven feet tall.

"We shall have many more experiences together. Now that I know the joy it brings you, we'll make a list of all the things you never believed you'd do or see. Together we can mark them off one at a time."

Ruby looped her elbow with mine as she shook her head.

"I can't believe this is my life," she gushed, her gaze taking everything in, her body leaning against mine.

I, however, was looking only at her, my future wife. The most stunning and refreshing woman I'd ever met. "Get used to it, my darling." I planned on gifting her nothing but new experiences that would in turn ensure that it was me she gave that look and smile to through the duration of our contracted marriage.

Maybe even longer.

Episode 82

I Need You

DAKOTA

I woke to the sound of the shower in our master bath turning on. Shortly following it was the distinct noise of a belt buckle hitting the floor.

Sutton was finally home from the hospital.

I closed my eyes for a moment as my stomach tightened. He'd left for the hospital shortly after his mother overheard my admission about The Marriage Auction. The memory flooded my mind with what had occurred earlier today.

"I'm sorry, Sutton. I'm so sorry I brought this to your life. You should have never bought me in The Marriage Auction. Your life would be so much easier if you hadn't."

He'd rubbed the back of my neck, attempting to knead the building tension. "Dakota, don't you start that talk. The day I bought you was the best day of my life."

The way he'd said it, with such love and loyalty in his expression, melted my heart where I stood. I couldn't have loved him more than I did in that moment.

Until I heard the distinct timbre of his mother's voice from not far behind us.

"Bought you?" Linda's tone was not only breathy and shocked, but achingly filled with confusion. "You bought Dakota in an auction? A marriage auction. What does that even mean?"

Sutton curled an arm around my waist, holding me close.

"Ma, don't worry about it," he'd grumbled.

"Son, don't take that tone with me. Dakota just stated you bought her in some type of marriage auction. Is that like when you bid on a date at a charity event?" She pressed her hand over her chest, clearly concerned.

"Yeah, Ma. Somethin' like that. Don't worry about it," he'd added, his frustration rising with every minute that passed.

"Don't you tell me what I can and can't worry about. Brody is at the hospital dying from a gunshot wound he sustained on the McAllister land. Everett has been cuffed and taken to jail. I came over here to check on my daughter-in-law after seeing her tossing her cookies into the bushes, and now I hear you bought your wife in some type of game auction. What in the world is going on!" she screeched.

"Nuthin' for you to worry your head about. This is my business. Dakota is my wife. The love of my life. That's all you need to know. You hear?"

"Son…"

He'd shaken his head and lifted his hand. "I'll not hear another word about it, Ma. I'm taking Dakota back home so she can see to her sister and the rest of her extended family. Then I need to get to the hospital and talk to Brody's wife. What I will ask is that my mother, the good woman I know her to be, help me in that effort and not hinder the progress we've made."

Linda clamped her mouth shut. "This isn't over, son." Her gaze flicked to mine. "Dakota."

I kept my mouth shut. I'd already messed up by spewing the truth out in the open, but now was most certainly not the time to address how Sutton and I came to be married.

Eventually she let it go, switching gears into nurturing mother mode immediately, asking me how I was doing, why I'd been sick, and so forth. She made coffee when we got back to our home. Then after Sutton, Erik, and Savannah left to go to the hospital to check on Jarod and Brody, she helped me get Erik's parents settled into the main farmhouse and found a local hotel for Madam Alana and her husband. Eventually, she made us all soup and sandwiches for dinner and then took her leave when the moon was high in the sky.

I climbed out of bed and padded to the master bathroom. Steam had already filled the air and fogged the mirror completely.

Sutton stood naked with his head down, the water beating on his neck as he braced himself against the shower wall with both hands. He didn't even notice I'd entered the bathroom. He looked like a man who'd been beaten to hell by life. I worried that meant he'd lost his friend.

Silently, I slipped off his T-shirt I'd worn to bed and slid my panties down my legs, leaving them both in a pile on the tile floor. Then I eased the shower door open and stepped into the soothing warmth of the heated space. I closed the door and moved the few steps to wrap my arms around my husband from behind. Water slid down my chilled skin, making me feel toasty warm.

When I plastered myself to Sutton's bare, slick back, he inhaled fully and let out a long breath of air. It was as though he was letting go of one of the most horrid days he'd ever had.

"How's Brody?" I asked, my voice small and soft against the noise of the shower beating down over us both.

"Alive." He said the single word as though it was ripped straight from his chest.

I tightened my hold. "Jarod?"

"He'll be fine."

I nodded against his back and just held on, giving as much silent support as I could.

Sutton stood up straight, covering my hands where I held him with his own. Slowly, he took one of my hands and dragged it down from his pecs over his muscled abdomen, down his happy trail of hair, and straight to his hardening cock. He groaned when I curled my hand around the base of his erection.

"I need you, baby," he admitted. "I need you so fucking bad right now." His voice was hoarse and gritty, filled with anguish.

My husband needed to feel something besides the horror of the day, and I wanted to be the one he went to in order to wash away his pain and suffering.

"I'm right here. I'll always be right here." I stroked his length and swirled my thumb around the slippery tip.

His breath caught as he thrust his hips forward. Together, we set up a delicious rhythm. With my free hand, I touched him everywhere I could reach. His firm behind, the rock-hard indents of each abdominal muscle he'd cultivated to perfection with all his manual labor. I teased and lightly pinched his nipples until he was humping my fist wildly, lost to the sensations.

Just when I thought he'd finish in my hand, he abruptly turned around. His eyes were blazing with lust, his chest rising and falling. He looked like a Trojan hero of centuries past, standing naked, his massive golden body on display for my eyes only. His nostrils flared at the sight of my naked body while his gaze traced every inch of me. Water droplets dripped down from the tip of his erection, making my mouth water with the desire to fall to my knees and take him in my mouth.

"I want to lick you everywhere. Bite you until your skin bears my mark for days to come. Imprint you with my cock until you scream." He snarled and fisted his hands in a way that proved the extreme level of restraint he had on his need.

I didn't want him restrained.

I wanted him wild.

"Do it," I taunted. "Take what you need."

Without even a second passing, he cupped my hips and walked me backward until my knees hit the bench at the very back of the shower. I sat down, and he fell to his knees. A king about to worship at the foot of his queen.

"Open," he demanded.

I split my legs wide open, showing him everything. Giving him my body, my trust, and the power over my pleasure.

He would not disappoint.

Sutton slid his hands up my spread thighs and tugged me to the edge of the seat, then tipped my hips to the angle he wanted.

"Hold on, wife," he grated through his teeth, his composure slipping completely.

I gripped the edge of the bench with both hands, and his mouth descended.

He was voracious in his need. He gorged on my sex, sucking, nipping, fucking me as deeply as he could go with his tongue. His hands were plastered on each side of my thighs, forcing me to stay wide open as he ate.

I came in minutes.

He didn't stop there. Doubling his efforts, sucking harder, swirling his tongue around and around my clit until I tumbled over the edge again.

"More," he rumbled against my flesh while inserting two thick fingers deep inside. He found the spot that made me sing and manipulated it repeatedly.

The buildup of a third orgasm had me wrapping my legs around his shoulders. I tunneled the fingers of one hand into his hair and forced him harder over my sex, riding him until I was about to go off.

He licked me from anus to clit one last time and pulled away. Before I could complain, he'd slid me off the bench and onto his lap where he'd settled on the floor. Thankfully our shower was large enough for two, even taking into consideration his well over six-foot frame that was stretched out over the floor.

I hovered over his hips while he centered me exactly where he wanted. The wide head of his length notched against my slit, and I impaled myself, taking his length in one harsh, downward thrust.

"Fuck yes!" I cried out.

Sutton's hands curled around my hips almost to the point of pain. "Ride me," he barked. "Ride me hard, baby."

After two delicious mind-bending releases, there was nothing more I wanted than to give my man exactly what he needed. With ease, I used my knees and shins to lift up and slam back down over him. I repeated the process until he was powering up, his mighty hips and quads bucking like a bronco, piercing me so deeply that I screamed with every plunge.

Sutton abruptly sat up, his cock going so deep I arched back on autopilot, trying to get away from the intensity of his girth and width splitting me open. He shifted his hands, curving one around my nape, his mouth going straight for my breast. He sucked one so hard, I mewled like a baby kitten as pleasure ripped through my chest. He repeated the process on its twin.

"Perfect fucking tits." He sucked at each one, making his point. "Perfect fucking cunt." One of his hands came around to my ass, where he squeezed one cheek roughly and held on, grinding his length exactly where I needed it most. "Perfect fucking ass."

"Baby," I whimpered, the pleasure building so huge I wasn't sure I'd survive another release of this magnitude.

He took my mouth in a soul-searching kiss. Our tongues tangled and danced against one another as we moved as one. Each of us vying for dominance, but neither giving in.

Before long, his body started to tremble with the beginning of his release. As it came over him, he bit into my bottom lip. I hissed, pulling back as he plowed into me over and over, mindless in his pursuit. I saw stars, then arched deeply as he continued to pound into me ruthlessly. His mouth fell to my neck, where he sunk his teeth in sharp little nips flowing down my chest. Each one striking a new, beautiful chord to fall from my lips.

And still, I needed more. A little more of something and I'd go over the cliff into nirvana with him. Desperate to fall, I lifted my small breast and fed it to his eager mouth. He growled like a wild animal, sucking and swirling his tongue around the tip.

"Harder, baby," I begged before he bit down on my nipple just hard enough to make me tumble over that final edge where pleasure and pain flourished.

The sound that tore from my lungs was guttural and barbaric as my entire body flushed with euphoric bliss. Pleasure unlike anything I'd ever experienced roared through my veins and pricked against my skin, while heat spread from between my thighs in a starburst of electricity.

Sutton wrapped his arms around my body in a vise lock as he held me in place. His release was hot within me as every ounce of pent-up tension exploded between us, shaking us both as hard as an earthquake.

I clung to him as my vision went in and out and the shower water turned lukewarm.

After a few minutes, he slowly lifted his head from between my breasts. There he placed soft little kisses all over my skin. His tongue slicked along my collarbone from one side to the other and then back up the column of my neck. I tilted my head so he'd have better access but didn't move anything else, as I felt entirely boneless.

He continued his worshipping kisses as he lifted me up and off his cock. His essence coated my thighs and dripped down to the tile, where it was quickly cleared away by the cooling water, disappearing down the drain.

Sutton set me on the bench once again before getting to his feet. He turned the water to full heat, which made it a bit warmer, but we didn't have much time before it would be ice cold. He filled a washcloth with soap and then washed my body quickly from my toes to my neck, making sure to cleanse himself from between my thighs. I sat there and didn't say a word, simply content to let my husband do whatever it was he needed to do. I was also completely spent.

He repeated the cleansing process on himself and rinsed us both off.

When he was done, he helped me stand and exit the shower, where he grabbed two towels. He wrapped one around me first, then the other around his hips.

"We didn't use protection," he announced, while drying every inch of my skin.

Protection.

My useless brain mulled over the word until it finally clicked.

Shit.

"Um, I mean, it was just that once," I countered, immediately thinking about how many hours I had before I could get the morning after pill. I was pretty sure we would be okay if I got one in the morning.

He shook his head as he reached for my panties, and I put one foot through the hole and then the next. He lifted them up and over my bum, settling them into place.

"That wasn't the only time, Dakota," he stated as he grabbed the T-shirt I'd worn to bed. "Lift your arms, darlin'."

I did as he asked, trying to make sense of what he was saying.

I thought about all the sex we'd been having as he put the shirt over my head. "What are you talking about? We've used protection every time."

He shook his head. "Not on our wedding night or the day after," he admitted.

No. No way. I thought back to that night, remembering we'd been drunk as skunks and hot as Hell for one another. We'd had a lot of unprotected sex that night and the next morning.

I stood perfectly still as he dried himself off, showing that beautiful body to me once again. It really wasn't fair how attractive he was. God shouldn't be that generous to any one particular human. I'd never seen a man so magnificent in my entire life. And that included models and actors. Sutton Goodall was the epitome of physical perfection. Thankfully, as he'd said several times while fucking me, he liked what I had too. That sure didn't fix the predicament we might be in, however.

"Dakota, when was the last time you had your period?"

I frowned as my entire body flushed with instant dread. I hadn't had my cycle since before the wedding. A solid ten days before that, and I hadn't had it since.

"No, no, no, no, no." I shook my head and waved my hand in the air. "There's no way. We've been so careful. And there's been a lot of stress. Women miss their periods all the time because of that," I tried.

"Baby, we haven't been that careful. And you've been feeling under the weather for a few days now. Don't think I haven't seen you sneaking off to the bathroom to vomit. Coming back smelling of toothpaste every time. And yesterday in the bushes too."

"I probably have the flu!" I fired back, fear fueling my response because I sure as hell hadn't felt sick outside of the random nausea that had come and gone the last few days.

"Darlin', I think you're pregnant." He looked at me with absolutely no hint as to what he was thinking or feeling.

I shook my head. It was too soon. Way too soon.

"I can't be pregnant."

Episode 83

She Is My Heart

ERIK

My gut tightened as violent, fiery waves skated across my skin. I ground down on my teeth as Savannah stood silent and pale as a ghost in the middle of the hospital lobby. She faced the woman who, a short time ago, was supposed to become her mother-in-law.

The look on Savannah's face clearly showed she was experiencing a living nightmare.

I knew what that felt like, and I wanted to lash out. To grab Savannah and hold her close, protect her from any hurt. Only this was a hurt I couldn't protect her from. She had to go through this trauma on her own. However, that didn't mean I wouldn't be the soft place she could land when she made her way through it. Unless she caved and ultimately chose Jarod and his family over me.

I shivered as I watched the reality of the situation come over her. It seemed her ex had not informed his parents that he and Savannah had broken off their engagement and were no longer a couple. I could imagine how hard this scene was for

Mrs. Talley, seeing her future daughter-in-law with another man. Especially a mother as devoted as this woman seemed to be. If my mother had been in this situation, she would have fought tooth and nail to ensure my happiness.

I took a few steps back but stayed close, determined not to interfere. If Savannah was truly to be my mate, she'd make the choice of her own free will. This was her battle to fight. As much as I wanted to pull her away, steal her from this inevitable heartbreak, it wasn't my place. Not yet, anyway.

"Mrs. Talley, I'm...um, I don't know what to say. Clearly Jarod has not been honest with you about our relationship. We broke up. Months ago, in fact." She'd told me as much. When she decided to enter The Marriage Auction, she'd ended her relationship with Jarod. He hadn't taken it well then, and his mother wasn't taking it well now.

The older woman's head jolted back, and she glared at Savannah, her lips twisting into a menacing snarl. "I simply cannot believe the words coming out of your mouth. You broke up with him," she rightly assumed. "After years of stringing my son along!" She pointed across the hospital lobby toward the emergency ward. "You mean to tell me my boy is being patched up from surviving a gunshot wound to the head...one given to him by *your* daddy..." She pounded her pointer finger against Savannah's chest accusingly. "...And I'm finding out that you broke off your engagement to my son and are already engaged to another man?"

Savannah winced, and that small gesture of discomfort was all it took to have me reacting.

I stepped up to Savannah, curved my arm around her waist, and pulled her back several feet before the woman could continue to physically attack her. "Don't touch her," I commanded in a tone I knew came across as low and threatening. I was a big guy, and my physical presence often made others uncomfortable. I'd use anything in my arsenal to protect Savannah. Even if the one hurting her was an irate middle-aged mother.

My action angered the woman further. "And who the hell is he? Your new fiancé?" She scoffed. "You've already attached your star to another man! What kind of hussy does something like that to a person who has been devoted to you for years! Years of his life wasted! Working on your father's farm, being treated poorly, making pennies, all in the hopes of marrying the beautiful Savannah McAllister. His perfect princess," she ranted.

Savannah sniffed against the tears falling down her porcelain cheeks. "Mrs. Talley, I didn't mean for any of this to happen," she croaked. "I'm so sorry."

"Sorry?" The woman's gaze turned glacial as her entire body seemed to vibrate with fury. "You're *sorry!*" she shrieked. "My son could be dead because of you! A two-bit hussy who left my son to go to some fancy college and ride the coattails of the next man you could capture in your snare. I'll just bet he's rich, too. Was he one of your professors? He fits the bill in that getup." She looked me up and down as though my mere existence was a stain on society.

I growled low in my throat and hung on to Savannah with both hands. Her body trembled in my arms, each new verbal barb striking its target.

"Don't listen to her, *elskede*. She is furious and lashing out," I warned.

"Damn right I'm upset! My son has been waiting years to marry the love of his life and start a family, only to be tossed aside by the likes of you! A rich foreigner. Probably don't even know your ass from a hole in the ground. Sweet Jesus. Get out of here!" she yelled.

"Mrs. Talley, please, if you'll just let me explain. I need to see Jarod. Make sure he's okay. And apologize for what my father did. I want to make amends." Her emotional turmoil was such that her body started to list to the side as though she might fall over.

I held her tighter, ensuring she kept on her feet.

"You are no longer welcome here," the woman seethed. "You're not welcome anywhere near our family. Don't you ever show your face around me and mine again. I won't be held responsible for my actions. And you better believe we'll be pressing charges against Everett. You think that farm was in trouble before? After he almost killed a man and attempted to murder my son! We'll be going after everything you love and hold dear. Especially that land." With her parting shot, she spun around and stormed over to the other members of her family.

Savannah slumped against my body, her hands covering her face as she sobbed into them.

I eased her to my side and walked her straight out of the hospital.

Savannah cried the entire time we waited for a member of Sutton's family to pick us up from the hospital and take us back to her family home. She cried when Dakota directed us to her childhood bedroom, and she cried herself to sleep with my arms tightly wound around her.

I didn't know what to do. What to say to ease her grief. Not only had her father been taken to jail for two counts of attempted murder, but her ex was one of the men he'd tried to end. She'd dealt with a long history of her father's abuse—something that I couldn't begin to unravel if I wanted to keep my cool. And now she had the fear of Jarod's family threatening to take her land. The very reason she'd entered into The Marriage Auction in the first place.

I watched Savannah breathe deeply in her sleep, loathe to

leave her, but I needed answers and a plan. Two things I'd find only by discussing the situation with her sister and her husband. From what I'd come to understand, Sutton Goodall had won over Dakota. They genuinely seemed to love one another. It was a full three-sixty from what I'd experienced at their wedding.

I distinctly remembered Dakota attempting to punch her husband after he kissed her when they'd been announced as man and wife. It was a memory I wasn't soon to forget. I'd have gone so far as to bet hundreds of thousands that the two would be the very first to divorce at the end of their three-year contract. And now, after seeing the way they clung to one another after a few short weeks...I was envious. The love within the words they didn't speak as their gazes caught from across a room was clear as day. The simple way in which they seemed to coexist in their farmhouse was everything I could ever want with Savannah. But I knew with my entire heart that I'd not have that same ease if we didn't get past the trauma of her relationship with Jarod and his family. And that didn't include the threats they'd just made to take what I believed Savannah held most valuable.

The land.

I slipped out of bed and tucked the covers around Savannah. She was unearthly beautiful with her long fiery locks, her pearlescent skin, rosy cheeks, and full, pink-tinged lips. Even now I wanted to kiss those lips, have her wake with my love on the tip of her tongue.

And it was love.

True love.

I'd known it almost since the moment I'd laid eyes on her, standing frightened and uncertain on that stage in Las Vegas. It was the first time I felt something other than extreme sadness. Before her, I was an empty husk swaying in the breeze in a dying corn field. I'd gone from place to place in search of the one thing she'd given me with a single look.

Joy.

I knew what intense loss felt like. I understood tragedy. As the man who wanted to love and honor her, it was my job to help make her feel whole again. I'd had years of feeling like half a person. Savannah made me feel complete. I wanted to be that safe place for her, but I also knew that it would take more than beautiful words of devotion and love. It would take action. Removing the obstacles in the way of our future happiness.

Silently, I grabbed my hiking boots and padded through the house, smelling the scent of coffee as I left the bedroom. In the kitchen, I found my mother. A vision I was unsurprised to find. If there was a place my mother could nurture her kin with food and other comforts, that was where she'd be.

"*God morgen, min sønn.*" My mother wished me good morning in our native tongue.

"Are you well, Mother?" I specifically reverted to English. I wanted my family to embrace my bride and her language until Savannah was fluent. It was good practice to speak in English more often than not.

"I am. How is Savannah?" She poured a cup of coffee for me into a travel mug.

I grinned at the sight. My mother knew me too well.

"Thank you. She had a hard day and night. I'm off to discuss the situation with Sutton and Dakota."

She nodded. "The sooner the better. Perhaps we can encourage everyone to come to Norway. The stench of unrest here is thick, my son. This is no place to have a wedding. Your nuptials should be a joyous event, not cloaked in the darkness this land exudes."

Mother was always sensitive to energies and had a keen sense of spiritual activity. I pressed my lips together, attempting not to laugh. "Are you insinuating this farm is haunted?"

She frowned and then shrugged. "I do not know. I can only feel the negative energy. After yesterday's tragedy and the fire prior to our arrival, I do not think you should start your married life here."

I clenched my teeth. "I will do whatever will please Savannah. It matters not where we marry, only that we do in fact come together as one."

"Why the rush?" She finally asked the question I knew had been burning on her tongue since I'd surprised my parents with my pending nuptials.

"Because she is my heart. It wasn't beating until we met. I should have died in that helicopter accident, Mother. It was a miracle I survived. And for over two years, my heart didn't beat. Nothing mattered. I was a living, breathing shell of nothing. Until her. She has filled me with hope. Made my heart beat again."

"I'm your heart?" Came the voice of my beloved from behind me.

I turned around quickly to find Savannah standing there barefoot, hair a mess, eyes puffy from crying, and looking absolutely breathtaking. I'd never tire of her beauty.

"Yes, *elskede*. You are my heart. I will do anything to bring you the happiness you have brought me."

Her bottom lip trembled. "You are too good for me, Erik. I don't deserve you." She shook her head and glanced away.

I took the few steps needed to reach her and cupped her cheeks.

"It is I who do not deserve you."

"Erik." She whispered the word, a plea I didn't know how to answer.

"Let me make you happy, Savannah. Take this all away. I know if you'll let me, I could be everything you want and need."

Her hands came to my chest, where she ran the flats of her palms up past my heart and curled them around my neck. "You are the only thing that has made me happy in a long time."

I dipped my head and kissed her softly. Letting her have the time to pull away if she desired.

She didn't.

Her fingers dove into my hair and tightened against my scalp.

I groaned into her kiss, canting my head to the side to taste her deeper. Our tongues tangled as our breaths intermingled.

The sound of a throat clearing snapped us both out of our connection.

"That's my cue. Good luck today," Mother said and then slipped out the back door, likely to enjoy her morning coffee while looking at the wondrous view.

Savannah giggled against my mouth and then tucked her head against my chest, hiding her face as she chuckled. I lifted her chin with a curl of my finger. Her cheeks were tinged a healthy pink, and her lips were swollen from our kiss, but her eyes stole my breath. They were dazzling. Happiness exuding from those endless blue depths. I could spend hours swimming in her gaze.

"I thought you might sleep longer. Yesterday was hard."

She frowned, her eyes losing that sparkle as she nodded. "I want to talk to Dakota. Make sense of all that's happened. And then there's what Mrs. Talley threatened. She needs to know we have yet another problem to consider. This one far more threatening than the bank liens and past debts."

I placed my hands to her shoulders. "Savannah, no one is going to take this land from you. Not with me in the picture. I'll have Jack touch base with our lawyers. Get you the best there is to fight the Talleys if that's what is needed."

She closed her eyes for a moment and shook her head. "I'm not sure that's the best plan. Everything's changed."

I took her hands and held them with my own. "Explain."

"I haven't been happy here in years. The barn has burned down. Several of the horses I bred and trained before leaving for school died in the fire. All of that pales in comparison to what happened yesterday. Dakota told me there's more to our mother's and grandmother's pasts that I don't even know." She shook her head and pulled her hands from mine and shifted to pace the kitchen.

She plucked at her bottom lip as she worried a line across the tile floor. "You know, Erik, I'm standing in the place I called home my entire life, and I feel like a stranger." She let her hands fall to her sides with a slap of her thighs as though she'd come to a new conclusion. "This isn't where I want to be anymore."

My heart pounded a heavy beat against my ribcage as pinpricks of nervous energy skated across my skin.

"Where do you want to be, *elskede*?" I asked, afraid of the answer but needing to hear it all the same.

For what felt like an eternity, she silently stood there, looking at the ground as if her cute, pink-painted toes had all the answers for her.

Then she lifted her head, and our gazes met. It was as if I was pierced directly in the heart by Cupid's love-tipped golden arrow.

"I want to be where you are," she whispered hesitantly and rather shyly.

I swallowed down the extreme hope that filled me to bursting, terrified to react too quickly or to say the wrong thing.

"I am right here. Standing in front of you. Within touching distance. Where I will always be when you need me, Savannah."

She licked her lips and smiled widely. "I know that now. Your parents were wrong." I frowned, not knowing what she was referring to, but waited for her to continue. "I'm not your safe space. You are mine."

A low hum settled at the base of my throat as the reality of what she'd just claimed filtered through the complicated feelings we were both wading through.

"Then come to me. Be mine. In every way. I'll be your home, Savannah. And you will forever be mine." I opened my arms wide.

It didn't take but a fraction of a second for the woman I wanted more than the sunlight in the sky or the breath in my lungs to jump into my arms. Her legs wound around my waist as she tucked her face to the skin of my neck.

I held her so tightly I wanted to imprint her into my skin, have her soul merge with mine until there was no Erik, no Savannah, just one perfectly whole entity that was us.

"I love you," I whispered against her ear, kissing whatever skin I could reach. "I will love you until I take my last breath on this earth."

Her hold tightened as she lifted her head, her lips pressed to my ear. "I love you too. I'm sorry I was afraid to admit it, but I do, Erik. I love you. And I want to marry you. As soon as possible."

"Then I shall make it happen. First, we need to discuss the most pressing matters with your sister."

"Do we have to?" she pouted.

"I'm afraid so. Much needs to be discussed, but I will be with you the whole way," I promised.

"Even when I tell her I want out of the farm?"

Pride and happiness flowed over me like a tidal wave. "Especially then."

She unwound her legs, and I let her fall to her feet. "I'll get my shoes. Will you get me coffee?"

"I'll provide anything you need, *elskede*."

Her smile was wide. "I believe you."

Episode 84

Faith & Joel's Wedding (Part 1)

JOEL

"Tonight? As in this evening?" The strangled voice of my resort manager filled my ear. I pressed the phone closer as I took in the show across the room.

Faith was bustling around the breakfast table, tending to our girls. Robert sat at the helm, teasing them both and telling jokes. Penny and Eden beamed under his attention. It made me realize that not only had I gained Faith and Eden, but Penny would now feel the love and respect of a grandfather figure.

The moment Faith finished loading up the girls' plates with food, Robert slipped an extra chocolate-dipped strawberry onto Penny's plate. She smiled huge, and he winked at her, then put his finger up to his lips in a gesture to keep quiet. Penny danced in her seat, happier than I'd ever seen her. My mother was a constant source of love and devotion for my daughter, but with Faith, Eden, and Robert, she had an entire family to dote on her, and my girl was thriving. Little Eden seemed to be happier this morning too with the addition of her grandfather.

"Yes, Melanie, I want the entire rooftop turned into a

magical evening wedding, complete with candlelight, decorations, music, and food."

"Um, okay, Mr. Castellanos. I understand, but this is a very quick turnaround. Almost impossible..." she blurted.

"Are you not the best there is? I seem to recall you handling many hosted events at my other resorts with aplomb and elegance."

"Yes, sir, but those events had much larger time frames. You want me to create a beautiful wedding in essentially twelve hours?"

I tapped my finger along the white weave of the textured armchair I sat in. I didn't speak, waiting for Melanie to come to terms with my request.

Suddenly the wheels of her creativity must have powered through the challenge, and she asked, "How many people will be in attendance?"

"Plan for no more than twelve. We'd like to marry under the arbor as the sun sets. You'll need to find an officiant, of which I'm sure there are many in this town."

"Any type of food you'd like to have?"

"Italian. Authentic."

"Authentic," she mumbled. "I'm sure one of our resort chefs can whip up a lovely Italian meal for a dozen people. I may have to pull in another chef to assist."

"I have complete faith you will conquer any challenge, Melanie. You have been in my employ for years. I trust you implicitly and understand that this is a unique situation. Your best will be far more than we expect, I assure you."

"One more thing. No, two more. What color scheme?" she asked.

"Hold on." I set the phone to my chest. "Darling?" I called out. "What colors do you want at the wedding tonight?"

"Honey, I don't care. I like all colors," Faith answered with a smile, her dazzling eyes sparkling against the morning light. She then bent over the dining chair and kissed Penny's forehead, then repeated the process with Eden.

"Ocean blue, silver accents." *Just like her eyes*, I thought.

"And what is your bride's favorite flower?"

I frowned, realizing I didn't even know something as simple as that.

"Darling, what is your favorite flower?"

She eased into the chair opposite the girls and rested her head against the tall back, her stunning face turned toward me, stealing every bit of my attention.

"I don't really have one. I love succulents and cacti, though. I mean, I was raised in the desert." She smiled.

"My bride prefers desert plants over flowers," I reiterated.

"You're kidding?" Melanie deadpanned.

I snickered under my breath. "No. My Faith is definitely one of a kind. I believe that is all. Unless there's anything else."

"Night wedding, cacti, Italian food, blue and silver. These are by far the most unique set of preferences I've dealt with, but I'll make it work. Plan to arrive at 6:30 p.m. According to my weather app, the sun will set at 7:46 p.m. That should give you enough time to view what's been done and get ready. Do you need me to call in a stylist for the bride?"

"I want the works set up for her. Cancel any appointments at the spa and gift everyone a free service for their inconvenience. I want the team taking care of all four of my girls. We'll be sending them down in the next hour or two."

"No problem."

"I'll make some calls to a few fashion designers in the area I know to send over everything they have. Thank you, Melanie. Pull this off, as I believe you can, and it will mean a hearty bonus on your next check."

"It will be an evening to remember, I assure you. Call if you need anything, sir."

We hung up, and I ambled over to the chaos that had ensued at the breakfast table. In the center were tons of different pastries and covered dishes which I assumed had eggs, bacon, and the like.

"Do you want me to make you a plate, Joel?" Faith offered.

"I'd love nothing more." I went over to her and leaned over her chair. "Today I marry my future."

She smiled widely and eased her head to the side to face me. "Today I marry my future." She whispered the words back to me.

We sealed the promise with a kiss.

The girls giggled and squealed. "Do we get to be flower girls?" Penny asked.

"Absolutely!" I said, reminding myself to text Melanie with that new bit of information so she'd be prepared.

"The four of you will be heading down to the spa to be pampered for the next few hours." I kissed Faith once more and reluctantly let her go.

"Mr. Marino..." I spoke but was cut off by the man himself.

"Now, son, you can call me Robert or Dad. We're going to be family after tonight."

I smiled and nodded. "Robert, it would be my honor if you'd accompany me to my resort tailor in order to secure tuxes for this evening's event. My treat, of course."

Robert grimaced. "I can pay for my own tux to my daughter's wedding, son. Don't you worry about me. I know a guy. I can have a rented penguin suit within the hour," he boasted.

"Um, Dad, I think what Joel is offering you is a gift, something a bit *fancier*." She scrunched up her nose, her face contorting into a sour expression.

The tailor and menswear boutique in my resort catered to the upper echelon of male clients. A single suit cost no less than three to four thousand, and that did not include the tailoring. A tux would be far more. The man had just lost his restaurant, his livelihood. I didn't want him to worry about a thing.

Robert scoffed and waved his hand. "My guy is the best

around. As a matter of fact, Joel, you should come with me!" He pointed to his chest. "I can get you suited up in no time."

Faith's eyes widened, and she pressed her lips together.

"I think I'll pass at this time, Robert. I have something in mind I'd like to wear when I marry your daughter. But there is a very important thing I need your assistance with."

"Oh?" His eyes lit up, eager to participate in his daughter's wedding.

"The ring."

Faith's cheeks flushed pink as she placed two pieces of bacon on a plate.

"A very important task indeed. I'd be happy to assist." Robert lifted his chest, pride exuding from the man in spades.

Faith continued to fill my plate with a bit of everything before setting it in front of me. She took the empty seat next to mine and curled her feet up on the chair.

I reached my hand out and took hers, lifting it to my mouth to kiss her knuckles. "By the end of the day, my sweet, we will be husband and wife."

Her entire face lit up. "I'm really excited," she admitted.

"Me too." I kissed her knuckles once more and then set about eating breakfast.

"First step for you, ladies: spa day. After, you will be brought back here where you will meet with the stylists and designers."

"They'll have dress options in my size?" Faith asked, her tone shy and uncertain.

I turned to the side and curled a finger around her chin, lifting her face until her gaze met mine. "They will have more than you can imagine available. I'm certain you will find something that compliments your incredible beauty. Though you could wear a sundress or a nightgown and I'd find you the most breathtaking woman there is." I ran my thumb across her plump bottom lip. "I'm marrying *you* tonight, Faith. The dress only adorns the body of the person I love. Whatever you choose will be perfect."

The light shining in her gaze was something I'd never forget, but her next words meant even more. "I love you, and I can't wait to marry you tonight."

I leaned to the side and kissed her, tasting the truth of her words from her lips.

"How about this one?" Robert pointed to a simple four-carat round brilliant diamond.

I sighed deeply and shook my head, not seeing anything that could represent the extreme love I felt for Faith and what she was bringing to my life.

The woman was everything I'd never believed I could have after losing Alexandra. The ring I chose, the proof to the world that she was in fact my everything, had to be just right.

"These are all too trendy and modern. Too...'rich man's wife.' Faith is her own person. I want something that resonates with how I see her." I scanned the rings my jeweler had laid out on two velvet trays. They ranged in price from six figures to seven. I had no problem spending millions on Faith as proven by the twenty million I'd bid in the auction. Not that the contract mattered anymore. Faith and I were far beyond committing to one another because of the auction. What money I had accrued to this point in my life was hers to have if she desired. I only wanted her.

I got up to pace the back room of the jewelry store. My jeweler had picked out what he thought were the best options, but none of them were right.

Without a word, I left the back room and entered the main

store. I went from display to display, ignoring the onlookers and other happy couples picking out rings. The more I looked, the more frustrated I became.

And then, across the room, I saw a small standing display behind the counter. A series of lights streamed down on a pedestal column. Behind the glass sat a series of five vintage rings. Right in the center was an impressive rose-cut, pear-shaped diamond ring that was set in platinum. The center stone had to be over five carats. It was completely see-through, just like my Faith's ocean eyes.

"Ah, I see you've found my vintage estate collection. All of these have been purchased by me personally through my years of estate shopping. They each carry a certificate of authenticity as one-of-a-kind rings."

"The teardrop. I must see it." My throat clogged, emotion coasting across my nerve endings in sizzling pinpricks of anticipation.

The jeweler pulled out a set of keys and unlocked the display. "These aren't technically available for sale as they are part of my personal collection..." he warned. I knew better. Just about anything in the world was for sale...for the right price.

I glared at him and picked up the most perfect ring I'd ever seen. When I placed it on the tip of my pinky finger, I could see my skin through the diamond.

"This is the Norristown ring, a six-carat diamond set in platinum with K Color and VS1 clarity. There is another full carat of diamonds around the base and sides. It belonged to an oil heiress whose husband was drafted and died in World War II before they could ever have children. She never remarried. Wore the ring until she died of old age. Claimed that he was the love of her life. The family was hesitant to sell me the ring because of its history. I promised that I'd protect the love that came with this ring by only selling it to the right person. I've had it fifteen years and have never once thought to sell it."

"I assure you I am the right person. And my Faith will adore the ring her entire life. And then it will be passed down to one of our daughters. This ring will grace the finger of a woman very deserving of the same everlasting love."

Robert sniffed and patted his teary eyes with a handkerchief.

"What do you think, Robert?" I showed him the dazzling ring. It caught the light, sending rainbows everywhere.

"It's more than Faith could ever wish for. She'll love it." He cleared his throat and set about pulling himself together. Knowing this ring had brought tears to my father-in-law's eyes sealed the deal in my soul.

I smiled and turned to my jeweler. "I'll give you double whatever you paid for it. And I'd also like to see about two single-carat diamond pendant necklaces for the most precious little girls in my world, and a diamond tennis bracelet for my mother."

"Absolutely, Mr. Castellanos. I have wonderful necklaces over here." The jeweler pointed.

Robert placed his hand to my shoulder. "You're buying the girls diamond necklaces?" His eyes practically bulged.

"It's my gift to them. I want all my girls to be showered in my love this evening. Tonight, we come together as a real family, for better or for worse, under the stars. I want to give them each a sparkling star of their own. An heirloom for them to remember the night by."

Robert pulled me into a hug in the middle of the store, clapping me on the back far harder than I expected. "You are an amazing man, Joel Castellanos. I couldn't have chosen better for my daughter and grandchild. Thank you. Thank you for loving them."

"It is I who am thankful to have their love." I smiled and patted his shoulder. "Come, we have much still to do before this evening."

After the ring purchase, I talked Robert into allowing my tailor to fit him with a tuxedo that would match well with my own. Ultimately, he demanded to pay for his tux, which I understood completely. That did not, however, prevent me from secretly having the retail attendant give him an eighty percent discount.

Now I was at the top of The Alexandra overlooking the Las Vegas Strip and the desert beyond as the sun crept toward the horizon, sipping on a glass of crisp, cool champagne. It helped to settle my nerves. I knew the girls would show up soon, and I was eager to see them.

"Okay, the ladies are ready and waiting in the rooftop lounge," Melanie, who was dressed in a smashing cocktail dress, stated as she approached.

"You look lovely." I dipped my chin.

She waved her hand. "Well, I couldn't wear one of my work suits to my first wedding at The Alexandra, now, could I?" she teased.

"I suppose not."

"Come, let's get you into place." She ushered me to the small platform, where the arbor was decorated with greenery and desert cactus shockingly in full bloom. Where she'd procured these plants in that stage of maturity, I'd never know. To see them all open and filling the space with their bright, prickly essence was impractical and uniquely special.

Melanie had outdone herself.

Three four-seater dining tables were set up in the back area, complete with candles and succulents in the center and fine china on full display. Another table had a three-tiered white wedding cake sitting atop its surface. There was a short blue velvet runner that led straight down the center of the rooftop, ending at the arbor. At each side of the aisle, two sets of silver chairs were draped with shimmery blue bows.

When I made my way to the arbor, I was shocked to find Bruno dressed in a tux hobbling up from a chair.

"'Bout time you showed up. My leg is killing me sitting here waiting," he grouched.

I reached my hand out and helped him to stand at my side. My cousin. My best friend. The man who had taken two bullets to the leg to save my woman's father. I owed him so much, and here he was, balancing on one leg to stand at my side while I married Faith. The same way he had when I'd married Alexandra.

I looked at him with deep appreciation.

"What? You think you can skip having your best man at your wedding?" He scoffed and grinned. "Not a chance. I was at the first, and now I'm at the last. You know I'm always down for a good party."

"You are the best man I know, Bruno. I am grateful to you for so many things. But mostly for always being at my side and having my back."

He grinned. "Shut up, Joel. The music is starting. Time to get married."

My driver and good friend, Carlo, walked my mother down the aisle, the two of them taking separate seats, one on each side of the aisle.

Surprisingly, Diego strode down the aisle in an all-black suit with a sultry Hispanic woman clinging to his arm wearing a fire engine red dress with a slit straight up the thigh. She was taller than him in her sky-high heels. I recognized her as the woman I'd pulled out of the burning car from our checkered past. She winked, and Diego grinned, giving me a thumbs-up gesture as he led her to a seat.

And then there were the girls. Two perfect little angels in white dresses with blue satin ribbons at their waists and matching flower halos on their heads. They were holding baskets and tossing white rose petals as they made their way to the front.

"*Baba!*" *Father.* Penny waved as she got to the end.

"*Baba!*" Eden copied.

My heart was filled to bursting with love at the sight of our two precious angels. And hearing Eden call me Father sent me reeling with pride.

And then Faith appeared. Standing at the end of the aisle like a living dream come true.

Our gazes met, and there was nothing but her.

She wore a sleek Grecian-style dress that made her look like a deity come to life. Her hair fell down her back in dark waves, a simple crown of small white roses mixed in as the rest was pulled back and out of her face. The front of the dress was a deep open V of lace that fluttered along her open skin giving a subtle, flashing hint of her breasts. The waistband was a thick, tiered design of fabric with lace showing skin through the middle. Lace sleeves graced her arms past her wrists delicately. The bottom flowed out like an evening flower, blooming as the sun set. She was exquisite.

A goddess.

Soon to be my wife.

Episode 85

Faith & Joel's Wedding (Part 2)

FAITH
Earlier that day…

The girls were positively buzzing with excitement when we entered the spa at The Alexandra.

"Ms. Marino, Ms. Castellanos, we are delighted to serve you today," a tall, full-figured woman with platinum-blonde hair announced as we entered. There were three additional attendants standing behind her, all of them wearing black scrubs.

"We are excited to be here." I reached out and shook the woman's hand.

"I'm Bella, the manager here at the spa, and these are my technicians, Sydney, Emma, and Heidi. We will be pampering you from top to toe as Mr. Castellanos has requested. First, I thought it might be fun to start with manicures, pedicures, and facials. Then you can soak in our Zen pool filled with natural minerals and essential oils that are great for the skin. We'll finish up with massages, and then bring you back up to your suite for hair, makeup, and styling. How does that sound?"

"Marvelous." Olympia grinned, her rounded cheeks turning a pretty rose color. She focused on Penny and Eden. "What color are my grandchildren going to get on their nails?"

"I wuv purple," Eden said shyly, clinging to my leg.

"Then you shall have purple, buttercup." I smoothed my hand over her unruly brown locks.

"I want to swim in the Zen pool!" Penny bounced up and down, her flip-flops clacking against the marble floor.

"Yay!" Eden perked up at the words *swim* and *pool*. The girls had loved swimming together back in Greece.

"It's not exactly a pool for swimming." Bella hesitated.

"I'm sure we'll figure it all out. Girls?" I called to get their attention. "We're going to be good and follow all the rules of this business, right?" I used my stern voice.

Eden nodded immediately.

"I thought my daddy owned all the pools? He would say I can swim if I want to!" she stated with pure confidence. "I won't hurt nobody, Mimi. I promise." She pouted.

"Let's start with manicures and pedicures and see what happens," I redirected her.

That seemed to mollify Penny, but I could now see how having the ability to do whatever she wanted whenever she wanted could pose a problem as she aged. I planned to nip that attitude in the bud before it became a problem in her teenage years.

A pang of regret squeezed my heart with the reminder that after the wedding, I might not be in the girls' lives for a while, if ever, again.

I shook my head.

No. I wouldn't go there. I had no idea what was going to happen when I offered myself up to Aiden. There was always a chance I could escape unscathed. I'd done it before; I could do it again. Besides, I was stronger. More intelligent. And I had a lot more to lose.

"Bella, lead the way," I said while shaking off the dread.

Today was about preparing to marry the love of my life. Whatever happened after that would be up to fate.

The Zen pool was indeed a small lap pool which the girls were enjoying enormously. Apparently, Bella had called the manager of the hotel to confirm whether the girls could swim in the Zen pool. As expected, the manager explained that it was the owner's wedding night and those were his children and to give them whatever they wanted as long as they didn't get hurt and stayed happy.

The girls were ecstatic. I was not.

"Joel is going to spoil them rotten, Olympia," I complained to Joel's mother.

She shrugged. "Probably, but does it actually hurt them? I don't think so." Her words were heavily accented and carried an air of wisdom.

"I think it's important to teach them that not everyone lives a charmed life." I tiptoed around what could possibly have been a hot-button issue between me and Olympia, seeing as she'd been the lone woman in Penny's and Joel's lives since Alexandra died.

"That is for you to share with them," she stated flatly as if it was all the same to her.

I took in the girls jumping up and down in the shallow water having a blast. Bella assured me there was nothing in the water that could harm them, even if they swallowed some or got it in their eyes.

"Eden has not had an easy life until now," I whispered. "Of course, she's had a lot of love from my father and myself, but it has certainly not been a normal experience for a small child. She understands disappointment, abandonment, and true fear."

"Don't you think that means she's owed this time of freedom? To play with her new sister free from worry that she'll lose a guardian at any moment?"

Tears pricked against my eyes at the reminder that she may indeed lose me again. At least for a while. I'd never stop trying to get back to her, Joel, and Penny. Not ever.

My stomach burned with the desire for action. I wanted to wipe Aiden off the face of the planet. Make him disappear so far away he'd never be able to reach those I loved. And yet the only way I could truly assure that reality would be to take his life myself.

I didn't think I could do it.

Take a life.

Even one as disgusting and vile as Aiden's. Murder was murder. And yet, if it was Aiden between me and someone I loved, I'd have no problem pulling that trigger. That was the dark side of my nature I was afraid of. Aiden could hurt and use me, but if he laid a finger on Eden, Penny, or Joel, I'd do anything to save them.

Olympia reached out and patted my knee. "Relax, Faith. Everything is fine. You are marrying my son tonight. All will be well. Joel will keep all of you safe. You just need to believe it."

I offered her a small smile. "I think I'm ready for my massage. You?"

She eased back into the cushy lounge chair and picked up her glass of cucumber and mint-infused water. "I'm going to let the girls play. You go ahead. You're the one who needs the stress worked out of you."

I grinned and got up. "Girls, Mimi is going to get a massage. *Yia-Yia* is here to watch you. Be good."

Two squeals of "Okay, Mimi!" echoed through the cavernous room.

I made my way to Bella, who was setting out some fluffy-looking folded towels.

"I'm ready for the massage. The girls and my mother-in-law are going to stay here if that's okay."

"I've been instructed that you have the run of the place. Let's get you on a massage table. We'll do a full ninety minutes."

"Sounds heavenly. Thank you."

The massage was as magical as I expected it to be, but it was what the stylist and makeup artist created that blew my mind as I stared at myself in the floor-to-ceiling mirror.

I was more beautiful in that moment than I had ever been in my entire life.

The wedding dress I chose from the plethora that had been brought over by Joel's designers was beyond perfect. It fit me as though it was made for me. Even Olympia shed a tear when she saw me in the Grecian-inspired gown.

It was pearl white with the most striking, decadent lace detailing and sleeves. It reminded me of Greek mythical attire worn by someone like Aphrodite, the goddess of love. I studied my frame from side to side, taking in the nipped-in waist and the deep V that hugged and accentuated my breasts in a provocative game of peek-a-boo I knew Joel would salivate over.

"*Cara mia.*" My father's voice rose in awe as he entered the rooftop lounge area wearing a tailored tuxedo. His gaze was glued to my image in the mirror.

I turned around and swished the dress from side to side, letting the fabric move with me. "What do you think? Not half bad for an Italian girl from the wrong side of the Las Vegas Strip, eh?" I teased, hoping he'd laugh.

He didn't. He was too busy taking in every inch of my dress.

"These are the times I wish your mother was here. To see you on your wedding day. To give you incredible words of wisdom to take into your life with Joel..." His tone was filled with sorrow.

"That's why I have you, Dad. If you could give me one piece of advice to take with me on my journey, what would it be?" I asked, feeling hopeful.

He rubbed the back of his neck, closed his eyes for a minute, and then cleared his throat. "I would tell you to let Joel keep you safe. He's smart, sweetheart. I haven't been able to protect you from the trauma Aiden continues to inflict on you. I wasn't able to years ago, and it's been proven I can't now. Let him protect you."

I frowned and turned back around to face the mirror, my soul bleeding at the reality that I was going to do the exact opposite of what my father begged me to do.

He came up to stand behind me, where he put both of his hands on the balls of my shoulders. "And tell him the truth..."

I flinched away. "You know I can't! Don't you think I would if I could? It can never, *ever* get out. You vowed *on my life* that you'd take my secret to the grave. I expect you to honor that promise."

My father scowled. "And I will. I am a man of my word. Your secret is safe with me. Still, I urge you to change your mind."

I shook my head. "Never," I whispered.

He jerked his chin as though he understood, even though he didn't agree. I didn't care if he agreed. I only cared that he'd keep his word.

Olympia bustled in with our girls in tow.

"Oh my goodness, you both look divine!" I crouched and

opened my arms. Both girls ran into them, and I snuggled them close. "Now remember, you have a super important job. When the music starts and *Yia-Yia* has walked down the aisle, walk slowly and drop the flower petals from your baskets."

Eden pulled out a wad of petals in her little fist and tossed them up into the air. "Wike that!" She screeched with glee.

We all laughed, and I nodded. "Ideally, you'll take a few at a time and toss them on the ground. Papa can help you," I encouraged. He moved into action, talking the girls through the process as Olympia came to me.

"I have been carrying this with me for too long. It's time it sees the light of day again," she announced strangely, her voice low and emotional as she removed a long necklace from around her neck. Dangling from the chain was a simple white gold ring with a line of black stones in the center.

Olympia unlatched the necklace and let the ring drop into the palm of her hand. "It was my husband's wedding ring. He would wish for his son to wear it on this day and for the rest of his life. Joel was the light in his father's eyes. Losing him was a deep wound that only compounded when he lost Alexandra."

"I couldn't... It's tied to your love." I gasped, grief consuming my response.

"Which is why it's important for my son to have this piece of his father with him on this day and for every day after. A token of the love we had for one another when we brought Joel into this world, and a token from his father and me for the love the two of you will carry long after we are both gone."

"Olympia..." I cried, wrapping my arms around the woman. "I'm so happy you are here."

She patted my back and nodded against my neck. "You will be as happy as my husband and I were. I know it as I know the sun will rise again tomorrow and the moon each night. You and my son were meant to find one another. It's in every look. Every touch. Every breath the two of you take when you're in the same room. The love between you lives and breathes, filling everyone with its glory."

Olympia took my hand and placed the ring in the center. She then patted the top. "Love him to distraction, my dear. You never know how long you'll have."

I swiped at the tears flooding my cheeks. "I will."

He stood at the end of the aisle looking more dashing and debonair than I'd ever seen him. The tuxedo wasn't the typical black and white. His was dark navy. The jacket a lush brocade pattern with a slight sheen I couldn't wait to run my fingers across. He had a matching vest, a white dress shirt with black buttons, and a dark bow tie. Joel was mouth-wateringly handsome and soon to be all mine. His green eyes blazed as he stared at me from the end of the aisle. His gaze taking in every ounce of my body, making me feel as if he was caressing me with his hands.

"You ready?" my father asked.

"I have never been more ready in my life," I admitted.

My father kissed my cheek. "Remember what I said earlier. Let Joel protect you from here on out. Make all decisions as a team. And think about sharing all your truths," he stated. "I love you, Faith, and I'm so proud to be standing here today giving you away to a wonderful man. No father could be happier than I am right now."

"I love you, Dad. Now take me to Joel." I tugged on his elbow, and he laughed.

The music rose and fell, but Joel never took his gaze off me as I got closer.

My father proudly announced that he was giving me away,

and there we were, facing one another, my hands in Joel's, squeezing for dear life.

"You are stunning. Blindingly beautiful, Faith." His voice was deep and sultry, a timbre that immediately made me clench my thighs.

I smiled widely as the tears started to blur my vision. "So are you."

Even though the officiant was speaking about love and honoring one another, he whispered, "Are you happy?"

"I've never been happier, Joel," I admitted.

"Now we will exchange rings," the officiant stated. Joel turned to his side and took a ring from a box that Bruno held.

The ring was splendid and caught the waning light as the sun was setting.

"With this ring, I promise to devote my life to making you happy. To wiping your tears. To holding you close. To protecting you and keeping you safe, all the days of my life." He placed the ring on my finger, and it fit perfectly.

I turned to the side to get the ring from Olympia, and then repeated the words the officiant said. Joel's eyebrows rose, likely not expecting me to have a ring.

"With this ring, your *father's* wedding ring, I promise to devote my life to making you happy." Joel's eyes teared up as he looked at the ring, his mother, who nodded and wiped at her eyes, and finally back to me. He swallowed and took a ragged breath, a tear slipping down one cheek.

I wiped his tears with one hand and continued. "I will support your goals, dreams, and desires. I will be a loyal wife and loving mother to your daughter and any children we bring into this world. I will love you all the days of my life."

Joel lifted both of our hands and kissed my ring finger. Then he let me go and turned to Bruno once more, grabbing the necklaces we'd discussed late last night when we'd made our plans for today. "May I please have Penny Castellanos and Eden Marino come stand with us," he announced to the small group.

Olympia led the girls to the riser, and they both stepped up, hand in hand. Joel crouched before Eden.

"Eden Marino, today I ask you to accept me as your father. I promise to love, support, and take care of you, all the days of my life."

"You want to be my daddy?" she asked point-blank, and my entire body convulsed with emotion.

I too crouched before her. "Would you like that, buttercup?" I whispered, my tears coating my words.

She nodded avidly.

Penny nudged her side. "You're 'posed to say *I do*," she instructed like the big sister she was turning out to be.

"I do!" Eden hollered, and everyone laughed.

"Here is a token of my love and commitment." He latched a diamond pendant around her neck. "I love you, sweetheart."

"I love you too, Daddy Joel." She beamed and fingered the necklace.

The tears fell, and I didn't even try to hide them. Then he handed a matching necklace to me. "Do you want to do the honors?"

I nodded and crouched before Penny. "Penny, I know you had an amazing mama who loved you very much. But I would like the honor of being your second mother. Never replacing Alexandra but honoring her by loving and committing to you all the days of my life. Will you take me as your mommy?"

Penny smiled wide, opened her arms, and crashed against me. "I do, I do, I do!" she cried against my shoulder. I wiped her tears and then placed the necklace around her neck. I repeated the vow Joel had said to Eden. "A token of my love and commitment."

Joel and I kissed and hugged both girls and then led them back to their seats. The officiant continued the remainder of the ceremony until he said those words we'd both been waiting to hear.

"You may kiss the bride!"

Joel swooped me into his arms, held my face with both his hands, and whispered against my lips, "I'm going to love you forever." Then he kissed me.

The kiss went on until we heard fireworks exploding in the sky over our heads.

The girls squealed and jumped out of their seats, *oohing* at the top of their lungs.

"I now pronounce you husband and wife. Congratulations, Mr. and Mrs. Castellanos!"

Tonight, I would fill my cup with love and happiness.

Tomorrow, I'd meet with the devil.

Episode 86

Scratching the Surface

RUBY

Dinner at the Gordon Ramsay restaurant was out of this world delicious. Not only was the food beyond my expectations, but my dinner companion was also scrumptious. I hummed at the memory of tasting the bits of chocolate crumble off Nile's fingertips as he fed me a bite of his dessert.

"Where to next?" I asked, placing my hand on his thigh and squeezing it with intent. The quads underneath his bespoke suit were finely honed muscles that I wanted to sink my teeth into. I loved the fact that I knew what beauty hid behind his *GQ* appearance. His body was worthy of worship, and I hoped the evening would end with us completing the next intimate step, especially in light of our verbal commitment. I was eager for more after the taste he'd given me. Or, I should say, the taste he'd had of me.

"You'll see." He smiled and covered my wandering hand, bringing it to rest near his knee.

I pouted and stared out the window, watching the London landscape pass by. We saw an enormous Ferris wheel spinning slowly around, gifting its patrons a spectacular view of the city.

"Would you take me to the Ferris wheel some time?" I pointed out the car window.

"That's called the London Eye. Would you like to go now? I can have the driver change directions," he offered, immediately tossing out his plans in order to give me a new experience.

I cuddled closer to his side and sighed. "Another time. I'm looking forward to going where you've planned to take me. Dinner at a celebrity chef's flagship restaurant was more than I could have ever hoped for."

He ran his thumb over the top of my hand. "Do you like to cook?"

I nodded. "Very much so, but I haven't had much time to practice. Back home, I worked as much as possible in order to pay the bills for my sister's tuition and room and board."

"And Opal did what exactly?"

"School," I stated flatly. "She needed to focus all her time and energy on her studies if she was going to accomplish her goals. And she was good at it. Highest grade point average in our high school all four years and at her community college."

"And what about your goals?" he asked, a sternness to his tone I hadn't heard before.

"She was my goal. *Is* my goal. Everything I've done is to give Opal and me a chance at having a life outside of how and where we grew up."

"Explain?" The single word was more a demand than a question.

I cleared my throat. "Well, we had a rough childhood. As you've now learned from my mother's vile attack against Opal, we never had it easy. Being older, I felt it was my responsibility to take care of my baby sister."

"Opal is hardly a baby. She's just under two years your junior. And yet you claim you are marrying me in order to give her a better life," he accurately explained.

I shrugged one shoulder. "I mean, obviously my marriage to you will benefit us both." I smirked. "And it's not as though you're a monster I don't want to be around. I enjoy your company. I had fun at dinner. I'm having fun now."

He stared at me through the streams of light breaking the darkness in the vehicle from the moon and the city lights. "Somehow I feel as though I've only scratched the surface of the woman I am about to marry."

I grinned huge. "Good thing you have three years to figure me out."

He lowered his head and took my mouth in a sensual, lingering kiss that continued to rise in heat until the limo abruptly stopped.

"We're here?" I whispered, out of breath.

"Time doesn't seem to exist when I'm with you. It just slips away along with all of my responsibilities." His breath fanned across my lips delectably. "It's refreshing." His dark gaze took in every inch of my face as though he was tracing it in a featherlight caress.

I trembled under the scrutiny, arousal warming my blood and making specific parts of me throb in anticipation of what was to come.

Nile alighted from the vehicle and stretched out his hand. "Come, darling," he requested.

I placed my hand within his and allowed him to help me out of the vehicle.

Shockingly, camera flashes went off in what seemed to be thousands of sharp, eye-piercing snaps of light.

I covered my eyes and wobbled on my stilettos.

"Sodding paparazzi," Nile grumbled between his teeth.

"Mr. Pennington. Nile!" One of the men holding a camera called out, "Who's the woman with you? Is she your girlfriend?"

I assumed Nile would rush us inside of the establishment, but instead, he curled an arm around my waist and twisted us to face the cameras. "Show time, love," he whispered in my ear. I shot right to attention. It was as if I'd been called on in school by the teacher when I wasn't paying attention. Straightening my spine, I plastered myself to Nile's side and lovingly placed my hand on his chest. Next in my arsenal, I whipped up my best fake smile. The same one I'd used trying to earn a bidder at the auction. The same one the governess had approved of during our practice sessions.

"Mr. Pennington! Mr. Pennington! Are you formally admitting that one of England's most eligible bachelors is officially off the market?"

England's most eligible bachelor?

That was a piece of information I did not know about the Pennington brothers. I assumed that Noah was also on that list.

Nile looked straight into my face and smiled. "That I am. Let me be the first to introduce my fiancée," he oozed in that debonair British accent that made Americans swoon. "Ms. Ruby Dawson. We are to wed at month's end."

I did my best not to let my fear show as the cameras went wild and the onlookers battered us with questions.

"Ruby, Ruby, turn to the front. Let us get a good look at you," a tall string bean of man asked in a creepy way. He reminded me of the men who attended the strip club I used to dance at. The same ones who tried to follow the dancers to their cars and ask for dates at the end of the night. "Ask" maybe not being the right word for the things they'd attempt. I'd always had to have a bouncer walk me to my car.

"She will do no such thing," Nile barked and curved me closer to his body in a protective gesture that made me feel all squishy inside. "You've got your pictures and your answers." Nile continued, "Let us have our privacy. Good evening." His unforgiving manner brooked no argument.

The doors of the building we'd been standing in front of suddenly opened, and bulky doormen ushered us inside.

"Mr. Pennington. Welcome," said a man in a pristine gray three-piece suit, hair slicked back with a bouffant style in front.

"It's always a delight to have you at Reds, sir."

"So much so that you alerted the media about my reservation?" Nile responded coolly.

"I assure you, sir. I was not the one who notified the press. I will promise, however, that said person on my staff will be reprimanded accordingly." He lowered his chin in deference to Nile's sharp and accurate allegation.

"Our table?" Nile asked while I stayed at his side, silently taking in the space.

Reds was well, red. Everything but the wooden tables, bar, and ceiling was dark brown, but the lighting surrounding the space gave a rosy hue to the entire room. Everywhere the eye could see were red velvet couches and chairs in cozy nooks lit by candlelight. There were even pretty crystal chandeliers throughout. Classical music was playing while customers waited, facing an empty stage where a glossy black grand piano sat.

The suited man led us to the front of the stage, but Nile tapped him on the arm and whispered something in his ear.

"A bit more privacy?" the man repeated. "Of course, sir." He promptly changed direction and led us to a darker corner that still had a clear view of the stage, but there were no patrons surrounding us. Each side of the booth had a divider, giving the impression of being alone.

Nile held his hand out to me, and I slid along the soft seat. My heart thrummed a solid beat as Nile made his way to the other side, settling his body smack dab against mine. He put his hand over the top of my thigh, easing the fabric of my dress back so he could caress more skin.

"Would you like anything to drink before the show starts?" the manager asked.

"Do you like champagne, darling?" Nile faced me but teased sensual figure eights around the skin just above my knee.

"Doesn't everyone?"

"Anyone with taste, yes." His gaze fell to my mouth and then came back up to my eyes. The fire and light in them heady and rife with sexual tension. "The Krug Brut 1988 if you have it."

The man smiled and pressed his hands together. "Right away, sir," he stated before practically jog-walking through the place.

"You make him nervous," I teased.

Nile slid his hand farther up my leg, his fingers dipping into the crevice where I had them pressed together.

I gasped at his brazen touch, looking around the room to see if anyone could see us. They couldn't. We were all the way in the back corner, covered not only by a very large table and the darkness of the room, but also by the tablecloth hanging over our laps.

"I make a lot of people nervous, love." His breath fanned across my ear and neck, sending arousal racing straight between my thighs. "Do I make you nervous?"

"No" came out in a needy gasp, hinting at the sexual tension that filled the space between us.

"Then open for me," he dared, his tone gravelly and direct.

Wantonly, I opened my thighs several inches.

He hummed in the back of his throat as his hand cupped my sex possessively.

My breath hitched, and my heart pounded as he started to rub me through my lace panties.

Arousal poured through my veins as I gulped and braced both my hands on the seat cushion, wanting his touch more than anything. Still, I worried we might get caught. "What are you doing?"

"Whatever I want. What you've been clamoring for all night." It was the first time I realized how much confidence he possessed. "Do you not approve?"

I whimpered and shook my head when his fingers dug into the front of my panties, slipping easily over my clit to dip inside.

I let my head fall forward as I thrust my hips in counter movements, losing myself to his touch.

"And here is the Krug 1988 as requested." The manager appeared with a metal bucket filled with ice, a bottle of champagne, and two tall, tapered crystal flutes.

I clamped my legs, caging Nile's hand as I went completely still, the fear of getting caught ramping up my desire a hundred times over.

"Darling, relax," Nile said out loud. It was a simple request, but I knew what it meant. He wanted me to let him touch me secretly, right in front of this stranger. "Tonight is all about your pleasure," he murmured against the skin of my shoulder.

Feeling the dare boiling between us, I did as he asked, opening my legs. Only I one-upped him by lifting my knee and thigh up onto the booth seat, still hidden under the tablecloth but giving him a wide-open playing field.

He hummed low and gravely from the back of his throat. "Oh, darling, you are going to be rewarded handsomely." He dragged his teeth along the ball of my shoulder as the manager set about opening our champagne. Right as the manager popped the cork, Nile found the hip string to my lace panties and snapped the fabric with a quick yank.

"Jesus," I gasped as Nile swirled two fingers around my clit until I was panting. I moved my hips slowly and dug my fingers into the velvet, keeping an eye on the manager.

It was thrilling, lewd, and depraved in a way that astonished me. I was getting off on the danger and exhibitionism of it all.

The manager filled our glasses and set them in front of us. "The show starts in a few minutes. Wave if you need assistance. Otherwise, we'll leave you alone."

Nile plunged two fingers deep within me. "Oh!" I cried out and then pretended to cough to cover my slip-up.

"Much appreciated. Thank you," Nile said and waved his free hand, his other fucking me slowly as we watched the manager walk away.

"Mmm," I hummed as he found that place inside me that felt so good I could hardly breathe.

"You are the most divine creature I have ever had the pleasure of touching," Nile complimented as he nibbled at my earlobe, his cologne mingling with the scent of sex in the air.

I thrust my hips against his fingers, now desperate to find release. "Nile," I pleaded, not knowing what more to do.

The stage lights went on, and the lights offstage dimmed further. This made Nile even bolder. He curved his body toward me, fingering me with more intent.

"I can hear how wet you are." His words were teasing my senses. "I can smell your delicious cunt." He ran his tongue down the length of my neck, and it might as well have been him licking between my thighs for how wild I became. My mind was a haze of need and want. Nothing but the two of us mattered. "Do you have any idea how much you turn me on? How hard you make me?" He sank his teeth into the spot where my neck and shoulder met.

"Nile, please," I begged, digging my fingernails into his thigh. "*Please.*"

"Please what, my darling? Fuck you right here, in front of everyone? Make you come? Lick your sweet pussy until you come so many times you pass out like last time?" he taunted, never letting up on the action between my thighs.

"Yes," I hissed, thrusting my hips against his talented, plunging fingers. They sank deep, and I arched into them, completely lost to what this man was doing to my body. I'd never had sexual relations where I'd felt wanton and restless with the desire only to get off. I had a difficult relationship with sex and stayed away from it. Not with him. Nile broke something open inside of me that no one had ever touched.

I *wanted* to fuck him. Wanted to do everything with him. Wanted to get on my knees under the table and suck him off. Every dirty thing girls my age thought about doing with a partner they trusted was what I wanted to do with Nile.

My fiancé.

The man I was marrying for money was suddenly

becoming the only man I wanted to be with. In every way.

Nile held me to him and manipulated my G-spot, fingers working deep, while his thumb swirled around my throbbing hot button in dizzying circles. I wasn't used to a person touching me with the sole purpose of bringing me intense pleasure. Not since he'd gone down on me.

"I'm going to..." I choked out.

"Yes, you absolutely are about to fall apart in my arms," he agreed. Then Nile worked me harder, the darkness hiding all as beautiful piano music filled the room and a sultry feminine voice started to sing "Fever" in a crooning, sensual tone.

The fire blazed inside me so strongly I knew I wasn't going to be able to keep quiet. The mewling and whimpering began. Just as the power of my release hit, Nile slammed his mouth over mine, muffling my cries of passion with his kiss.

He ravished my mouth as I convulsed in his arms, the orgasm seeming to go on and on in a powerful burst of energy.

When it calmed, Nile's kisses slowed, turning more sensual and lingering. Our tongues explored one another for a few minutes before he eased his hand from between my thighs and pulled far enough away that he could lift his hand between us. Then he boldly sucked the two fingers he'd had inside me. He closed his eyes and moaned as though he was tasting the finest aged spirits.

"Just as I remember. Divine." He licked his lips, then pressed his thumb to my mouth. "Taste," he challenged.

I took his thumb into my mouth and swirled my tongue around the sensitive pad. The flavor was rich earthiness mixed with a hint of salt.

Nile's eyes blazed with desire. "You are absolute perfection, Ruby. I cannot wait to take you home and continue our play."

"Then why don't you?" I argued.

His brows rose. "Good things come to those who wait."

"No, good girls *come* when you take them home and fuck

them silly, which is what we should do right now."

He smirked. "Is that so?"

"Are you saying you don't want to fuck me?"

"Oh, my darling, there are many things I want to do with you. Fucking being one of them. More than that, I intend to keep you in my bed, where I will ravish you until we both can't walk. Alas, this is supposed to be our first date."

"When did I ever say I wasn't the type of girl to put out on the first date?" I scoffed.

"Are you?" He took his glass and sipped the champagne neither of us had touched.

"I am for you."

He practically purred. "This pleases me. Almost as much as it pleases me to make you wait. Enjoy your drink. It's a very good year. We'll be home soon enough."

I grabbed the champagne, lifted it to my lips, and drank it down in one go. I set the glass back down a little harder than was necessary. "Yummy. I'm ready to go."

Nile burst out laughing. "Ruby, love, you never cease to amaze me."

Episode 87

Falling on the Sword

NOAH

"I'm not only celibate, I'm a virgin."

The statement Opal had made in the car a couple days ago was on rapid repeat in my mind.

A celibate virgin.

To find out she was a virgin wasn't really that much of a shock. A lot of men and women waited to sow their wild oats until they were in university. And I was pleased that she would turn twenty in a few days. Something about leaving that "teen" title behind made me feel relieved. It was silly seeing as we were only six years apart in age.

The celibate part was what I wanted to further discuss with the outspoken woman. If she'd never had sex, how did she know she did not want to partake of it? What could cause a young person to come to such extreme principles? Perhaps she was religious? Maybe instead of celibate she meant abstinent? Abstinence by choice I could work with.

Either way, I'd need to get to the bottom of it. As much as I wanted a wife, I planned on fully committing to the brash, outspoken woman for a period of no less than three years. I would not be abstaining from sexual activities during that time, and I did not fancy myself a womanizer. I'd not force her to do something she didn't want to do, nor would I sneak around behind her back. Mistresses and back-door dealings were not part of my repertoire. I intended to be faithful to the woman I chose to share my life with and expected that same loyalty in return.

Speaking of the devil, she came padding down the staircase, her melted-chocolate gaze on me where I relaxed in the dining room. She wore a simple pair of blue jeans, a white tank top, and an oversized butter-yellow jumper that paired well with her tan skin. She had scuffed white trainers on her feet and a scowl on her lips.

I grinned widely. "Good morning, poppet. How did you sleep?" I asked, wanting to break the ice and get to the real reason I'd been waiting for her to come down to breakfast.

Opal lifted her hand and ran her fingers through her thick, espresso-colored hair and sighed. "Don't you have a job you need to go to?"

As expected, her snarky side came out to play. "I am master of my own universe. I choose my work schedule." I stood and pulled out the chair directly across from mine, as much to give her space as to be able to look her directly in the eyes. "Sit. We have much to discuss."

She sighed under her breath but took the seat I offered.

"We're ready!" I announced.

Within moments, one of the kitchen staff entered with two steaming plates of fried eggs, bacon, beans, sausage, sliced tomatoes, black pudding, and toast. Another server carried a tea kettle and a basket filled with a variety of jams.

"Goodness gracious, this is a ton of food," Opal wheezed. "I would have been good with an English muffin."

I chuckled. "Eat what you like and leave the rest."

Opal's expression soured. "I don't appreciate wasting food.

Too many in the world go hungry as it is. I know what that feels like all too well, and I..."

"You've gone hungry? Truly?" I interrupted, eager to learn any bits and bobs I could about the enigmatic Opal Dawson.

She slumped back against her chair and thanked the servers after they poured her tea and placed a napkin on her lap. "Yeah. Ruby did her best, but it's not like a ten-year-old can go out and buy food alone. There were a lot of times when the only meal we had was at school. Until Ruby was around fourteen and started to pick up odd jobs like raking the leaves from lawns in the nicer neighborhoods, getting a paper route, offering to help the single mom in our trailer park clean houses while I watched her kid. That type of thing."

A surge of anger flooded my veins as I imagined a ten-year-old Ruby and her eight-year-old sister sitting in a trailer park with no food on the table while Nile and I had servers dishing out more food during a single meal than we could eat in a week.

It was dawning on me, the more I spoke with Opal, how vastly mistreated these sisters had been. It also highlighted how much Ruby had left out over the past weeks of us getting to know her. She hadn't been forthcoming in the slightest.

I realized then that I didn't know Ruby Dawson at all. Every day it seemed something new was being unraveled about the mysterious woman. Then again, I imagined Nile had learned far more intimate details since they'd recently shared a bedroom and gone out on their first official "date" last night. Neither having risen yet from said event.

"Even more reason for you to ensure that you and Ruby never have to live that type of lifestyle again. Marry me, and all of your problems will be solved. You'll have school, your sister, a husband, a sizeable bank account, and a new life in London, far away from any of that."

Opal prodded at a circular slice of black pudding, turning it from front to back. "What is this?"

"Blood sausage," I answered.

Her head jerked back. "I'm sorry. Did you say blood sausage?"

"Yes." I clapped my hands, wanting to get the show on the road. There was a lot to do if we were to move forward on our plan to dupe my brother and get Ruby off the hook for marrying a man she didn't love. "My lawyers have drawn up the marriage agreement. It is almost identical to the one Nile and I signed for The Marriage Auction with Madam Alana."

"What does that mean exactly? Blood sausage? Is that referencing its color, because this is, well, mostly black." She inserted the tines of her fork into the sand dollar-sized patty and lifted it up to her nose for a sniff.

"It means it's made with pork or beef blood, fat, and grain such as oats or barley. Now, unfortunately, in order to marry in England, we are required to submit our intent to marry to the Register's Office at least twenty-eight days prior to the wedding. Madam Alana took care of that but supplied Ruby's name. I won't be able to pull any strings to make it faster for the two of us."

"You eat this? Blood mixed with fat and oatmeal?" Her nose crinkled, and I finally saw something that distinctly connected the sisters. They crinkled their noses the same way when they didn't like something. It was endearing and adorable in a way that I thought I might enjoy seeing regularly from the two women.

"Yes, poppet. It's a very common dish."

"It's gross. What would make someone think, oh, I know what sounds good! Meat mashed with blood mixed with oatmeal. Yum, yum. Gobble, gobble." She continued ranting while inspecting the sausage.

I laughed and then let out a long breath. "Darling, we really need to hash out these things if we are to move forward with our plan prior to Ruby and Nile's wedding."

"I haven't agreed to marry you yet. I'm still not sure it's the right choice." She pursed her lips. "Why do you have baked beans with eggs, bacon, tomatoes, and the gross blood sausage?" She continued inspecting her breakfast. "It's a really odd combination. It's like breakfast and an outdoor barbeque had a baby and *voila*...this." She gestured to her plate as though she was highlighting an item up for sale.

"Opal, forget about the meal. Back up to the part about not having agreed to marry me. I have believed since our chat in the car that we are on the same page. Are we not?" My heartbeat pounded a rapid rhythm in my chest as sweat beaded at my hairline. I needed her to agree, or all would be lost.

"I mean, it's one idea. I'm just not sure. Ruby's already put everything on the line..."

"Which is all the more reason why you should take that burden off her," I countered. "She's carried the brunt of sacrifice for your lives for as long as you can remember. That is the concern you've shared. You also made it seem as though you wished to relieve her of that burden."

Her head snapped up, her gaze meeting mine. "I do. I want to be the one who falls on the sword for us."

I grimaced, not enjoying the analogy that made marrying me akin to falling on a sword.

"Then you will marry me?" I reiterated, wanting her to finally say the words: that she would indeed become my wife.

"You yourself just said that we couldn't get married because of the twenty-eight-day wait. How do you propose to get around that?"

"Excellent question. I'm so glad you asked." I grinned.

She glared, pushed aside her sausage, and picked up her toast, sinking her teeth into one of the triangular slices. Her response, "Go on, enlighten me," came out muffled as she chewed.

"We'll marry in Denmark. The day I asked you to marry me, I had my legal team submit the required paperwork. It only takes a few days. If you agree, we can be man and wife by this Sunday, exactly one week before Ruby and Nile are set to wed."

"You want to fly to Denmark?" she asked.

"Indeed."

"This weekend?"

I nodded.

"My birthday is Friday, and you want to get married on Sunday?" Opal confirmed.

"Yes. We can celebrate both."

"And what about the, um, thing I told you?" Her voice lowered to almost a whisper.

"About being a virgin?" I cocked a brow.

She looked from left to right when I said the word *virgin* as though it was a naughty word.

"Yes," she hissed. "And can you keep your voice down? I don't want anyone to know what we're talking about."

"It's a nonissue." I picked up my tea and sipped the warm liquid.

"How is it a nonissue? You're going to be okay with not having sex?"

"No. It's a nonissue because I will take your virginity as the gift it is."

She blanched, her entire face turning ghost white.

"I will be gentle. We'll go slow. And I promise, you will feel nothing but pleasure when we consummate our marriage on our wedding night." I smiled gently, wanting her to feel at ease.

"I told you I am *celibate*." Her voice shook with extreme emotion, not fear, leading me to believe I knew exactly why she claimed to be thus.

"Poppet, you are celibate because you are a virgin. Likely scared of what might occur with a man such as myself. But I assure you, I am a man you can trust. If you grant me the honor of taking you as my wife, of sharing my bed, I will have you begging me to fill you. Completely out of your mind with more pleasure than you could imagine."

She dropped her fork on the table. "I'm not celibate because I'm a virgin who doesn't know what sex is, asshole."

She stood so quickly her chair slammed back and fell to the ground. "I'm celibate because I watched my mother whore herself out multiple times a day to one stranger after another. I'm celibate because I listened to my sister be raped over and over by disgusting men our mother sold her child to while I hid in the closet. Sex has only ever been ugly, violent, and despicable," she sneered. "You'll never convince me otherwise. Go find someone else to marry." She turned around and raced to the stairs, taking them two at a time.

I sat for a long time as what Opal shared burned through my mind. These sisters had been through absolute Hell. Nothing I'd ever seen, heard, or experienced in my lifetime came even close to the things Opal had shared today.

Ruby had been raped. Repeatedly. Whored out by her own mother. And if what Opal had said was true, that she hid in the closet during those attacks, it meant that Ruby had taken the abuse for both of them so Opal wouldn't have to.

Ruby Dawson was a fucking saint. A living angel. The respect I had for her grew a hundredfold. To be able to carry on, work a job, plan to get married, continue on day after day in spite of such a tragic past proved the depth of her character. And even though she'd protected Opal from the physical abuse, she too had suffered. They both had, in such extreme ways that it was hard to swallow down the bile that climbed my throat. It was an even harder truth to hear and sit back and do nothing.

But I could do something. I could give Opal everything she'd ever missed out on. Show her what a good man looked like. Earn her trust. Hell, maybe that trust would one day turn to respect, compassion, and love. I was open to anything life offered me. I didn't close myself off to feeling love when our parents died, like Nile did. I'd just never trusted anyone enough to give the same type of love in return. Seeing what Ruby was doing for Opal, knowing more about the pieces and how they fit together, I was even more determined to let Ruby off the hook. To allow her the chance to make her own choices when it came to her life and the man she wanted in it. She may have chosen Nile over me, but would she have done so if she didn't have to get married in order to secure a better life for her and her sister?

I thought not.

I made my way out of the dining room, up the stairs, and to Opal's room. I could hear her crying through the door. I knocked softly and tried the handle, finding it open. I entered and closed it tight. Opal was sitting in a chair facing the estate grounds, her knees folded to her chest, her arms wrapped around them. She was in a literal knot, protecting herself from the demons of the past.

I came to her side and kneeled down before putting my hand over one of hers. "I'm sorry, Opal. I'm sorry for what you and Ruby endured. It's not okay. There is no world in which those experiences are acceptable. All I can do is apologize and tell you that I'd like to help. The family stuff between me and my brother is not for you and Ruby to worry about. But I do want to give Ruby the opportunity to live whatever life she wants. I want that for you as well."

She frowned and wiped away a tear that slid down her cheek. "What are you proposing?"

"I'll give you the money you need. You can both start new lives here in England. Neither of you need to get married. What's happened to you both is atrocious. I want to duel with my brother, and I want to win. I will win, but not at the price of your well-being or Ruby's."

"You don't want to marry me because of what I told you?"

I nodded. "Exactly."

"So what? You're going to find someone else to marry then?" Her tone held reproach.

I shrugged. "Perhaps. I don't really know."

"I'll do it."

I shook my head avidly. "You don't understand. I'm setting you and Ruby free. I'll have my financial team transfer over enough money for you both to get a healthy head start. Pay for your schooling. Get you a home. Whatever it takes."

"And I said I'll do it." She frowned. "Are you not listening? I said I'll marry you."

"What? I'm so confused." I slumped onto my shins.

She licked her lips. "The fact that you are willing to help us without anything in return shows you're the type of man I *could* want in my life. A man I could trust."

"In what way?" I hedged, not sure if I understood all that she was offering.

"Everything. Marriage. Sex. Being in a relationship." She looked down and away. "I'm afraid, Noah. So damn afraid it makes my gut sink just thinking about being vulnerable with a man. But I'm also smart enough to know that if I don't start somewhere, I'll never escape those fears. I'll never be free of my past and the pain it's caused. Those wounds will continue to haunt me."

"You want to try to be in a relationship with me? Get married and pull one over on my brother while I introduce you to…uh, the more intimate, sensual side of life?"

She chuckled. "Exactly."

I hooked a thumb toward the door. "Before, you were angry with me…"

Opal grabbed my hand. "That was before. This is now. I want to learn. I want to try to be open with a man. I want to be vulnerable with you. I…I trust you."

Her saying she trusted me made me feel ten feet tall.

"Okay," I gulped, not sure what else to say. The woman

had my head spinning like a merry-go-round.

"Ask me again." Opal brought her knees down, her feet to the floor, and sat up straight. "Ask me to marry you again."

A whirlwind of emotions battered my mind, and yet one message kept coming back. Opal *trusted* me. It was the most powerful treasure anyone had ever handed me. And I found I wanted to be worthy of her trust. Wanted to be the man who could change her life in so many beautiful ways.

"Opal Dawson, will you marry me?" My voice cracked.

She swallowed and smiled shyly.

"Yes."

Episode 88

The Cowboy and the Viking

SUTTON

The distinctive sound of someone vomiting woke me from a dead sleep. The reminder of last night's discussion with my wife flooded my mind as I wiped the grit from my eyes.

"I can't be pregnant."

She'd said it as if carrying my baby was the worst possible thing that could ever happen to her. In my mind, it was the exact opposite. I'd always wanted children, a whole house full. That was why I'd built this home with plenty of extra bedrooms and room enough around the property for my kin to roam.

I flung off the covers and followed the sound of my wife heaving her guts out. She wasn't in our bathroom, but in the guest bathroom farther down the hall. Probably didn't want me to hear her.

There I found my girl, curled over the rim of the toilet, her hair a strawberry-golden mess clutched in one fist while she clung to the porcelain throne as though her life depended on it.

I came up behind her and curled my body around her smaller frame.

"You don't want to see this," she blubbered, and then spit into the bowl.

The stench wafted up, and I breathed through my mouth. "I've seen far worse than a beautiful woman working the sickness out of her stomach. Let me help." I unfurled her fingers from her hair and pulled the locks away from her face as her body went tight, convulsed, and she dry-heaved.

I wrapped an arm around her stomach and held her close, not adding pressure but making sure she didn't feel alone in her misery.

When the worst of it passed, I flushed the toilet, rubbed her back, then stood and ran cool water over a couple washcloths. One was for her face and the other I alternated pressing against the back of her neck and forehead until finally she relaxed against me. Easing us both away from her shrine, I rested against the opposite wall with her curled in my lap. She laid her clammy cheek to my chest and sighed.

The poor thing reeked of vomit and the hint of wildflowers that always clung to her skin.

I cupped her cheek. "I think we should get you an appointment to see Doc Blevins."

She stirred in my arms, her body going stiff. "Can't we get a test first? I don't want everyone in town knowing our business."

"And you think Doc Blevins is going to share? That goes against the oath he took. 'Sides, Doc is a good, honorable man."

"Yeah, but his wife who hangs out at his office to chit-chat with everyone and their uncle is not held to the same oath. Mary Beth flaps her gums to anyone who will listen."

I hummed, knowing what she said was the damn truth. Mary Beth was a kind woman, but she did have a reputation for being the town gossip.

"You're sick, possibly pregnant, and that needs lookin' into," I said, firm in my conviction.

She lifted her face, her brown eyes pleading. "Let's confirm we're pregnant first. Then I'll consider going to the doc, okay?"

I frowned and cupped her cheek. "Dakota, you're the most important thing to me. If you're sick or hurting, I need to know that you're being seen to. I just wrapped my head around the fact that I've finally got you. In my bed, in my heart, and in my life for good. I can't bear to think something is hurting you and not doing anything and *everything* in my power to fix it."

She pressed her forehead to my chin. "And we will. First step, let's find out if we're going to be parents. Jesus, I can't believe I'm even saying that," she groaned.

I lifted her chin with my finger so I could see her eyes once more. "I thought you wanted children?"

Dakota sighed deeply. "Down the road, I do want them. I just believed we had more time. Time to plan for them. To be excited. To worry about maternity clothes and a nursery. We've been together less than *a month*. One month, Sutton. We haven't even had time to deal with my family's farm or my father's actions, and we've possibly got a child on the way?" Her voice caught. "It's like we're being hit with one life-changing event after another, and I...I don't know if I can keep up. It's too much."

"Hey, hey, now." I wrapped my arms around her in a full-body hug. "I'm here. We're going to face any challenge together. You are not alone. Not ever."

She slumped against me, wet drops falling on the skin of my shoulder as she silently cried. "Why do these things keep happening?" She half-hiccupped, her breath sawing in and out as more of her tears slid down my back and dried against my skin.

I held her close. "I don't know. But what I do know is that a baby made out of love is not a bad thing. I don't care how long we've been officially together. All I care about is that we are a family. Me and you. And if you are pregnant, that just means our family grew."

She laughed dryly. "It almost sounds like you're hoping I

am pregnant. Happy even."

I ran my hands up and down her back. "I am happy. I've got everything I could have ever wanted. *You*."

She sat up, straddled my lap, and wiped her tears using the bottom of the T-shirt of mine she wore, clearing away the snot dripping from her nose. "You really are good at this husband stuff." She pouted as though it irked her to admit such a truth.

I stared at my wife's ratty bedhead, clammy skin, snotty nose, swollen, teary eyes, and smelling of vomit. Right there and then, I thanked the good Lord for giving me such a boon. Even at her worst, she was the most beautiful thing I'd ever had as my own.

With reverence, I covered her stomach with my hand.

"We might have made a baby." My voice was low, tinged with awe.

She covered my hand with hers and took a deep breath. "Yeah."

"It's going to be okay." I answered with as much raw pride as I could muster in order to keep her calm. My mind was a jumble of wild emotions that I too needed time to work through. But I'd do that once she was taken care of.

It was possible I was going to be a father.

Definitely not something we'd planned, but it was an honor I'd wanted for as long as I could remember.

"You're going to make it all okay?" she whispered, hope in every word.

"I am," I promised. I'd do just about anything to make this woman happy.

She bit into her bottom lip and dipped her head, setting her forehead against mine. "I believe you."

We cleaned up and dressed, and I made her fluffy scrambled eggs and toast. I noticed she mostly pushed the food around her plate rather than put the nourishment into her body. I clenched my teeth, about to chastise her with the reminder that she could be eating for two, when there was a knock on the door.

"I'll get it. You eat. Meaning put the food *into* your mouth," I warned, pointing at her plate.

She snarled. "Maybe I don't want to puke all over our table. My stomach is still unsettled." She glared.

I grumbled but went to the door and opened it swiftly. Savannah stood there wrapped in an oversized knitted men's sweater, her hands mostly covered, just the tips of her fingers peeking out. Erik stood behind her, a solemn expression on his face.

"Um, can we come in? I need to see my sister," Savannah asked softly.

I tapped on the doorframe, wanting to slam it shut, take my wife to the pharmacy, get a test, and then spend the next week glorying in the very likely fact that we were going to have a baby. What I did not want to do was deal with her sister, the Viking, his family, or that damn Madam Alana. All of whom I'd forgotten were here after spending most of the night in a waiting room to see if my friend was going to make it. After all that had happened in private with my wife...as Dakota had suggested, we needed time. Time to process all of it. The one thing we didn't have.

I sighed and opened the door. "Come on in. Hungry? I just made eggs and toast."

"We already ate. Thank you," Erik answered.

Savannah silently walked in, her gaze taking in our modest home. It still lacked a woman's touch, which was another thing we should have had the time to do. Since I'd brought Dakota back from Las Vegas, it had been one disaster after another. I couldn't blame her fear of bringing a child into this. Nothing was settled or consistent, and children needed a solid home environment to thrive.

"We just moved in. Haven't had the chance to make it our own yet. Come on. Dakota's in the kitchen."

They followed me into our kitchen where Dakota was standing. Savannah went straight into her sister's open arms and burst into tears.

"Everything is so messed up, Kota," she bawled.

I set about making coffee for the two of them, finding out from Erik how they preferred it.

Eventually Dakota got Savannah to calm down. Which was when Savannah went straight into the story of what happened when she met with Jarod's family at the hospital. I hadn't stayed for their meet and greet yesterday, too focused on getting information on Brody. Now that I was hearing the details of what had occurred, I was fuming.

These two sisters couldn't seem to catch a break to save their lives.

Not only were they dealing with their father in jail. A burned down barn. Lost horses. Debt up to their eyeballs on their family's land, now they had townies threatening to sue? And Dakota hadn't even shared the violent and rather despicable history their grandmother had suffered at the hands of their beloved granddaddy.

The issue with the Talleys I could handle on their behalf. I knew them well. They were considered good people, well-respected in the community, maybe a bit hungry for more in life, as anyone would be in a small town. I'd heard Jarod's father griping at the local watering hole about how he'd been taken for a ride on one deal or another over the years, keeping them stuck in a modest home with little to call their own. Still, that didn't give them the right to threaten taking away someone else's land.

I gestured to Erik, and he came around the kitchen table and followed me out to the porch, leaving the women to it.

I stood against the railing and looked out over the tree line. Erik leaned against one of the wooden pillars and waited for me to speak.

"Man of few words?" I asked.

He shrugged and sipped his coffee. I waited for him to add something. To let me know where he stood in all of this mess.

"I want to take Savannah far away from here," he stated flatly. "I've been here less than twenty-four hours and I've seen more heartache and tears from her than I have the entire time I've known her."

I nodded. "Feeling is mutual. Except this is Dakota's home. She's made it clear this is where she wants to be. The only thing threatening that is her father."

"And what about the threat made to Savannah by Mrs. Talley?"

I waved a hand. "I can handle the Talleys. They're angry. Hurt most likely that they didn't know Savannah wasn't going to be in their family. I'm sure when Jarod hooked his lead to Savannah and the McAllister farm, he thought he was moving up in the world. Boy found a pretty girl and the possibility of more. That's been taken away by the likes of you." I lifted my chin. "He'll get over it."

"You've had more time to assess the situation with the farm than I have. What's your plan?" Erik asked.

"To get old man McAllister off the deed," I answered.

"Does it matter now that he'll be facing life in prison for attempted murder?" Erik added.

I sighed and set my mug on the railing. "I suppose not. Then again, nothing is ever black and white. There are always plenty of shades of gray." I knew better than most that you couldn't count on any one thing happening. Hard work, sacrifice, and commitment usually did the job, though.

"What do you think is the best plan of action?"

"We find out what the sisters want and support 'em in it. I'm assuming they're in for a fifty-fifty split, being the only living McAllisters, once their pa goes to prison."

Erik rubbed at his cropped beard, his long hair hanging down around his ears. "I'm not so sure Savannah's interest lies in keeping the farm anymore," he confided.

"Really?" I asked, surprised. "She wants to be bought out?" A million ideas burned through my mind at the possibility. Dakota and I could easily combine farms, add more ranch hands, and start the process of truly making the farm something she could be proud of again. A fresh start for everyone involved.

"She might. Told me today she didn't feel as this was her home anymore." Erik focused his gaze out over the horizon. "I'd like to take her back to my home, have her finish her studies, and do whatever brings that smile back. Show her my farms and the brewing business, travel, make a family..."

I smiled widely and moved closer to my future brother-in-law. "You keepin' Savannah for good?"

Erik frowned. "As opposed to?"

"Don't play coy, brother." I clapped him on the shoulder. "The contract is for three years, remember?"

"Is that what you plan on doing? Divorcing Dakota after the time is up?" Erik's expression was horrified.

"Hell, no!" I reassured him. "That feisty woman is all mine, and I am all hers." *Especially now*, I thought. "There's nuthin' that's going to tear us apart."

"I have no intention of letting Savannah go," Erik said.

I grinned. "Does she know that?"

Erik clenched his jaw, a muscle ticking in his cheek. "She will soon enough. When I've had more time to convince her. First, we get married. Something we were supposed to do here." He reminded me why they were in Sandee.

"Bad luck," I hissed and shook my head. "What about our farm? My parents have a huge deck looking out over thousands of acres of nothing but land, cattle, trees, and wildflowers. We could do it up right. Clear out space in the barn for a reception."

Erik smiled. "Yeah? You'd do that for us?"

I gripped him by the shoulder and squeezed. "We're family. Those women make us brothers. I take that role seriously."

"Thank you. It sounds incredibly generous. I'll have to discuss it with Savannah, but our window of time is waning. And I know she'd like her sister present for our nuptials. I'd be in your debt."

"Nah, man…" Then an idea hit. "But I do have a favor to ask."

"Anything." Erik stood up straighter, a man ready to pay back a kindness he believed he owed.

He didn't owe anything. Allowing him and Savannah to get married on Goodall land would make my mother the happiest woman on Earth and get her off my back. It would also win me serious points with Dakota. Double win in my book.

"I need to go into town and have you purchase something on my behalf, without anyone knowing who it's for. I'm talking stealth job, brother. I figure no one will question a stranger that looks like you." I laughed, loving the idea more and more.

His eyebrows rose up his forehead. "And what will I be buying?" he asked in a leery tone. It took all I had not to burst out laughing.

"A pregnancy test."

Erik's eyes widened, but he didn't say a word. He simply nodded. More proof he was a good man.

"I'll get the keys." I gestured to the work truck my parents had loaned me yesterday that was still sitting out in front of my house.

"I'll tell Savannah we're taking a ride into town," he stated.

I held up my finger to my lips in a shushing motion. "This

is between me and you. Brother to brother."

Erik turned, put both of his hands to my shoulders, and looked me straight in the eyes. "Brother to brother."

"I think I'm going to enjoy being related to you, Erik," I offered, wanting to express how much this chat meant to me.

"The feeling is mutual, Sutton. Get your keys. We have a stealth mission to complete." He grinned.

"Damn straight we do."

Episode 89

Maybe Baby

SAVANNAH

"Enough!" I held up my hands, palms facing out. "Kota, I seriously cannot handle any more." I stood, grabbed the mugs and her mostly uneaten breakfast plate, and took them to the sink.

"I'm sorry, Savvy," Dakota apologized. "I know our family's sordid past isn't what you wanted to hear after everything that happened yesterday, but it would have been wrong of me to keep our history from you."

I flipped on the faucet and rinsed the dishes, my insides feeling completely wrung out and numb as all the chaos piled up one thing right after the other.

My grandmother had been forced to marry her rapist.

Our beloved great-granddaddy had cared more about business and profit than his only daughter's happiness.

I gritted my teeth as revulsion clawed painfully at my heart. I clumsily put the plate into the dishwasher, my hands shaking at the news I'd learned. "I can't believe she was in love with Duke Goodall Senior, Sutton's granddaddy. And now here you are, married to his grandson."

Kota ran her fingers through her loose waves a few times, pushing the locks out of her face. "Yeah. It seems everything has come full circle." She tapped her fingers on the kitchen table and snuck a furtive glance at me.

"I'm not going to freak out. I mean, I am freaking out, on the inside, because it's a lot to digest. Finding out the man we loved more than any other wronged our grandmother in such a way is devasting. I mean, I based what a good man should be on the way our great-granddaddy treated us. How he doted on us…" I gagged as the coffee I'd drunk started to climb its way back up my throat.

I braced my hands on the lip of the sink and breathed through the disgust and shame. I couldn't even cry anymore. I'd cried all the tears I could yesterday and this morning. My eyes physically hurt. They were swollen, itchy, and dry at the moment.

"Our family is so fucked up, Kota," I said while breathing through the madness swirling in my mind.

An arm wrapped around my shoulders. I leaned my head against Dakota's as the two of us stared through the window over the sink out at the land beyond the back porch. It was unbelievably beautiful.

"We're changing that, Savvy. Have a little faith. We can bring the farm back to its glory days and leave it to our children. Make something special out of it."

The thought of raising my children on the same farm that had such tragedy and strife tied to it made my chest tighten even more. As the concept evolved and changed, it spread across my body like red fire ants.

"Kota, I don't want that," I whispered, barely getting the truth out and into the open.

Her hand moved from my shoulder, and she started to play with a lock of my hair. "What don't you want, Savvy?"

"I don't want to raise my children here. I don't want my

kids knowing any of our history." I admitted the reality I'd only just begun to accept myself.

Being here with Erik after having spent time with him in Norway had shown me everything I needed to know. I'd thought coming back where I had roots would make me happy. It didn't. Everything I'd ever disliked about myself and my life had happened on McAllister land. I'd lost my mother here. My grandmother. Experienced emotional and physical abuse at the hands of my father. Watched my sister hurt repeatedly. Good memories were few and far between.

Dakota eased to the side and rested her bum against the counter.

"I don't want anything to do with the farm," I admitted, fear thickening the weight of each word I spoke.

"But it's the entire reason we…" Dakota blinked rapidly.

I lifted my finger to stop her train of thought.

"I know we entered into The Marriage Auction to save our family's land, but after almost a month of living a completely new life, I've realized something."

Dakota canted her head to the side.

"The farm has never been what I wanted. I believed it was what was *expected* of me. To come back from school and stay here."

"But you love farm life…"

I nodded. "I do. Absolutely. Love training and breeding horses. Love working with the animals. Love the smell of hay. But I can work on animals and live just about anywhere. Ever since we were little, you wanted to work the land and make our family's farm the best it could be. You always had a vision for it. One I didn't actually share. I just tried to fit in like a mismatched puzzle piece."

"Savvy, your contributions are important. Don't sell yourself short," she contradicted instantly.

I smiled and took her hand. "I know you feel that way, and I agree. I worked my butt off to do everything I could to help, but what I'm really passionate about is the animals. Seeing to their health and well-being has always been my calling."

"And you can still do all of that here. We have the money from the guys, and our father is likely going to prison for the rest of his life, meaning we'll finally have full authority over the land."

I lifted her hand and rubbed my cheek against it. "I'm sorry. That's not what I want."

"What do you want?" Her voice dipped, concern filling the air around us.

"I want Erik. I want to move to Norway. Finish my studies and get my degree. Travel the world. Maybe set up a practice somewhere. Honestly, I don't really know. What I do know is that Erik is willing to support me in whatever I decide. He just wants me to be happy."

"And that happiness means you're going to move a continent away from your big sister?" she choked out.

I tugged her into my arms and hugged her tightly. "Don't be that way, Kota. You know with rich-ass husbands, we can travel whenever we want. Hell, Erik has a private plane and more money than God. He won't care if we want to travel every few months to visit."

"And if there are children involved... Then what?" she asked randomly.

I shrugged. "Then we'll make it visits once every other month. And calls. And video chats. The world isn't as closed off as it once used to be. Even though I know technology and you aren't the best of friends, I can teach you how to stay in contact without feeling so far apart."

Dakota pulled back and sighed. "You really want out of the family business? Entirely?"

The mere thought should have brought me feelings of dread and sadness. Instead, the idea lifted an incredibly heavy anvil off my chest. Relief poured through my veins, filling me with a lightness I hadn't felt in...well, ever.

"I really do." I smiled widely, the decision fortifying itself in my mind.

"Savvy, you know I won't be able to buy you out right away. And you've already spent your first installment from the auction to pay down the debt and the bank liens against the land."

I grabbed both of Dakota's hands. "Keep it. I don't want anything back nor do I want to be bought out. I just don't want to be part of any of it going forward. I'll sign whatever you need to ensure you get everything."

"But, Savvy, in ten years you might feel differently. Heck, in three years when you get divorced, you'll want a safe place to land."

I frowned. "First and foremost, who knows what my marriage will bring? I'm not going into it with an end date. Second, are you telling me that if I leave everything behind and need to come home, you won't offer me a place to live?"

Dakota's head snapped back, and a horrified expression tore across her face. "No! My God. How could you say such a thing? I'd never leave you out on your ass. And I'll be the first one to bail you out of any trouble."

"Exactly. And I would do the same for you. It's always been us sisters against all the odds."

Dakota pouted. "And now you want to leave…"

I cupped her cheeks. "It's not that I want to *leave*, Dakota. It's that I want to *live*. I want to give this marriage I'm entering a real chance. I want to give Erik that chance. The feelings he stirs in me…" I shook my head. "Are unexplainable. I feel like I could climb Mount Everest. Paint a masterpiece. Learn how to play an instrument. Erik doesn't put limitations or obligations on his care for me or the life we could live together."

"And I never will," came Erik's accented voice standing at the arch of the dining area, two plastic bags in his hands.

Both Dakota and I jumped at the sudden intrusion of our men, neither of us having heard them come in. My cheeks flushed with embarrassment as he'd obviously caught my response, though the smile on his face said he liked what he'd heard.

Sutton came barreling in with another few plastic bags and set the lot on the table.

"What is all this?" Dakota asked.

Sutton's eyes widened. "Um..."

"Pregnancy tests and items that are supposed to decrease morning sickness," Erik answered.

Sutton shoved Erik. "Brother! What part of 'stealth mission' did you forget?"

"Pregnancy tests?" I spun around and faced Dakota. "You're pregnant?"

She pulled the length of her hair to the top of her head and let out a long breath. "Maybe?" she admitted.

"Holy. Fucking. Shit. You think you're pregnant!" I screeched at the top of my lungs, excitement, worry, and a heavy dose of disbelief bleeding into every word.

Sutton pushed past me and Dakota face-planted right against his chest as though she'd done it a thousand times before. He instantly started to rub his hands up and down her back in a soothing gesture. "I'm sorry the Viking let the cat out of the bag."

"I'm not a Viking, *Jesus Kristus!*" Erik cursed in his language.

I went over to the table and looked through the first set of bags. There were crackers, lemon-lime soda, popsicles, yogurt, applesauce, bananas, and more. The other bags held a variety of prenatal vitamins and a dozen or more pregnancy tests.

"Why are there so many tests?" I asked, pulling them out and lining them up on the table.

Erik groaned. "The first store in town only had one kind, and it was generic. Sutton did not like this, so we drove to the next town over that had a larger selection. Which is when I grabbed two of everything they had. How am I to know which is best? And then some of them talk of false positives, so I figured it was better safe than sorry."

Dakota chuckled and left her husband's arms to check out the plethora of tests.

"Wow. Electronic. Plus and minus sign. One line, two lines. Jeez Louise, I didn't even know they had this many options," Dakota groaned.

"Pee on one of each, and we'll compare them," Sutton suggested.

Dakota turned around, exasperation clear on her face. "You want me to pee on a dozen sticks at the same time? Are you nuts?"

He shrugged, and then went to the fridge, grabbed a bottle of water, and brought it to her. "Feel like you need to pee yet?"

Dakota glared. "No!"

"Then drink up. You've got a lot of testin' to do, darlin'." He grinned wickedly.

"Goodall, I swear you're going to be sleeping alone tonight if you keep pushing. Maybe I'm not ready to test. You might not realize this, but it's *scary*, okay?" she huffed.

He sighed. "It's not that you're afraid to test. You're afraid of the outcome. I'll come into the bathroom with you. We can kick out your sister and brother-in-law."

"Oh, hell no!" I snapped. "If my sister is taking a pregnancy test for the first time in her life, I'm going to be ready for the fallout, whichever way that goes."

Sutton pointed at me from across the table. "I'm the husband, in case you forgot. She may be carrying *my* baby, not yours."

"Shares my blood," I fired back with all the sass.

He squinted. "It's my job to take care of all of Dakota's needs. If there is any 'fallout'"—he used air quotes with his fingers—"then I'll be the one handling it."

I was about to nail him right in the kisser when Erik wrapped an arm around my waist and backed us up. He put his mouth to my ear. "*Elskede*, this is a major life moment."

"I know, which is why I need to be here. For my sister!" I hissed in Sutton's direction.

He snarled back, surly as ever.

"If the roles were reversed, would you want an audience?" Erik asked.

My smart guy had a point. I slumped against him. "But I want to know right now," I whined.

"On that we agree!" Sutton crossed his arms.

"Fine! Here's how this is going to go. Sutton, you're coming in the bathroom with me," Dakota announced. I hunched deeper against Erik, feeling pushed aside. "Savvy, you put all of this away"—she gestured to the bags—"and wait for me to come out and share. I want you to be the first to know, *after* my husband and the father of this maybe baby."

"Maybe baby? Aw, super cute. I hope it's positive." I clutched my hands together in a prayer position while Erik tried and failed to hide his laughter against the back of my head.

"Of course you do." Dakota rolled her eyes and grabbed one of the electronic tests and a plus sign one. "Wish me luck?" she asked, but I wasn't sure if we were hoping she was or wasn't pregnant.

I was darn excited about the possibility of my big sister being pregnant. Our family was so small. Having a little one to love would bring hope and good tidings to an uncertain future. We both needed something wonderful to look forward to. And there was nothing more monumental than bringing a baby into the world.

Dakota held her hand out to Sutton. "Come on, big guy. Let's go see if we're about to become parents during all of this crapola."

Sutton grabbed her hand, and they started up the stairs. When they got a few steps up, he turned back around and stuck his tongue out.

"You suck!" I yelled back.

"I do. Very well. Just ask your sister!" he hollered before

entering their bedroom and closing the door with a loud smack.

I stared for a solid minute at that door, glaring, wishing I had Superman's laser eyes so I could blast my brother-in-law right in the behind. Erik let me go and started to put the cold items they'd purchased in the fridge.

Waiting for them to come back down was absolute torture.

I paced the kitchen after we'd put away the groceries and extra tests. When they still hadn't come down, I paced their living room, glancing longingly up the stairs. It had been at least twenty minutes.

"Do you think it's positive?" I fiddled with my fingers, nervous energy flooding every nerve ending as we waited.

"*Elskede*, come here," Erik commanded with a low tone that spoke directly to all my girly parts.

I shuffled over to where he sat in one of the dining chairs. He patted his lap, so I sat in it, wrapping my arms around his neck.

"Why are you so stressed? Hmm?" His voice was a soothing rumble.

"I'm used to being the one Dakota goes to for these types of things." I slumped within his embrace, feeling completely left out of such a huge moment and hating every second of it.

"Pregnancy scares?"

"No. Well, yeah, but we haven't had that problem before. At least she didn't. I had a scare once with Jarod, and she was Johnny-on-the-spot with a test, ice cream, and a chick flick. Obviously, it came out negative, but having her there for me during a frightening time was everything. I want to be that for her."

He pushed a lock of hair behind my ear and stared into my eyes. "Because the two of you were all you ever had. That's not how it is anymore. Now she has Sutton. And it is his honor, his right to be there for his wife. To be there in a moment such as this. I don't want anyone around us when we share this experience."

"*When?*" I gulped.

He frowned and stared intently into my eyes. "When you are carrying my child, it will be the second happiest day of my life." This statement was not only confounding, but surprising. Mostly because I didn't think we'd be discussing a family when our marriage contract was short-lived. When children were involved in a relationship, things were more complex and complicated, not to mention came with a hefty time constraint. Translation: our entire lives.

Children were forever. Planning to have them with a person was a colossal decision that I wouldn't ever make lightly. Not that Dakota was, either. She was very clearly shocked by the possibility and didn't exactly seem elated about the prospect. Even though I knew she'd handle whatever the outcome was with grit and a take-charge approach. But for me and Erik, our impending marriage wasn't supposed to be like that.

"If having a child with me," I gulped, hardly able to speak the words, "would be the second happiest day of your life, what was the first?" I asked, nervous to hear his answer.

"It hasn't happened yet." His beautiful eyes danced with mirth.

I pursed my lips as my brow pinched tight. "I don't understand."

He curled his finger around my chin. A move I was beginning to adore. "The happiest day of my life will be the day you marry me."

I closed my eyes and put my forehead to his, pushing the discussion of having children with him to the back of my mind. We didn't need to discuss every possible outcome of the next few years. I was content with simply living in the moment. Something I hadn't had the opportunity to do before Erik entered my world.

"You are the most wonderful man, you know that? I truly can't wait to marry you and start our new lives." I ran my fingers through his gorgeous hair, loving that I was allowed this intimacy.

"Speaking of…" He went through the conversation he'd had with Sutton about the possibility of us marrying on their property.

"He offered their home and land? For us?"

He nodded. "Said we're brothers now. I think it would be lovely." Then he looked up toward the stairs right as Dakota and Sutton started to come down. Dakota's face was unreadable, but Sutton let all his emotions hang out, his entire face beaming with glee.

"We're pregnant!" Sutton hollered and fist-pumped the air as though his favorite football team had just won the Superbowl.

I gasped, removed myself from Erik's lap, and flung my arms around my sister. "No more maybe baby! You're having a child! This is awesome!" I breathed.

Dakota nodded, eased back, and covered her belly with both hands. "I can't believe it."

I could hear Erik hugging and clapping Sutton on the back, sharing his congratulations.

"You know what else I can't believe?" I said as the tears finally came back at hearing such beautiful news. "Sutton offered to let me and Erik get married on the Goodall farm. After this sign of good things coming to our family"—I covered her belly with my hand—"I'd like nothing more than to get married right here. The same place you're going to make me an aunt."

"Really?" She turned to Sutton. "You offered that option?"

He nodded. "Ma would love hosting a big bash, and I knew with all that you have been dealing with, you could use something fun to turn your attention to."

Dakota reached out and curled her arm around my shoulder, then did the same with Sutton. I reached out to Erik and wrapped my arm around his waist. Sutton stretched his arm around Erik's back. We stood in a four-person huddle.

"To our growing family," Dakota whispered.

"To our growing family," I mimicked.

"To our growing family!" the guys chimed in.

That day was the moment we cemented ourselves as true family members. The Goodalls, the McAllisters, and the Johansens.

I'd never forget that moment as long as I lived. And I'd do anything to keep our small circle intact and safe.

Episode 89B

God's Plan (Bonus Scene)

Twenty minutes earlier...

DAKOTA

"Darlin', you're squeezing the life right outta my hand," Sutton complained as we entered the master bedroom.

I let go of his hand, tossed the tests onto the bed unceremoniously, and then immediately started shaking out my arms, frantically trying to release the sudden burst of chaotic energy.

"I can't do this." I shook my head and paced. "Nope. Can't. We could just wait, I don't know, another month or two. What would it hurt?" I nodded to myself. "Yeah, that sounds good. Figure out the barn fiasco, my father's hopeful imprisonment, get Savannah and Erik married off..." I kept rambling and pacing, looking for a way to sink my head right into the proverbial sand.

Sutton stopped me mid-pace from behind by putting his hands around my waist and tugging my back to his chest. "Breathe, baby. You're going to hyperventilate," he warned.

I sucked in a sharp breath and let it out as the waterworks started. "I can't believe this is happening." I slumped against his chest as he held me. "It's too much. It's too damn much."

"I know. This scenario was not what we were expecting. At least not for a couple years down the road. But that doesn't mean we won't be able to handle it. You're not alone, Dakota. You have me. You have Savannah. If what we think is true, my entire family will be beside themselves with glee."

I huffed. "And my father will want to disown me."

He snorted against my neck, and I could feel the warmth from his breath as he chuckled. "Do you really care what your old man thinks?"

I shrugged and let out a sigh. "And what about the townsfolk?"

"Since when have you given two fucks about what anyone in town thought of you?"

"I mean...you have a point there," I begrudgingly admitted.

His big body shook with quiet laughter. "What else you got up in that head of yours making you think crazy thoughts?"

"My mother chose to leave her children, Sutton. She chose to end her life because she couldn't handle the cards that were dealt to her. What if...what if something in my mind clicks after having a baby, and I suddenly don't want to exist either?"

"Kota..." His hold tightened. "That isn't going to happen."

"But it could." My breath hitched as the tears fell.

"No, it won't. Because you're forgetting one extremely important thing in all of that worry."

"Yeah?" I asked it as a question, needing the reassurance only he could give.

"You're forgetting that I'm this baby's father." One of his hands slid down to my abdomen and stayed there. "I'm going to be there for everything. Right by your side for the highs and lows, the good and the bad. And your ma, darlin', had a man abusing her for years. Physically, emotionally—in every way possible. That is never going to happen to you. All you have on the horizon is a good future with a man who loves you, an extended family that would bend over backward to help during the tough times, and a sister who would give her life for you. Your ma had none of that support. So there's no comparison between what you're experiencing right now and what she had to deal with."

He was right. One hundred percent correct. And though I was scared out of my mind, there he was with kind, soothing promises that I believed he'd follow through on. He was the type of man who would dote on his child. Hell, he doted on me, and I wasn't even nice to him most of the time.

I spun around within his arms. "I love you, you know that?"

He looped his arms at my waist. "I do know that. I also know that if you're pregnant, we'll figure it out together." He pushed a lock of unruly hair behind my ear. "Let's start by taking the tests so we know one way or another, yeah?"

I pouted. "Fine. Let's do this."

He let me go, and I grabbed the tests and passed one to him. "You read the instructions on this test. I've got the electronic one. Seems like the easier of the two." I scrunched my nose together and focused on the information included in the box. Sutton did the same, and after a couple minutes we entered our en suite bathroom.

He handed me a test after removing the pink cap. I removed the gray cap from the electronic one and took the one he handed me.

"Okay, since you need to pee for a few seconds on each, maybe we should have you go in a cup and then submerge them?" he wisely suggested.

"Sounds smart."

He handed me the cup we used to rinse our mouths out when brushing our teeth.

"Gross," I cringed.

"Just use the damn cup. We'll wash it."

"You mean we'll throw it away," I corrected.

He looked up at the ceiling. "Give me strength," he grumbled. "Get on with it. The longer it takes, the more you're going to freak out." He suddenly grinned devilishly. "Then again, the longer you take, the more your sister has to wait."

"Don't you start with my sister. You will be friends with her." I pointed the unused sticks at him.

"Definitely frenemies," he amended.

"A word I never thought I'd ever hear a man like you say. Frenemies." I went to the toilet and pushed down my pants and underwear.

Sutton stared openly, not at all weirded out by me undressing to sit on the pot. "You can turn around now. Or better yet, wait in the bedroom."

He made a gruff "not happening" noise. "Married couples piss in front of one another all the time, darlin'. Get with the program and pee in the cup."

"Well, I can't if you're watching me. Call it stage fright. Pee-fright. Whatever. Turn around."

He laughed and did as I bade. "Okay. Go ahead."

I sat down, put the cup where I needed it, and tried to go, but nothing happened. I groaned and then sighed. "Turn on the water."

"Really? You're stalling," he complained, though humor filled his tone.

"I am not! I just can't force my body to urinate whenever I want. I have to be ready. Or in the mood. Whatever it is, the sound of water will help. Now turn on the damn tap or get the heck out and let me do what I need to do!" I snapped.

He turned on the water. "Better?"

I thought about it for a good ten seconds and felt the

telltale tingle. "Yeah, I think so. Just talk to me."

"What do you want me to talk about?" he asked.

"Anything. Nothing. Whatever. Just make noise so I'm not focused on you being all up in my business when I need to pee in this stupid cup."

"Okay, um, where have you traveled in your lifetime?"

"Uh, Montana and Nevada," I stated instantly.

"You haven't seen any of the country besides where we went for the auction?" he clarified.

"Yeah, and I didn't see much of that either. We got off the plane, had dinner, went to bed, and started our meetings and makeovers the next day. Then you bid on me. Now we're back home. So yeah, that's it."

"Jesus, your father is a piece of work," he griped.

"We both knew that. You said you traveled a lot for work?" I asked, then finally was able to relax enough to go in the cup. I plopped the two tests in with the stick side submerged and set the cup on the counter before I finished up.

When Sutton heard the toilet flush, he turned around, his gaze going straight to the cup. I washed my hands and turned off the faucet. Then I grabbed a clean washcloth and set it on the counter. Next, I put a cap on each stick and then laid them on the cloth. I eased my back against the opposite bathroom wall and let myself slide down it until my bum was on the cool tile. Sutton kneeled and then sat down next to me.

"Three minutes?" he asked cryptically.

Then it dawned on me that he was referring to the amount of time needed for the results. "Yeah."

He took my hand and interlaced our fingers. "I've seen most of the West Coast and the middle of the US. Cattle ranching and farming tend to be most profitable in calmer climates that don't get blanketed in snow. Therefore, a lot of the land we bought and transformed into high-functioning farms and ranches are in states with good weather."

244 / Audrey Carlan

"I'd like to do visits with you sometime. I mean, if that's something you do," I clarified.

"We can. Ma knows now that I'm settled down, it's Junior's turn to take up the heavy lifting with the travel and startups. I'll be available and heavily involved in the purchases and will share in the site visits and planning, but the bulk of the travel should be done by someone who's unattached. And I am most certainly attached to my wife." He grinned and bumped my shoulder.

"And if I'm pregnant?"

"More reason to be home. Besides, Bonnie's been dying to get out in the field. She's smart and capable. I'll suggest Junior and I take her along to learn firsthand as I transition out of that portion of the Goodall business."

I nodded. "And what about me?"

"Well, if all works out as it should, you'll have your hands busy with the McAllister ranch, the rebuild, and then if those sticks turn out positive, which I think we both know they will, you'll be a momma. I want the mother of my children to have a choice in what she does with her time. If you don't want to be 100 percent with our baby all day long, we'll get help. Though my mother will lose her ever-loving mind if she isn't chosen to be the regular care provider, so you might want to start wrapping your head around that possibility now. If you really don't want that, we can discuss it with her."

"Why wouldn't I want family helping raise our baby? Linda is an amazing mother. She's raised three of her own who are pretty damn great."

"She's going to be pushy about spending a lot of time with her grandchild. I'm warning you now." He smiled sweetly.

"There are worse things than an actively involved grandmother. Besides, you're talking as though we're already pregnant," I whispered, fear and maybe even a tiny hint of excitement weaving through my statement.

"Let's say I'd be shocked if you weren't. We had a lot of unprotected sex, and I regret absolutely none of it. I also know you've been sick a while, and it's not a cold. The most likely conclusion is you're good and knocked up."

"Ugh, I'm a stereotype." I let my head bang lightly against the wall as I sighed. "Quickie wedding in Las Vegas to someone I barely knew. Unprotected sex. Now we're probably pregnant. This is every romantic comedy romance novel that is based in Vegas ever."

Sutton chuckled. "Because you've read many?" he inquired, half-joking.

"Actually, yeah, I have," I admitted, absolutely no shame in my reading preference.

"When?" he scoffed.

"We've been quite busy with a lot of unexpected things, so I haven't had time to read, but I usually read a book a week, and romance happens to be my favorite genre."

"I must say I'm surprised. First, you don't seem like a romantic. Second, you don't have the bookish-girl way about you. Mostly because you are so active. Constantly moving or finding something to do."

I nodded. "True, but when things were more settled, I'd read at night while I ate dinner or while the sun set in the evenings. Then I'd read before bed. It wasn't like I had a man to keep me warm at night or to fuck me so good I crashed promptly after." I pressed my lips together in an effort not to laugh.

"Don't expect to be getting back to having much time to read at night in the future either, darlin'. I like our private time together too much to give it up."

I grinned, leaned close, and kissed him.

Eventually he pulled back, licked his lips, and smiled. "You ready?"

"No. But with you here, I can handle it."

"Good answer." He got up and offered me his hand.

I let him help me to my feet and then we stared at the two tests. The results were not hard to decipher.

The pink test had a big fat PLUS SIGN in the window. The electronic test clearly stated PREGNANT in capital letters.

"Welp, we're going to be parents." He smiled so big and stood so tall I couldn't help but smile in return. Then I burst into tears and laughter at the same time.

He held me while I let it all out, whispering little words of praise and gratitude into my ear.

It's going to be okay.

I'm here.

You're going to be a beautiful momma.

I'm excited to see what we made.

I've never been happier.

I love you, and I love our baby.

His sweet nothings were exactly what I needed as I breathed through the reality that I was going to be someone's mother. I clung to his body and then tilted my head. "Don't ever leave me. I need you." I admitted my deepest truth. I didn't want to do this alone. I didn't think I could. But with Sutton, I knew I could handle anything.

"I won't. You're mine until I leave this world. And then you'll be mine in our next life." He smiled so gently I wanted to imprint it into my mind. "You're making me a father, Dakota. Thank you. It's the best gift I've ever been given."

I cupped his jaw. "You really think so?"

He nodded. "Besides you, I've never wanted anything more. I feel like everything I could have ever wanted and dreamed is coming to fruition as each day passes."

"I don't think I've ever met a better man. There is no one on this earth I'd rather be sharing this with." I got up onto my toes and kissed his neck, then his jaw, and then his lips. We kissed for a long, long time. Cementing this as one of the best moments I'd ever had with him.

Was I any less scared? Maybe a little. Knowing he was going to be there for it all changed my perception of what was to come. Why couldn't we be the best parents the world had ever seen? Just because we didn't expect it or plan for it didn't mean it wasn't exactly what fate intended.

Sutton put his hand over my belly, and I placed mine on top of his.

"We're going to be parents." He said it again with such awe my heart swelled.

I nodded and laughed out loud, enjoying his happiness.

"Yes, we are," I confirmed, still uncertain how to feel about it all. I wasn't upset, but I was still scared.

"I can't wait to find out what it is! Or do you want to be surprised?" he asked.

I frowned. "People still want to wait to find out? No way. I'm all about instant gratification."

He chuckled. "Me too. That's how we got into this situation in the first place," he teased, referring to how enthusiastic we both were to consummate our marriage—not at all thinking about the possibly of this moment down the road. I couldn't say I'd change our wedding night, though, because it had been the best sex of my life. I'd never felt passion or lust that strong before Sutton. The man made my knees weak and my body ache with need and desire. He was an incredible lover, extremely gifted and giving in bed. Apparently too giving, since he'd given me a baby along with unforgettable orgasms.

When it came right down to it, this was bound to happen. Sometimes a person needed to just have faith. Trust in fate. Perhaps this was all just a big part of God's plan.

Whatever it was, it was happening. I just needed time to wrap my mind around it.

"Let's tell Savannah and Erik but keep things between us for a little while. At least until after the first doctor's appointment. I think we could use some time to adjust to what is to come."

He nodded. "Okay. As much as I want to scream it from the rooftop or call a family meeting to make the announcement, we've had a lot of change in a short amount of time. It's good to let it simmer. And it's fun to have a little secret just for us."

"And Savannah," I added.

He groaned dramatically. "Fine. And your sister."

I chuckled and kissed his chin. "Thank you, husband."

He took my hand and led me out of our room. "You're welcome, wife."

Episode 90

I Want In

MADAM ALANA

The first thing I did after I woke was check my phone and sigh with relief when I saw a text from Faith.

From: Faith Marino
Sooooooo sorry I didn't respond to your last message. I got married tonight! The last few days have been crazy. We're back in Las Vegas and got married on the rooftop of Joel's hotel The Alexandra. It was magical. I'm so happy.

With the text was an attachment. I clicked on the image and was delighted to find a stunning photo of Joel and Faith, him in a debonair navy tuxedo and Faith in a Grecian-style wedding gown that made her look like Aphrodite. Two little girls in pretty dresses stood in front of them, one with red hair, the other with medium brown, big smiles on all their faces.

My heart fluttered with joy at the sight as a pair of arms wrapped around me from behind. Christophe's overnight scruff tickled the skin of my neck and shoulder as he planted several pecks and nibbles.

"Good morning, *mi amore*. I love to see this serenity on your face in the morning's first light. It makes my wife look like a goddess," he rumbled against my skin, sending a new type of flutter throughout my body.

"Speaking of goddesses, look at this, Cristo." I showed my husband the image of the happy family.

"Aw, they got married. This is good news, no?"

"*Oui*, it is very good news."

Christophe dragged his hands up from my middle to cup my breasts. "We should celebrate." He nipped at the ball of my shoulder as I sighed, leaning back against him.

"We absolutely should," I said breathily and turned my head, aching for his kiss.

He didn't disappoint, taking my mouth in a deep, soul-affirming kiss that bolted through my system like lightning.

I turned around with a fervor and need that had my husband falling back onto the bed. I straddled his hips and ground down over his impressive morning erection. With a quickness he didn't expect, I grabbed his wrists and shoved them beside his head on the mattress.

"You had your fun last night." I nuzzled his nose with the tip of my own, my breath fanning his face. "My turn." I flicked my tongue against the seam of his lips until he opened on a groan.

"Far be it from me to deny my wife her fun. I am all yours to do with as you wish." Christophe stretched his beautiful body and sighed as I sat on top of my love and planned my attack.

We arrived at the Goodall home as Savannah, Erik, Sutton, and Dakota were piling into an SUV. Savannah waved and told us to follow them farther onto the property.

"This place is right out of an American Western movie," Christophe said, overjoyed.

I reached across the seat and rubbed my husband's arm, loving that he was having this moment. The land was sprawling, picturesque, and did in fact resemble paintings such as those done by Charles Marion Russell, an artist I knew my husband favored.

"*Cheri*, I am getting so many ideas for my next sculpture! I'm thinking the title 'American Prairie' would do my vision justice."

"I look forward to watching you work on it." I smiled, paying more attention to him than the view. When my husband's muse was piqued, the results were often extraordinary.

The driver led us up to an expansive all-white home, at least twice the size of Sutton and Dakota's more modest farmhouse. There was a massive red barn with a perfect white wooden "G" in the center. Out in front stood Erik's parents, Irene and Henrik, who were talking to a man and woman dressed from top to toe in Western attire. A younger man and woman also exited from the home to meet up with them. They were similarly dressed.

Sutton and Erik alighted from their vehicle and went around to the passenger side, both opening the doors for their women. My heart swooned at the chivalrous gesture as my own gentleman did the same for me.

Hand-in-hand, Christophe and I approached the group already speaking animatedly with one another. Savannah had glued herself to Erik's side, nodding at whatever her sister and Sutton's mother were saying.

Then abruptly Sutton's mother clapped her hands, and everyone stopped talking.

"All right, I know everyone is excited, but someone has to lead the charge if there is to be a wedding here this weekend." Her tone was all business.

I gasped and made my way over to Savannah, Christophe following at my heels. "Darling, you are to wed this weekend?"

She beamed, her smile so wide I could see her gums. Her eyes were lit up with sheer excitement. That sparkle in her eye and the aura surrounding her made it very easy to see that I was looking at a woman who had fallen in love.

"The Goodalls are going to let us get married *here*, on their property." She bit into her bottom lip as though holding back her joy so as to not embarrass herself.

"*Magnifique!*" I put my hand to my chest, remembering how she'd planned to marry on her family's farm after they made their way from Norway to Montana. The shift in location likely had to do with the barn burning down and the events that had occurred there recently.

"What we need to do is divide and conquer." The older woman's voice rose over the chatter between each small group of people standing around. "The men can get the barn and ceremony set up with tables, chairs, linens, and the like. We'll need a DJ…"

"I know of a good band a couple towns over I could probably secure," a man who looked a lot like Sutton announced.

"Good idea, Junior." Mrs. Goodall pointed at him. "You get on that." She tapped her lips with a finger. "Next, we've got to pretty things up a bit. I'm thinking twinkle lights, candles, and flowers."

Savannah finally spoke up. "We know the florist in town." She glanced at Dakota. "I'm sure if one of us visited, we could get the things we needed."

"Excellent," Mrs. Goodall said. "Food. Who's on food?"

"Woman, you know if we're having an event, I'm grillin'," Sutton's father growled with impatience.

She put her hands to her hips and glared. "It's not *your* wedding, Duke. How do you know Ms. Savannah and her fella there want you grilling their first meal as husband and wife?"

I watched as Savannah poked Erik in the ribs and whispered something to him.

"Who wouldn't want a fresh, juicy steak made by a master?" he touted, his chest puffing up.

"Oh, I don't know. Maybe a woman who grew up all her life on a cattle ranch." She slapped her denim-clad thighs with both hands. "Maybe she wants chicken? Ever think of that?"

"I can grill chicken with the best of 'em, and you know it. And taters, and even that fancy bacon-wrapped asparagus you all seem to drool over every time I make it."

Savannah poked Erik in the ribs again.

"Excuse me, Mr. and Mrs. Goodall. All that food sounds wonderful. Both Savannah and I love a good steak, potatoes, and vegetables. We'd be honored to have you share your gift of grilling with us."

"Well, there you go, Linda," he responded with bite. "I'm grilling. Which means you are making those amazing stuffed mushroom caps and gooey cheeseballs with that peppered jelly stuff. Shee-it, this is going to be a night to remember," Sutton's father prattled on.

"It's true. I do make delicious stuffed mushroom caps and cheeseballs. Would you like that, dearie?" She addressed Savannah, who promptly nodded.

"This is all so generous of you. We can't begin to thank you. And of course, we'll pay for any and all expenses."

Linda and her husband waved their hands back and forth

as if they were swatting away flies. "Bah, we're family now. This is just a fancier version of family dinner with more people to stuff full of food and booze. Speaking of…"

Sutton raised his hand. "I'll get the booze and drinks."

His mother nodded. "Who's got the decorator's eye?"

I raised my hand. "My husband is an artist, and I am well known for my soirees. We'd be happy to assist."

Savannah cut me off. "You're staying?" she asked, hope in her voice.

I smiled softly and reached out my hand. She placed hers within mine, and I squeezed, trying to imprint as much support as I could offer.

"You know I love a good wedding." I winked, and she giggled sweetly. "And since I missed your sister's…" I side-eyed Dakota, who hooked a thumb accusingly at Sutton.

"What? If I didn't wrangle you in Vegas when you were willing and able, we might have never got hitched. With your sass?" He let out a sharp breath that sounded like a horse braying while he rubbed at his jaw dramatically. "I'd have never locked you down."

She crossed her arms and glared at her husband. "Sounds 'bout right!"

"Point proven." He looped an arm around Dakota's waist, hauling her against his chest. She looked up at him, adoration and spice flowing through her body language. The spiciness dissipated the instant he put his lips to hers in a loud, lip-smacking kiss.

She tried to push away, but he held her close and mumbled around her mouth. "Nuh-uh. Not done getting my fix."

The crowd cackled and laughed as eventually Dakota gave in and kissed him back.

"Let's focus, friends. We've got a wedding to get underway." Mrs. Goodall brought everyone back on track. "That means we have location, food, booze, decorations, music, and flowers set. Do you have a gown, dear?" she asked

Savannah.

"Oh, yes. I have the perfect dress. But of course, my matron of honor will need something. Dakota? Shopping this afternoon after visiting the florist?"

Dakota nodded while snuggling against Sutton. The man was constantly taming his bride's attitude, but he seemed to love it even more than she enjoyed dishing it out. Then again, after watching Duke and Linda, I wasn't surprised. This family seemed to appreciate a good verbal tussle. Not my preferred mode of communication, but I wasn't one to judge. Christophe and I had a connection that seamlessly existed. We were one another's other half. It's what I wanted and wished for in all my pairings, and I had a stellar record to date.

"Bonnie, we're going to need a cake. Can you visit the bakery and see if Ruthie can pull something beautiful together on such short notice?"

"Yes, Momma." Bonnie answered.

"All right, everyone, let's get to work."

A dark-haired man approached me and Christophe. He held out his hand. "Hey, I'm Jack Larsen. We didn't get to meet officially. I'm Erik's best friend, best man, and the CEO of his company."

I shook his hand after Christophe. "It's good to meet you, Mr. Larsen."

"Jack is fine," he said while putting his hands into his pockets and rocking back on his heels awkwardly without saying any more.

"Is there...something we can help you or Erik with?" I hedged.

He glanced over his shoulder. "You run the uh, the auction, right?"

I allowed my surprise at his question to show as I raised my eyebrows. "I do." I lowered my voice as I didn't believe it was common knowledge that Erik and Savannah had met in my auction. Not to mention Sutton and Dakota, whose family was crawling all over the place.

"Yeah, uh, I want in," he stated nervously.

"In?" I tilted my head as if to better hear him.

"I want to bid on a wife," he rasped and once again looked over his shoulder to see if anyone was close.

They weren't.

"I see. Obviously, Erik has shared with you some of his experience," I surmised.

He waved a hand. "Oh yeah. There are no secrets between us. Well…" He shifted his head nonchalantly from side to side before continuing. "Technically there was. I had Savannah checked out. Confronted them, and they shared their story."

I narrowed my gaze and pursed my lips, wariness fueling my nerves. "My clientele is rather discreet, and my process takes time."

He shrugged. "Whatever it takes. When is it?"

Christophe nudged me. "I'm going to go help the rest of the guys get things situated in the barn and on the back porch. You two chat, *oui?*" He kissed one cheek and then the other before nodding at Jack.

"Mr. Larsen, we'll need to sit down and have a full conversation. Not a rushed conspiratorial chat as we prepare for a wedding. These things take time…"

He shook his head. "Whatever it takes. I want in on the next auction."

"The next one is in three months' time. Las Vegas. I'd be happy to discuss this further *after* the festivities and within the confines of a private location. Though I must say, you seem flustered and rather eager all of a sudden."

He sighed and let out a breath. His dark hair with layers on top, scruffy jaw as though he hadn't bothered to shave in a day or two, paired with his melted chocolate gaze had a mysterious slant I rather liked.

"I don't know. I just feel itchy. Like I've been wasting my time." He rubbed at his jaw. "Watching Erik with Savannah…

I've never seen him happier. Not ever. And it dawned on me when we came here that I've never felt anything more than a passing interest in a woman before. I mean, I take women out for business, but my life has been…"

"Lonely?" I provided.

He nodded. "I didn't notice it until I spent time with them." He pointed to Savannah dangling her arms around Erik's neck, their foreheads pressed together as they whispered secrets to one another.

"My entire world is work. The Johansens are my family, the only family I know. Erik and I, we've always been one another's person. He has Savannah now, and I…I need to focus on my own future. Find a woman to settle down with. Create a family of my own."

"And you don't want to attempt to do that yourself? The old-fashioned way?" I asked, needing to know the rationale behind his interest. In the business of matchmaking, money, and marriage, the reason behind wanting to participate in the auction was often the most important factor to finding the right candidates to auction.

It was rare that I would enter into an auction not having any idea who would be most likely to bid. It was the reason I'd fast-tracked Sutton's entry into the auction. The McAllister sisters had already been accepted. I'd had a feeling one of them would be absolutely perfect. Though I had assumed he'd have gone for Savannah because she was sweet and innocent looking. Little did I know he preferred his woman with sass and grit. Regardless, it all worked out in the end as could be seen by how effortlessly Dakota and Sutton were with one another.

"Family is important to you?" I asked, hearing something behind his answer.

"I don't come from a good upbringing. It's why the Johansens mean everything to me. I want what they have. I want what my brother Erik has found in Savannah."

"And what do you think it is that he's found?"

"A future worth living for."

"Good answer." I reached into my purse and pulled out a card. It was shiny, black, and had *Madam Alana* written in silver script on one side, my cellphone number in the same on the back. "Call me after the wedding, and we'll set up a time to meet and discuss this further, if you're still interested by then."

"Oh, I never go back on a plan. I only work harder to achieve my goal."

"And the goal would be?"

"To secure myself a wife who wants to build a family."

"Jack, you realize the term limit on the marriages I bring together are three years. They don't include the promise of children. I can work to find a candidate who is not opposed to the idea, though I imagine the fee would go up astronomically."

He grinned. "Money isn't important."

"Money is always important. It's what you do with it that matters," I countered.

"Jack! Can you help move these tables?" Erik called out, breaking into our discussion.

"I'll be in touch, Madam Alana." He read the card and then shoved it into his back pocket, grinning boyishly.

I watched him walk away, mentally going through my database of possible candidates and not finding a single woman from the list who wanted to have children with their bidder. I'd have to go scouting for just the right bride.

A sliver of excitement bloomed at the base of my spine and spread out through my nerve endings. Jack was a wildcard and his request unusual. Unique situations didn't deter me, they only fueled my desire to get to work. Alas, there was a wedding to be had, and my attention was needed in the present.

Later, I'd research a woman for the mysterious Jack Larsen...after I had him fully vetted. Then the hunt would begin.

Episode 91

Your Wish, My Command

JOEL

I could hardly wait until we'd finished the typical wedding festivities to get Faith *alone*.

Faith.

My wife.

Happiness coated every inch of my body as I watched Faith spin around the dance floor, holding hands with both of our girls. And they were absolutely ours. Eden may have been her niece and Penny her stepdaughter, but the way she treated them, the devotion and love that came so naturally, was meant to be.

I looked up at the sign over the bar. I'd named the rooftop hotspot *Astéri*. It meant *star* in Greek and specifically referenced a conversation I'd had with Alexandra before she passed.

"Just look up at the stars, my love. That is where I will be. Watching you and Penny from above. Always there for you."

I could feel her presence all around as I watched my new wife and our girls. Alexandra had chosen well.

"Einai teleia." *She is perfect.* I heard the whisper against my

ear like a melody, the sound disappearing with the wind.

I spun around to see who'd spoken, the hair on the back of my neck standing up straight, my heart pounding at that subtle, recognizable lilt. It was Alexandra's voice. I knew it deep within my soul, the same way I'd known Faith was the one for me the night she'd walked out onto the stage. I'd spent countless nights speaking to my late wife. Actually hearing her voice was startling, but not altogether unwelcome. Though it was what I'd heard that moved me so.

She is perfect.

That was what the voice had said, and I agreed wholeheartedly. Faith was the woman I was supposed to spend the rest of my life with. The woman I'd have more children with. The woman I'd grow old and gray with. Alexandra taught me what it was to love. What it felt and looked like and how to recognize it when it happened. There was no doubt in my mind that Alexandra was here, blessing this union.

"I will always love you, Alexandra," I stated softly, letting my admission filter into the music and jovial harmony happening all around me. "Thank you for showing me how to love *you*, so that I could one day love *her*." I allowed the heaviness in my heart to disappear, replaced with my gratitude.

A wave of warmth settled over the skin of my jaw, reminding me of the times that Alexandra would cup my cheek before she'd kiss me. It was something she'd always done.

And then I felt it.

A feather light pressure against my lips. Gone before I could truly react.

My heart squeezed, and I swallowed down the emotion I felt as I gripped my hands into fists.

"Goodbye, Alexandra," I said for the last time.

I would always remember my late wife fondly. Would always love her and the time we'd shared together, the child we'd made. But it was now the time to jump into my marriage with my entire heart and soul. Faith was my present and my future. I'd allow nothing and no one, not even the memory of Alexandra, to come between us.

I approached my wife slowly, watching Faith's body shift from left to right, her ample bosom bouncing with her movements. Her long hair flew with the breeze as she twirled, and I imagined wrapping the length around my fist, forcing her head back as I moved within her. My cock hardened behind my slacks, and I had to grind my teeth and breathe through the carnal reel flashing across my mind's eye.

"May I cut in?" I asked right as a slow song started to play. "Perhaps you little ones would enjoy the bubbles they just brought out." I pointed to my mother, who was speaking with the attendant who had games for the children.

"Bubbles!" Penny cried out. "*Yia-Yia*, wait for us!"

"*Yia-Yia!*" Eden screeched, dashing after her new sister.

I bowed before my beauty. "Hello, wife," I murmured.

"Hello, husband." She giggled girlishly and then came freely into my arms.

I pressed her against my chest, one hand around her waist keeping her close, the other holding her hand. I soaked in her delicious scent of coconut and citrus, breathing it deep into my lungs where I hoped it would never leave.

"Have you enjoyed this night?" I asked.

She hummed, "Mmm-hmm," deep in her throat. That sound stirred my cock back to life, once again making it hard to concentrate on anything but getting her out of there and into our marital bed. "You?" she asked with a hitch.

"Everything I could have hoped for, but now I'd like to take my wife to a place where we can celebrate a bit more...privately." I dragged my lips lightly up the column of her neck.

She gripped my hand tighter and pressed her body closer. "Oh?"

I placed several kisses leading up to her ear, where I spoke candidly. "I want to whisk you away to our bed. I want to watch your pretty dress puddle at your feet while I lie naked before you, enjoying the show. Then I want you to crawl across the bed, where I will remove anything you have under this delectable dress…with my *teeth*."

Faith stopped moving completely, my shoulder in a vise grip, her nails digging into the fabric.

"Um, there is a problem with that plan, husband." Her lips grazed my ear, and a shiver ran down my spine.

"I'm an excellent problem solver," I boasted. "Tell me what it is, and I will figure out a solution."

She hummed once more, the rich purr filtering through my nerve endings, making me feel antsy and ready to haul her out of the room caveman style.

"You see, the problem is…" She dragged the words out, then nipped the edge of my ear.

I grunted, my hand going lower to tease the open skin at her lower back with my thumb. "Yes?" I grated out, the control on my desire slipping with every breath.

"I'm not wearing anything underneath my gown," she breathed.

I couldn't be held responsible for the bruising, open-mouth kiss I laid on her in the middle of the dance floor. Our tongues wove in and out, each of us desperate to taste the other.

"We should go," I rumbled as I pulled away, sucking in air.

"I-I would like that very much," she replied, her eyes alight with desire. "What about the girls?"

"My mother and security team will take care of them. You and I are going to the honeymoon suite across from the penthouse. We will be close if the need arises, but nowhere near hearing distance for what I have planned for us."

She made a strangled sound. "Can we go now?"

I chuckled and nodded. "Your wish, my command, darling."

Faith smiled wide, then patted my chest. "Remember you said that when I want my wicked way with you," she teased.

"Sounds like a threat I can get behind," I taunted before lifting her hand and kissing the center of her palm, flicking my tongue against the sensitive flesh as I did so.

She gasped, and her eyes lit with arousal.

It took no more than fifteen minutes to thank everyone and ensure the girls were settled with my mother.

I led my bride to the elevator and pressed the button to go back to the penthouse level. I entered the access code, and we were off. The very second the elevator doors closed, I had Faith up against the wall, my mouth on hers.

We were starved for one another. Her hands already tugging at the buttons of my vest. I pushed aside the deep V of her dress and palmed her luscious, bare breast. She groaned as I dipped my head and teased the tip with my tongue. The elevator dinged, and I promptly pulled my mouth away and covered her nudity.

I gripped her hand and tugged her to the only other door on this level, across the hall from our penthouse. I entered the code and pushed open the door. Then I whisked Faith up and into my arms, princess style.

"Whoop!" She squealed and laughed as I carried her over the threshold and set her down, slamming the door.

She smiled widely and walked backward. "Now that you have me all to yourself, what are you going to do with me?"

My nostrils flared, and I clenched and unclenched my hands, not knowing what I wanted to do first. Bend her over the leather couch, lift up her gown, and rut into her like a wild stallion was option one. Option two: Take her to the king-size bed and lick, kiss, and bite every inch of her skin until she begged me to fuck her. Then of course there was option three: Fall to my knees and taste her cunt until her fingers tore the hair from my scalp with her release.

My cock rose to full mast behind my pants at the visuals.

"What are you thinking?" she whispered, her eyes filled with such love and devotion I knew I'd have to start with an entirely new option.

"I'm thinking about how to best fuck you." I yanked at my tie, undoing it and tossing it to the floor.

"Oh? And what have you come up with so far?" She licked her lips, bringing my gaze to those succulent bits of flesh I wanted to devour.

"Option one." I undid my jacket, removed it, and tossed it over a nearby chair. "To fuck you right here, right now, from behind, while we're both still wearing our wedding attire."

Her eyes heated from love to lust in a nanosecond.

"What else?" The question was a breathy, greedy sound that had my balls drawing up tight.

I inhaled sharply as I undid my cufflinks. "Option two was to take you to the bedroom and lick every inch of your skin until you beg for my cock to fill you."

She gasped, her hands going to her chest, where she fiddled teasingly with the lace of her gown that covered her breasts. "That's a good option as well. Is there a third?"

I removed the vest and let it fall, not caring about the expense of the tuxedo or how it was treated, needing more than anything to get naked as quickly as possible.

"I drop to my knees and worship you until you come on my tongue. An appetizer, if you will."

She swallowed slowly, her chest rising and falling at a quicker pace as goosebumps rose on the exposed skin of her arms.

"And what did you decide?" she asked softly, her question filling the air with an added dose of the sexual tension already crackling between us.

"Option four." I smiled and unbuttoned my dress shirt.

Faith watched as each new bit of my chest was revealed, an audible whimper leaving her lungs when the shirt too fell to the floor.

"Option four?" she repeated.

I took the few steps toward her and cupped her cheeks.

"Option four is I make love to my wife. I love you, Faith. There is nothing I wouldn't do for you. No challenge I wouldn't best a thousand times over so I could be right here with you."

Her eyes teared up, and two drops fell over my thumbs. "I love you, Joel. No matter what happens in our lives, know that you and the girls are everything to me. I want a long life with you more than anything."

"That life starts today." I sealed the promise with a kiss.

She moaned as I took her mouth and lifted her up into my arms once more. I carried her to the bedroom, turned around, and sat with her on my lap.

Eventually, she stood, and I did the same. Her hands went to my belt. She made quick work of removing my pants and underwear as I kicked off my shoes and toed off my socks.

"Get on the bed and lie back," she demanded, her hand on my chest. "I'm going to make your first wish come true, baby."

Eagerly, I sat down and moved backward across the mattress until my back hit the pillows and headboard. Faith stood across from me still wearing her wedding dress. She was just as beautiful with her hair rumpled from my fingers running through it as when she'd stood at the end of the aisle. Not being able to contain my need, I wrapped my hand around the thick length of my cock and stroked.

I hissed between my teeth as Faith watched me pleasure myself.

"You are the sexiest man alive, Joel Castellanos." Her voice was a sultry siren's song.

I thrust harder into my fist a few times, loving not only how good it felt, but how it seemed to turn Faith on.

"Are you ready for me, Faith?" I asked, rubbing the slippery tip of my cock.

Instead of answering, she unzipped the side of her gown, shrugged her shoulders, and let the entire dress slide down her body. She was exactly as I'd imagined. And then she crawled across the bed on all fours, her bare tits swaying, her skin looking sun-kissed and shimmery. I couldn't wait to get my hands on her.

Before I could do anything, her head went down, and her mouth covered the bulbous head of my cock.

"Fuck!" I cursed as she sucked.

I let her use her mouth on me until I was dizzy with the hunger for a taste of my own. Using agility and speed, I hauled her body forward as I slid flat to the bed, her thighs perfectly straddling my head as I'd hoped. When she realized what had happened, I was already tongue-deep in her core. Her hands scrambled to gain purchase on the headboard as I curled my own around her hips, using them as leverage to rock her lower half over my face.

She cried out as I gorged on her sex, merciless in my need. I humped the air as I ate, my cock painfully hard as I worked her until she clenched around my tongue with her release. I groaned and drank deep, sucking up every ounce of my wife until she started to lose her ability to hold herself up. That's when I curled an arm around her waist and flipped her to her back.

I took my time kissing and licking my way up her beautiful form, spending time nibbling her ribs and sucking on her nipples until she started to move restlessly against me, wanting more.

"Spread for me, Faith. I want to make love to my wife," I panted against her lips, my forehead resting against hers.

She opened instantly.

I centered myself where I needed to be and slid slowly into ecstasy. When I was seated deep, Faith wrapped her arms and legs around my body as her sex clamped down around my cock magnificently.

I took her mouth with mine and set up a rhythm that had us both barreling toward bliss. I moved one of my hands to her ass and used it to grind further inside, rubbing against the tight knot of need that made her moan nonstop. I shifted and swirled my hips until she gasped and cried out, her entire body arching. My cock slid against that magic spot within her. I doubled my efforts, lost to my desire to give her pleasure, lost to the pure nirvana that was being inside her.

Finally, her entire body locked around mine, her heels digging into my ass as she let out a scream. Her orgasm triggered the start of mine, and I ruthlessly slammed into her, chasing my release like a madman. I tucked my face into her neck, both of my hands to her juicy ass, and plowed into her several times until I finally came, flooding her with my essence and groaning against her skin. She held me tightly, her sex throbbing as my own slowly started to soften.

That was option four.

Later, we completed option one through three before falling into bed, exhausted and whispering sweet nothings to one another about our future.

When I fell asleep holding my beautiful wife, my life was perfect.

When I woke up, she was gone, a note on the pillowcase where her head should have been.

She'd gone after Aiden.

Episode 92

Your Time is Up

FAITH

The morning after the wedding…

I woke with a start, lifting onto my elbows, Joel's arm lovingly slung over my middle. He didn't so much as stir at my movement. He was zonked out, as I should have been after four rounds of amazing sex.

My husband.

Joel Castellanos was my real-life *husband*.

I was now Faith Castellanos.

Pride, pure and sweet, swam through my veins, warming me from the inside out. That did not, however, stop my bladder from screaming its need for relief. I slung my feet over the side of the bed and stood, stretching my naked body, hands above my head. I yawned as I glanced at the end table. I tapped my cell phone that was charging, the front display telling me it was only five in the morning. We'd gone to bed just a few hours ago. I definitely needed more sleep. The six message notifications, though, caught my attention. Since we weren't with the girls, I figured I could check the texts, make sure everything was okay, and then crawl back into the cave that was Joel's chest and arms. Joel was a maximum touch sleeper. He liked to cuddle me the entire night, and I found with him that I didn't mind being held tight, his heavy limbs locking me in place.

Joel was comfort.

Safety.

Even though I was scared of Aiden and what seemed to be his endless reach, I trusted Joel to keep me and Eden safe. I'd initially planned on meeting Aiden tomorrow before Joel could, but after last night, after committing my love and loyalty to him under the most perfect evening possible, I couldn't do it. I couldn't let lying and deceit color our first day of marriage.

I was going to tell him what I'd overheard between him and Diego. Make it known that I wouldn't be left out of the plans to take down Aiden. I didn't want to be the consolation prize or the princess hiding away in her flashy penthouse tower while the prince risked his life. I wanted to be a team. An unbreakable wall that Aiden couldn't get past. We just needed to put our heads together and come up with something that would save us all.

I grabbed my phone and brought it with me to the bathroom. While I took care of business, I clicked through the texts. Several were from Madam Alana attempting to check in. I'd ignored her messages the last couple days but knew she'd take matters into her own hands if she didn't hear from me. Quickly, I typed out a text and attached a picture from last night of me, Joel, and the girls wearing our wedding attire. Hopefully it would keep her happy for a few days. God willing. That woman was a dog with a bone if she didn't get her way, even though I knew it was all to protect us. She took the role of "Madam" seriously, and I had to respect that.

Next, I scanned through the rest of the texts. Savannah and Erik were on their way to Montana to meet up with Dakota and

Sutton. They planned to have their wedding on her family's ranch. I didn't know much about the sisters, but they were super nice in their texts, all of us dutifully checking in with one another like we'd agreed.

I grinned as I opened a text from Memphis Taylor, the hunky gentleman we'd connected to at the auction. He was the man who had taken himself out at the last minute to chase after Jade when she left in tears. I read through his long update.

Ladies, I'll be joining your ranks soon! I've signed up to be in the next auction three months from now. And it could not happen soon enough, let me tell you. The family really needs my help monetarily. One of my sisters just got accepted into Harvard. Can you believe that? Harvard. She'll be the first in my family to finish college. Keep your fingers crossed there's a fine Black queen who wants to marry my broke ass. I sure don't want to tell my sister Paris that she can't go to her dream school. Anyway, hope you ladies are busting some rich balls like the warriors you are.

Peace.

Memphis

I shook my head as I finished up, then washed my hands. I was just about to brush my teeth when I noted the next message was from an unknown number.

With a shaky feeling in my gut, I clicked on the message. It was a picture. I squinted and then expanded the image, gasping as I saw a bloody image of my sister, Grace. She was suspended by her wrists, which were tied together with thick rope. Blood poured down her gaunt face from the top of her head. She was either passed out or dead. I couldn't tell from the image no matter how hard I strained to see every detail. I could see both her eyes were black and her nose coated with dry blood. Her lip was split while her head lolled to the side and forward, chin to her chest.

I flicked the screen up and read the words below the image.

Meet me at our place. 8:00 a.m. You know where. If Castellanos or his men come with you, Grace dies. Do not test me, Faith. I've had enough of your games. Your time is up. Choose. Your life for your sister's.

I let out a half sob before I smothered it with my hand, trying desperately not to wake Joel.

Fuck. Fuck. Fuck. This can't be happening.

I'd planned on working through the situation regarding Aiden with Joel later today. Now, if I did that, Grace would die. I had only three hours to get where Aiden wanted me, and that would take some serious sneaking about. Unfortunately, I was no stranger to sneaking around. I'd spent years on the run. My mind was constantly assessing situations and locations, always finding the easy way out, usually having to take the hard way in order to truly disappear.

Though I didn't want to disappear this time. I wanted to crawl back into bed with the love of my life and celebrate our marriage. And yet, visions of my sister's body hanging lifelessly swam through my mind like a sickening movie reel.

My hands shook, my mouth watered, and I had to push down the need to be sick. I took a full, long breath in, holding it at the tippy top of my lungs before letting it slowly glide out.

"You've got this, Faith. We've been here before. One step at a time. First step, figure out how you're going to get past Joel and the guard at our door and leave the resort without anyone being the wiser."

I splashed water on my face, brushed my teeth frantically, and grabbed the robe off the door. Thankfully, sitting on the bench in the bathroom was one of my suitcases. Joel had planned everything perfectly, moving what we might need to the honeymoon suite yesterday. I swear I could have fallen to my knees and praised Jesus right then, but I knew my time was limited. I'd have to focus to stay quiet and not wake Joel. As it was, the longer I wasn't in his arms, the more likely it was he'd feel my absence and wake up, ruining my escape.

With practiced ease, I opened the suitcase, found a bra and panty set, and put them on. Then I pulled out a pair of yoga pants, a tank top, and a light hoodie. Once I was dressed, I rolled the yoga pants to up above my knees. I left the hoodie open and pushed up the arms to my elbows. After, I grabbed a pair of ballet flats and shoved one in each pocket before I donned the big fluffy hotel robe, concealing my attire completely. I pulled up my hair into a messy bun and then rifled through my purse, making sure I had my wallet and phone, which I tucked out of sight in my robe pocket.

As quiet as a mouse, I padded barefoot out of the bathroom and through the master bedroom. I stopped at the door and looked at my husband's sleeping form.

Joel was not only the most handsome man I'd ever known, he was the kindest. He didn't deserve any of what was about to happen to him, but I didn't have a choice. Aiden would kill Grace. I knew that fact to the darkest depths of my soul.

I took in Joel's dark hair that I'd spent so much of the last evening clinging to. His beautiful lips I'd kissed over and over. The strength in his frame that made me feel protected. It was my turn to protect him and the ones I loved.

"I'll find a way to make it back, my love. I swear it." I whispered so softly I could barely hear myself.

Across from the master bedroom, there was a living space that included a desk with pen and paper. Not wanting to waste time but knowing this could be the last moment I shared words with the man I loved, I sat down and picked up the pen.

Dearest Husband,

I'm sorry.

I didn't want to leave your side. Didn't want to slip away from the comfort of your arms or our marital bed. However, I had no choice.

Aiden has Grace.

He's hurt her, Joel. My baby sister is being tortured by a madman. I wouldn't be able to live with myself if he killed her, and he threatened to do just that. He said if I told you, or if any of your men followed me, he would kill her.

So please, don't come after me. Stay safe. Protect the girls. Protect my father.

I know I have no right to ask this of you, but I know I must. If I don't make it back to you, I want you to raise Eden as your own. Show my father this letter, in my own words and in my handwriting. He'll believe it and he'll grant me this wish. Eden will be happiest and safest with you.

I'll miss you, Joel. I miss you even now and you're only in the other room. Please know, last night was the best night of my life. It was the night I married the only man I'll ever love. I will try my best to make it back to you and our girls.

Until then, I love you.
Forever yours,
Faith

Tears dripped down my face and onto the thick paper. As I attempted to get my emotions back together, I slipped into the master bedroom and placed the note on the pillow I'd used. I blew a silent kiss to my husband and left the room.

When I exited the honeymoon suite, I knew who would greet me. Both the guard in front of our room and the one across the hall in front of the penthouse.

"Morning, gentlemen." I smiled and walked barefoot over to the penthouse door. "Just want to grab something before I head to the spa level. Can one of you take me down when I come back out?" I asked sweetly.

"Would be happy to, Mrs. Castellanos," a blond, burly lumberjack of a man stated.

I nodded, slipped into the penthouse, and made my way silently to the girls' rooms. I couldn't leave without one more look at my girls. I'd need that image imprinted on my mind in the weeks, months, maybe even years to come.

I entered the room and found it no surprise that they were sharing one of the queen beds. I went to Penny first and pushed her pretty auburn locks off her forehead before planting a featherlight kiss.

She hummed, but didn't wake. "I love you," I mouthed, and then kissed my lips and touched her little hand.

By the time I got to Eden, tears were filling my eyes once more. I wiped them away, crouched, and cupped Eden's warm cheek. Her eyes flickered open, and she grinned. "Hi, Mimi," she said groggily. "Time to get up?" she yawned.

I shook my head. "No, buttercup. I just wanted to kiss you and your sister before I took a shower. I missed you last night."

She smiled widely and wrapped her little arms around my neck, tugging me to her. I inhaled the scent of apples from her shampoo and soaked my soul in the comforting smell. I pressed kisses to her cheek and her forehead. "Mimi loves you more than all the stars in the sky."

"That's a lot." She yawned, her eyes closing again.

"It is. Go back to sleep." I ran my thumb over her cheek.

"Love you, Mimi. See you soon," she mumbled before her breathing evened out and she fell back into slumber.

I wiped the wetness from my eyes and left the room.

Joel will take care of them. They will have the best life possible. I reminded myself of this as I made my way back to the entrance. I slipped out and smiled at the burly blond guard.

"Shall we?" I asked, heading to the elevator.

"Should I double check that it's okay with Mr. Castellanos?" he asked.

I jerked back, my hand going to my chest. "I'm sorry, are you insinuating that I'm a prisoner in my husband's hotel?" I chuckled. "Don't be silly. Let's go." I played it off, and the guard shrugged and followed me into the elevator.

"I'll be back when she's done. Tell Bruno where I am if he comes looking for me, yeah?" he said to the other guard, who gave a chin lift then leaned back against the wall with his arms crossed.

"Feel like I need to soak a bit in the Zen pool, ya know? After last night's festivities?" I played up my exhaustion by cracking my neck.

He made a rude, snort-like sound. "Mmm-hmm."

My cheeks heated instantly, but I kept quiet.

The guard cleared his throat as the elevator dinged, bringing us to the spa level. I was thrilled to see Bella, the woman who'd catered to my group the other day, standing behind the desk.

"Mrs. Castellanos, I hear congratulations are in order!" She smiled widely.

"Yes, thank you. It was a long, glorious day. However, I'm a bit sore. Do you think I could take a dunk in the Zen pool?"

"Of course, it's all yours. You have carte blanche, and if you need a massage when you're done, I don't have any appointments for another two hours. I'd be happy to work any kinks out."

"Sounds like Heaven." I turned around to face the guard. "You can go back to your watch or wait here." I pointed to the chairs. "I'm going to be naked in the pool, so…"

Burly blond lifted his hand. "Nuff said. I'll be here to escort you back when you're ready."

"Thanks." I waved and then made my way to the room. I knew it was connected to the locker room, which had a door that led outside.

When I got to the locker room, I pulled out my phone and called the hotel. Once they answered, I asked for the manager onsite.

"Yes, this is Sheila, the day manager of The Alexandra, how may I assist you?"

"Hi, I'm so sorry to bother you. This is Mrs. Faith Castellanos. Can you have one of the taxis out front drive around to the staff section near the spa's rear exit? I have a surprise planned for my husband. A secret mission if you will that I want to achieve without anyone being the wiser. Can you help me out?" I laughed, making it sound as though this was something fun I was working on.

"Oh, of course, Mrs. Castellanos. Not a problem. We always have drivers ready to take our VIPs wherever they want…" She started to prattle, but a driver that could be tracked wasn't what I wanted.

"No, I need a taxi. I'm going completely incognito. As I said, it's a surprise for Mr. Castellanos."

"Absolutely. One will be around the block just as soon as I can run out front and tell them to pick you up."

"Excellent, thank you!"

"Not a problem. Keep your eyes peeled for the taxi."

I hung up, flung off my robe, put on my shoes, unfolded my pants, and lifted up my hood to cover my hair and face.

Without a second glance, I pushed through the spa's exit just as the sun was starting to chase the dawn and light the sky. In the distance, I watched a taxi roll around the other side of the building. I had my hand on the handle before the vehicle was even fully stopped.

I jumped in and slumped in the backseat.

"West Wind Las Vegas Drive-In. Please hurry." I lifted my head above the back seat and scanned the parking lot as we drove away.

Something felt off even though I'd made a seamless escape. Which was when we reached the corner of the building and I turned my head, my gaze meeting a pair of dark eyes set within a face that was so similar to Joel's my breath caught in my throat.

There leaning against the wall stood Bruno, a cigarette dangling from between his lips, a puff of smoke leaving his mouth. I watched the burning ember tip fall when his mouth opened and he screamed, "Stop!"

I pounded on the driver's seat. "Faster! Go, go, go!"

The driver slammed his foot on the gas pedal, and we were off.

Episode 93

An Ocean of Tears

NILE

Sunlight pierced through a crack in the drapes, making the backs of my eyelids so bright I squeezed them closed tight and shifted my head, not wanting to let the day pull me from the incredible dream I was having. It was of Ruby, swimming naked in our indoor pool. I'd just dived in and saw her incredible body move and sway beneath the water, the teal backdrop highlighting her tanned skin deliciously.

A silky, featherlight touch ran from the top of my forehead down the bridge of my nose, over the indent above my top lip, and ended at my chin.

Sexy dream Ruby slowly faded as I opened my eyes and got a gander at real-life Ruby. Her hair backlit by the sun, a halo of light giving her an angelic appearance. She had her head propped up on her hand, elbow on the bed, her other hand resting on my chest. Her lips were puffy and pink, eye makeup smudged in a smoky appearance I quite enjoyed. Waking up to this woman naked, her hair a mess, lips swollen from my kisses, had pride filling my chest. I stretched my body, finding her leg tucked between both of mine, most of her curved toward me.

"You're a tease," Ruby stated, a hint of a smile curving her pretty lips.

I cocked a brow. "Oh?" I answered, intrigued by her statement.

"You promised sex," she noted flatly and clamped her mouth shut as though waiting for my response so she could blindside me with something that would either make me laugh or make me hard. A state I found myself in regularly when I was around my intended.

I pursed my lips together, trying to ward off the laughter bubbling up my chest, and lifted one of my arms above my head, getting even more comfortable. I could hardly wait for the verbal sparring we were about to have while naked in bed together.

Ruby Dawson had become my obsession.

Talking to her, pleasuring her, spending time with her. It was refreshing to be with someone who was a constant surprise. The way her eyes lit up with each new dish delivered at dinner last night. How she'd boldly allowed me to be intimate with her out in public, nervous but still eager. How she walked with a sway to her hips that wasn't blatantly sexual but definitely caught the attention of every eye in a room. Her constant desire to learn about her environment. How she'd thrown herself in headfirst with the governess in order to learn more about the lifestyle to which she would soon become accustomed.

In the circles I traveled, the women I met tended to be rather dreary or entirely focused on social hierarchy. Many scheming for the most palatable matches that would benefit them and their family's reputation. It was rare that a woman's personality shined so completely that it was hard to see anything else in a room but her. Ruby's personality was a golden beacon of light, drawing me and everyone around her in like moths to a flame.

"Hey, are you awake?" Ruby waved her hand in front of

my face.

I chuckled, grabbed her hand, and kissed each of her fingertips, swirling my tongue around a couple of them. Her eyes lit with a lust so intense I wanted to roll on top of her and give her all of me.

But not yet.

"I said you are a tease," she pouted.

I grinned. "How so?"

She squinted and crinkled her nose. Every time she did that, I wanted to lean forward and kiss the crinkle, smoothing it out with my lips.

"Do you have, um…" She pulled her hand from my grasp and pointed her index finger to the sky then crooked it down and up several times. "You know…performance problems?"

That did it. I lost my hold on my laughter and let it fly. The hilarity of her concern so wonderfully refreshing I could hardly breathe with how long and hard I laughed. So much so, my abdominal muscles were flexing and releasing as if I'd just done two hundred crunches with no break in between.

When I got myself under control, her hand was back on my chest, this time rubbing it back and forth. "You know it's okay if you do. A lot of men can get it up but not keep it up…"

I pressed two fingers to her lips. "Darling, whatever would give you the idea that I am incapable of satisfying you in every way possible? Including, 'keeping it up,' as you so helpfully described."

"You didn't…we didn't…I mean…" She blew out a frustrated breath, a lock of her hair flying up and away from her face with the effort. "You didn't fuck me," she blurted. I watched her facial expression change as she swallowed and looked somewhere over my shoulder but not at my face as her cheeks turned a rosy color that very much matched her name.

"Darling, I fucked you many times last night. With my fingers at the restaurant." I reached out and teased a lock of her hair, spinning the golden strands around and around my finger before tugging it tight. "The best date I've ever had, bar none."

Her breath caught, and her sleepy gaze finally came to mine.

"I fucked you with my mouth when we got back here." I let the strand of hair go and petted her bottom lip with my thumb as I cupped her cheek. "You came twice, if I remember correctly. Begged me not to stop after the first one, so I gave you a second. Rather greedy, if you ask me," I taunted.

Her eyes were molten lava, her lips opening as she inhaled sharply, my thumb dipping into the wet cavernous space of her mouth until she flicked her tongue around it and sucked...*hard.*

My nostrils flared as I released her face and pushed her hair back over her shoulder so I could see her bare. The pink peaks of her nipples were darker this morning, flushed with color as she became more aroused.

With one finger, I teased a tip, circling around and around until she sighed. Then with thumb and index finger, I lightly pinched and plucked. My reward was a sharp intake of breath as she gasped and moaned.

"Remember when I fucked your pretty tits while you teased the head of my cock with your tongue until I came all over these beauties?" I palmed one globe, its weight and shape a perfect fit for my hand. Even more perfect pressed together so my cock could tunnel through them like last night.

"But..."

I let her breast go, leaned forward, and took her mouth in a long, leisurely good morning kiss. Our tongues danced and greeted one another as if we'd done this a million times before. When I pulled away, her eyes were still closed, a contented purr of a sigh leaving her chest.

"I have no such performance issues, my darling. I just haven't wanted to give you my cock yet."

Her eyes snapped open, and she glared. "Why?"

I smirked. "Maybe I'm feeling a bit old-fashioned. We're to wed in just over a week. Perhaps I'd like to take my wife's cunt for the first time on our wedding night."

"You're kidding," she deadpanned, clearly not at all keen on the idea.

The more the concept bloomed within the confines of my mind like a lotus flower unfolding, the more I liked it. Saving that final step for when we became one legally and within the eyes of the church had merit. Not that I was a religious man by any means, but there was something special about tradition. Leading up to such a moment, especially for two people with enough sexual tension to fill a cathedral, would be deliciously agonizing.

The wanting.

The waiting.

The payoff would be explosive.

I grinned at my intended, decision made.

"We're waiting for the wedding night."

She pushed up and onto her knees, her bum resting on her heels in a position that reeked of supplication but would reveal the opposite as her fury filled the air, choking me where I lay.

"You don't just get to decide that for the both of us!" she snapped, her arms crossing over her chest, showing her indignation.

I pushed up and shoved myself backward until I rested against the headboard. "Ruby, love, think of how exciting it will be on our wedding night. The anticipation, the desire."

She dipped her chin down, letting her arms fall, resting her hands to her thighs.

"I guess it is kind of romantic," she admitted.

I grinned, knowing I had her. It seemed my bride-to-be hadn't been courted conventionally. Frankly, I hadn't spent much time catering to the opposite sex myself. My dates in the past were usually women within my circle or one-night stands who I'd met at a bar and who wanted the same thing I did. Mutual release.

I wanted the relationship I had with Ruby to be different.

Because everything about her was unique and called to a part of me I didn't know existed. I found that with her, I, too was different and wanted to be thus.

"Ruby, we'll positively set the honeymoon suite on fire with how badly we want one another." A truth I believed wholeheartedly.

Her cheeks tinted a berry color once more. "You're sure I can't persuade you?" She bit into her bottom lip, reached out her hand, and tugged the sheet down, revealing my naked lower half. Instantly my cock started to harden.

I lifted my leg to a ninety-degree angle and let it fall to the side. My length becoming erect right under her heated gaze.

"Oh, darling, I'd be disappointed if you didn't at least try," I murmured, seduction teasing at the edges of my taunt.

The determined and confident smile she gifted me in response before she crawled between my legs and wrapped her hand around the base of my cock would be one I'd never forget.

After, we lie there panting, our bodies sticky with sweat, each sated with another round of creative coupling and lost deep within our own thoughts.

"That thing you did with your tongue…" I shook my head and kissed her temple. "Positively inspired."

She giggled against my chest, her fingers drawing imaginary lines between the muscles of my abdominals.

"I'm glad you enjoyed it." She hummed against my pec. "Can I admit something without you going all macho man on me?"

I ran my fingers along her arm from elbow to shoulder and back. "I have never in my lifetime been convicted of 'going macho man,' so I think it's safe to say yes."

Ruby rubbed her cheek against my skin in a manner I believed was meant to comfort her more than me, but I enjoyed the intimacy all the same. And anything that would get her sharing was a windfall. My fiancée was rather guarded, preferring to ask questions about others than to share of herself. Something others had used to describe me as well.

"Sex has never been an act I initiated or enjoyed in the past and…" She circled my belly button with her fingertip. "I just, well, this is going to sound stupid, but thank you for showing me how fun and exciting it can be."

I hugged her side. "My pleasure. Truly. It's *my* pleasure." I chuckled.

She smiled and rolled her eyes in a move that demonstrated that her comfort level around me had increased astronomically. We'd vaulted over one of her many walls, getting ever closer to the real princess hiding behind the castle fortress. Before I could celebrate this momentous occasion, she cleared her throat, dug her nails into my ribcage, and grabbed hold.

"My first experience with sex was when I walked in on my mother giving a stranger a blow job. I was five or six."

"Jesus!" I clung to her, wrapping my other arm around her and holding her close, feeling instantly protective of her.

"The man liked me seeing it so much, he said he'd pay her an extra twenty dollars if she'd finish him off while I watched. And we were dirt poor, so…"

"Fuck!" I growled. "That's despicable, vile behavior. I'm sorry that happened to you."

She closed her eyes. "I don't want to enter into a marriage with you, Nile, without you realizing what you're getting."

"I know exactly what I'm getting, Ruby." I'd planned on fueling her ego with endless praise and compliments of her beauty, wit, humor, and what seemed to be a miraculous amount of strength, but she cut me off at the quick with her next admission.

"You don't, Nile. I'm damaged goods. Not like those perfect royals with rich upbringings and all kinds of pomp and circumstance the governess talks about."

"Pomp and circumstance?" I reiterated. "Darling, I don't give a flying fig about royals or the women who come from those backgrounds. If I did, I'd have married one of them." I tugged her body against my chest more completely so I could look into her eyes. "None of those stuck-up socialites could hold a candle to your beauty, courage, and determination."

"You don't understand," she whispered, tears filling her eyes making them look like freshly blown glass still shimmering from the heat of the forge.

"Then make me understand," I begged, wanting her to finally open up to me.

She closed her eyes and let it all out. "The first time I was sexually assaulted, I was eight years old."

My arms tightened around her so hard she squeaked.

"My apologies. Continue," I grated through clenched teeth. Even though I wanted to hear none of it, I knew it was a burden I needed to share if Ruby and I were to have more than just a marriage contract. I wasn't exactly sure what that more would be, but the mere hint of it was enough to want it.

"I lost my virginity before I'd ever even menstruated, and not by choice," she confided, a wicked sharp nail piercing the coffin that I manically imagined putting her still-breathing mother into.

"And how long did this abuse last?" I asked, the words sitting like ash on my tongue.

"Until I could work it off. Bring in money from odd jobs that would supplement the money she received from pimping her daughter."

I closed my eyes, my mind a scramble of all the things I wanted to do to her mother. She'd tried to kill Opal in her sleep. Now I learned she'd trafficked her own child for *years*. Made a living off the back and abuse of a child. The woman should have been hung up by her toenails, covered in sugar, and left outside for the birds and the insects to slowly peck and eat away at her flesh until she took her last breath. And still, that death wouldn't have been harsh enough for such a monster.

With every new horror Ruby revealed as we sat in the cradle of our bed, I fell deeper into the abyss.

Love. Lust. Want. Desire. Hate. Rage. Sorrow. Hope.

A myriad of emotions flowed between us as she shared. Through it, the tears came, and with them some of my own. I hadn't cried since my parents died. Not even when we lost our beloved grandfather. Feeling the need to be strong, show I was a male of worth who could handle any hardship, even grief, I'd held back.

For Ruby, I cried an ocean's worth of tears.

When she was done sharing, I rolled her onto her back. There I hovered over her beautiful body and looked straight into her eyes, hoping I'd reach her soul.

"Ruby Dawson, you are not damaged goods. You are one of the finest humans I have ever met. And in just over a week's time, you will be *my wife*. And I will stand at your side, holding your hand, feeling nothing but extreme pride and gratitude that you are mine."

"You're going to make me fall in love with you, Nile," she confessed, fear clear and present in not only her words but her eyes.

Love wasn't part of the deal.

"There are worse things that could happen," I breathed, the admission surprising us both, if her raised eyebrows were any indication.

She smirked, and I could see her facial expression changing to one with sass. "Maybe you'll be the one to fall in love with *me*," she countered, lifting her legs and wrapping them around my waist, my length rubbing delectably against where I knew she wanted me most.

"Stranger things have occurred, I am sure." I placed a wet kiss to her plump lips as I rubbed along her folds.

"Nile, *please,*" she pleaded.

I grinned wickedly, kissed her forehead, the apples of her cheeks, and then finally her lips before I pulled away. "Not until the wedding." I wagged a finger and got off the bed.

She sat up and waved her hand in the air. "After all of that, you're going to leave me hanging? Rude!" She scrunched up her nose, and my heart clenched at the familiar sight.

I started to walk backwards. "Now I never said I would leave you hanging. Fancy a shower shag?"

"Will there be a happy ending?" She flung off the covers and stood up, gifting me the most succulent view of her naked silhouette against the daylight streaking in.

"Guess you'll have to join me in order to find out." I turned around and quick-stepped to the master bath.

"Wait for me!" I heard her small bare feet slapping against the wood floors as she chased after me.

There was definitely going to be a happy ending.

Episode 94

Trojan Horse

OPAL

Not even a second went by before Noah grabbed my hands and hauled me up and into his arms in a full-body hug. He spun me around so wildly that my legs flew out behind me as he roared with absolute glee.

"Opal, you will not regret this. I'm going to be the best husband you will ever have!" he gushed and then stopped suddenly.

I clung to his shoulders as my body continued to sway from the force of our spinning.

Before I could protest, he cupped my cheeks and laid his mouth over mine. I stood still, unmoving, until out of nowhere, as though a match had been struck deep within my chest, I reacted to the pressure against my lips and kissed him back. I gripped his shoulders as his tongue came out and swiped along the seam of my lips. A rush of adrenaline poured through my veins, heating my blood and setting fire to my soul. On instinct, I opened my mouth just a centimeter.

It was all he needed.

One of his hands left my face and wrapped around my back, crushing me to his frame as he tipped my head to the side. I was clay in his hands and he the sculptor. He slid his tongue into my mouth on a groan. When his touched mine, I gasped, never having felt something so carnal, so...*real*. Tentatively, I flicked my tongue against his to see what would happen. Another sound left his lungs, this one more of a moan as he teased that bit of flesh along mine, tasting of tea and the vanilla scone I'd seen him bite into at breakfast.

I relaxed against his hold, allowing my hands to leave his shoulders and travel up to his head, my fingers combing through the dark, silky strands. The kiss went on and on, morphing and changing the same way the ocean tide ebbed and flowed against the shore. Heat curled at the base of my spine, spreading out like pleasure-soaked ribbons fluttering along my nerve endings.

Just as fast as the kiss started, he ended it, pulling back, eyes sparkling with excitement as he stared down at my bewitched face.

"I knew one kiss would spark a flame so bright, neither one of us would want to put it out." He dipped his head and kissed me softly once more in a simple, affirming touch of lips that meant maybe even more than the languorous one.

Feeling shocked, a little overwhelmed, and a lot silly, I pushed away from his warmth, giving myself much-needed space.

That kiss was... Wow. There really weren't words for the experience, as I had nothing to compare it to. I'd never been kissed before. Never had a man look at me with gratitude the way Noah did. And yet as I stared at his smiling face, I could finally understand Ruby's attraction to the two men and how she'd ended up between them, both vying for her hand in marriage.

Noah Pennington had a boyish, edgy charm that would appeal to any heterosexual woman, me included. Maybe that's why I'd changed my mind about becoming his wife. About attempting real intimacy with the opposite sex. If it was anything like that kiss, I was entirely unprepared. As it stood, I felt twitchy, my skin sensitive to even my own touch and my lips swollen. I pressed my legs together, noting the tender throb of arousal simmering underneath my clothes.

This was what true *lust* felt like. Real, unabashed desire.

I wanted to crawl into the bed across the room and spend hours detailing everything that happened, how I felt about it, surmise what he might have felt, and put it all into a list of pros and cons so I could decide whether or not I wanted to do it again.

Except I already knew I wanted to do it again. Chase that feeling of flying without having wings. Of diving into the murkiest water but seeing the beauty within from the moonlight shining above. Noah had given me that experience, and a part of me wanted to throw caution to the wind and demand more, drown in the experiences he could show me, while the tarnished and broken child I also was sought the safety and protection of her locked closet.

"My wife-to-be is an excellent kisser." He clapped his hands jovially. "Somehow, everything is turning out exactly how it's meant to."

His musings reminded me of what was on the table.

Marriage to him for a period of three years, intimacy practice, school, and true security for me and Ruby in the form of a lot of money. More than anything, the fact that Noah was willing to help me and Ruby without anything in return sealed the deal. It was by far the most decent and kind gesture either of us had ever received. And after that kiss, I was definitely in over my head; but with Noah, I just knew I didn't need to be afraid.

He'd earned my trust.

When Ruby told me she was entering herself into The Marriage Auction, I thought she had lost her mind. She'd been used and abused her entire life. Why would she put herself into a situation where she could be trampled by someone she was legally bound to for no less than three years? It was certifiable. Then she explained more of the concept, the contract involved, and her trust in Madam Alana specifically, and as much as I detested the idea of my sister giving up her life for another lengthy period of time, I could see the same light she'd seen at the end of the tunnel.

We'd be rich.

Money and security were the two things we'd never had enough of. Ruby was ensuring that we'd have both by going through with marrying a stranger. Thankfully, that stranger turned out to be the Penningtons. Well, one of them, anyway.

Noah started to pace the room. He rubbed his hands together as though he were plotting some grand plan and had just solidified the most important piece. Which I guess, was technically...me. I was his Trojan horse in the battle to gain his family's holdings.

When it came down to it, I knew Noah and his brother were good men. They'd already proven their true colors by not forcing my sister into anything tawdry or debauched. The worst she'd experienced was etiquette training with the insufferable governess. But that didn't change my desire to finally be the one to give her everything she needed. It was my turn to give back.

Ruby deserved the world, and I wanted to be the one to hand it to her on a silver platter. By marrying Noah, I'd do just that. Plus, the bright side being she wouldn't have to marry Nile. Sure, they seemed to be getting along famously, but my sister was an incredible actress. She could pretend she was having the absolute best time while spilling her tears under the noise and quiet comfort of a shower. I'd heard her do that more times than I could count after one of Momma's men used her up and spit her out like old gum that had lost its flavor.

The more I thought about it, the more I agreed with Noah's plan. It was perfect. He'd get what he wanted, and my sister and I would finally come out on top. I could already imagine house hunting with her. Helping her get set up, decorating my room in whatever house we chose so it would be ready when I divorced Noah. She'd go to art school, and by then, I'd hopefully be able to use my husband's social connections to secure a position as a museum curator.

The plan couldn't be more perfect.

"When do we leave for Denmark?" I asked abruptly.

Noah's stride shuttered to a halt. "Now who's the eager beaver?" he prattled, grinning like a loon.

I crossed my arms, rolled my eyes, and tapped my foot. "Well, you said it yourself. We don't have a lot of time to prepare. Not to mention, we don't know how we are going to convince Nile and Ruby to let us fly off to Denmark."

His dark eyes sparkled with mirth. "I do not ask for permission in anything."

"Meaning you take the 'ask for forgiveness instead of permission' approach. I'll have to remember that fact for after we say I do," I huffed.

Even talking about our impending nuptials made me twitchy and off-kilter. I didn't know if it was irritation or anticipation of what would happen when we were married that made my palms sweat, my skin feel prickly, and my nipples tingle and become erect behind the lace bra I wore. Or maybe it was simple fear of the unknown. Perhaps a bit of both. Either way, I knew the longer we talked about it, the more freaked out and uncertain I'd become.

Once a decision had been made, I found it best to follow through as quickly as possible.

"I'm being serious, though. Ruby is not going to be okay with you whisking me off to another country," I reminded him.

He crossed his arms over one another and then brought a

hand up to tap a finger against his chin. "I've got it." He snapped his fingers and pointed at me. "We're going to tell them it's for your birthday. That after everything you've dealt with, you need to get away and do something fun. My brother knows I'm always out for a good time, and besides, I'm constantly popping in on my businesses. I have clubs there. Nile will believe it and be happy that I'm leaving him alone with his fiancée prior to the wedding."

I mulled over his idea. "It could work."

He smirked. "And in the meantime, you and I can work on the other, more intimate part of our agreement." He stepped forward, his eyes back to sparkling. I swore the light clung to him like he was a multifaceted cut crystal. It dazzled me for a moment, making it to where I didn't realize he'd come closer, was practically hovering over me until I could suddenly feel the heat of his body.

Noah cupped the back of my neck. "Do you have any idea how beautiful you are? How soft and elegant your features become when you don't think anyone is looking?"

I inhaled sharply as he filled his hand with a chunk of my hair, letting the strands spear through his blunt, masculine fingers. He had nice hands. Squared off at the tips, neatly trimmed nails, and long fingers. He played with the strands, touching the lengths as though it was his right.

I, on the other hand, stood perfectly still, unsure of what I was supposed to do, how I was expected to respond.

"You have gorgeous hair." His voice was low, like thunder moving in from the horizon. A warning and a promise rolled into one.

I swallowed down the dizzying emotions swirling through my mind as I tried to figure out every possible outcome, to anticipate what he would touch next.

"*Breathe,* poppet. At some point you'll have to get used to my touch, my nearness," he warned.

I licked my dry lips and nodded noncommittally.

"We'll work on it," he murmured, his fingers lazily weaving through my hair in unhurried strokes. "What are you afraid of when I touch you?" he whispered, his thumb curling around my chin to tip my head up so I'd be forced to look him in the eye.

"*Everything,*" I confided, letting the admission slip from between my lips as though it were a sacrifice.

I didn't like to admit weakness. Weakness meant pain. The moment someone stronger discovered a weak spot, they would pounce. Use that vulnerability to hurt you. I'd seen and experienced it time and time again.

Noah hummed but didn't stop running his fingers through my hair. "I'd never lay a finger on you in anger. Never allow another to do so either." He proved his point by sliding his thumb along the apple of my cheekbone in a delicate caress that had me trembling.

"That may be true. But you can't always be everywhere. There is far more ugly in the world than there is good. Until you've seen what really lies beneath the masks people hide behind, you'll never really understand true fear. I've seen it, Noah. Stared it in the face. Suffered under its wrath. Watched Ruby suffer even more. I'm not sure I believe that people are genuinely good underneath it all. Not when I've only ever been shown the worst."

My admission sank like dead weight in the air between us. When I thought Noah would back away, try and push aside my fear as the negative musings of an abused girl, he surprised me again. He didn't back away, didn't leave me swallowed up by the burden of the truths I'd shared. Instead, he pulled me into his arms and pressed my ear to his chest, right over his heart. There he rested his chin on the crown of my head and held me close.

"You're right, the world can feel like the ugliest place, the people within it nightmares of their own making. But I believe that each and every last one of us holds the power to make change. To right wrongs. To clean up the ugly. To load it all into a rubbish bin and start over. That's what you and I are going to do, Opal. We're going to make your world a beautiful place to live. I swear it on every dime I've ever made. On my mother's and father's graves. I will show you how good it can be, how there's always something amazing to live for."

"The only thing I've ever had to live for is Ruby. She's the only good I see. The only good I've felt."

"Even still?" He locked his arms around me. "Even after that kiss?"

I bit down on my bottom lip, closed my eyes, and listened to Noah's heart beating.

"Maybe not all the good is lost...but the jury is still deliberating," I conceded.

He chuckled, and I could feel his laughter seep deeply into my bones, taking away some of the heavy weighing me down.

"I'll take that seed of hope and turn it into a forest of nothing but beauty as far as the eye can see, Opal. Just you wait. It will be glorious."

I wanted to believe him. Wanted to believe that he alone could change years of damage, but hope was a fickle thing. Hard to hold on to when you'd been proven wrong so many times.

"I want to believe you" was all I could offer.

"It's enough...for now," he said.

With those final words, a kernel of hope broke open within me and started to bloom.

Continue along with the entire cast in the fourth book of The Marriage Auction, available now!

Madam Alana: A Marriage Auction Novella
By Audrey Carlan

From *New York Times* and *USA Today* bestselling author Audrey Carlan comes a new story in her Marriage Auction series...

I run the most elite auction in the world.

Candidates and bidders come from all over the globe hoping to change their lives.

And I deliver.

I'm in the business of bringing couples together in a mutually beneficial and legally binding marriage. The terms are three years for no less than a million dollars a year, not including my commission. Once a pair signs on the dotted line, the contract ensures there is no going back.

Most couples find over time they are a love match, but not all.

Before I took over The Marriage Auction, there wasn't an extensive vetting process. Some candidates were subjected to horrors that haunt my every waking moment.

I vowed to change that. To stand up for those who deserve more and to release them from the wrongs inflicted upon them by circumstance and chance.

What my bidders and candidates don't know is that I understand exactly what they are experiencing.

I wasn't always known as Madam Alana.

Once upon a time, I too was purchased in The Marriage Auction... And this is my story.

Acknowledgments

We are almost to the finish line, friends! I know I've said it before but THANK YOU, readers, for making this saga the success it is. I'm humbled and honored you have committed to this journey. Big virtual hugs to every last one of you.

To **Team AC** for being my ride or die. My sisterhood of some of the most incredibly talented, compassionate, thoughtful, and supportive women. My stories are a thousand times better because of your contributions and feedback throughout the process. I love each and every one of you. I'm so blessed to call you my tribe.

Jeananna Goodall – World's Greatest PA, Emotional Support Guru, Work Wife

Tracey Wilson-Vuolo – Alpha Beta, Disney Freak, Proofer, ADA Expert

Tammy Hamilton-Green – Alpha Beta, Rock Chick, Educational Expert

Elaine Hennig – Alpha Beta, Brazilian Goddess, Medical Expert

Gabby McEachern - Alpha Beta, Dancing Queen, Spanish Expert

Dorothy Bircher – Alpha Beta, Mom Boss, Sensitivity Expert

To **Jeanne De Vita**, I'll bet when you signed on for this project you had no idea it would be five thousand rounds of editing. I think you know the characters as well as I do at this point. <wink> Thank you for your endless commitment to this saga, to me as an author, and to my stories. I'm better for it. My story is better for it. We're a stellar team.

To **Michael Lee**, you've been one of the best things that have come out of the pandemic for me and my business. Your ability to share my story out across the masses is beautiful to watch. Your technology prowess second to none. I have no idea how you do it, but I love that you do it for me! I'm glad to be a small part of your career trajectory. You're going to do amazing things with your talent, my friend. Happy to have a front row seat as you soar.

To my literary agent, **Amy Tannenbaum** with Jane Rotrosen Agency. Girl, you are the best thing that ever happened to me and my career. I love you.

To **Liz Berry**, **Jillian Stein**, and **MJ Rose** from Blue Box Press: How did we get here!!! I have never had a better experience working with a publisher before. You've ruined me for other pubs. Now I'm going to expect every future project to be handled with grace, elegance, and commitment to my artistic vision. Being able to pick up the phone and call every single owner directly, and have them not only answer but know what's happening with the process, have thoughtful considerate input, and be just as excited as I am about the story? It's unheard of. You three are the diamonds in this industry. I am so lucky to be with Blue Box Press.

About Audrey Carlan

Audrey Carlan is a No. 1 *New York Times*, *USA Today*, and *Wall Street Journal* bestselling author. She writes stories that help readers find themselves while falling in love. Some of her works include the worldwide phenomenon *Calendar Girl* serial, *Trinity* series and the *International Guy* series. Her books have been translated into over thirty-five languages across the globe. Recently her bestselling novel *Resisting Roots* was made into a PassionFlix movie.

NEWSLETTER

For new release updates and giveaway news, sign up for Audrey's newsletter: https://audreycarlan.com/sign-up

SOCIAL MEDIA

Audrey loves communicating with her readers. You can follow or contact her on any of the following:
Website: www.audreycarlan.com
Email: audrey.carlanpa@gmail.com
Facebook: https://www.facebook.com/AudreyCarlan/
Twitter: https://twitter.com/AudreyCarlan
Pinterest: https://www.pinterest.com/audreycarlan1/
Instagram: https://www.instagram.com/audreycarlan/
Tik Tok: https://www.tiktok.com/@audreycarlan
Readers Group:
https://www.facebook.com/groups/AudreyCarlanWickedHot Readers/
Book Bub: https://www.bookbub.com/authors/audrey-carlan

Goodreads: https://www.goodreads.com/author/show/7831156.Audrey_Carlan

Amazon: https://www.amazon.com/Audrey-Carlan/e/B00JAVVG8U/

Discover 1001 Dark Nights Collection Ten

DRAGON LOVER by Donna Grant
A Dragon Kings Novella

KEEPING YOU by Aurora Rose Reynolds
An Until Him/Her Novella

HAPPILY EVER NEVER by Carrie Ann Ryan
A Montgomery Ink Legacy Novella

DESTINED FOR ME by Corinne Michaels
A Come Back for Me/Say You'll Stay Crossover

MADAM ALANA by Audrey Carlan
A Marriage Auction Novella

DIRTY FILTHY BILLIONAIRE by Laurelin Paige
A Dirty Universe Novella

HIDE AND SEEK by Laura Kaye
A Blasphemy Novella

TANGLED WITH YOU by J. Kenner
A Stark Security Novella

TEMPTED by Lexi Blake
A Masters and Mercenaries Novella

THE DANDELION DIARY by Devney Perry
A Maysen Jar Novella

CHERRY LANE by Kristen Proby
A Huckleberry Bay Novella

THE GRAVE ROBBER by Darynda Jones
A Charley Davidson Novella

CRY OF THE BANSHEE by Heather Graham
A Krewe of Hunters Novella

DARKEST NEED by Rachel Van Dyken
A Dark Ones Novella

CHRISTMAS IN CAPE MAY by Jennifer Probst
A Sunshine Sisters Novella

A VAMPIRE'S MATE by Rebecca Zanetti
A Dark Protectors/Rebels Novella

WHERE IT BEGINS by Helena Hunting
A Pucked Novella

Also from Blue Box Press

THE MARRIAGE AUCTION by Audrey Carlan

THE JEWELER OF STOLEN DREAMS by M.J. Rose

SAPPHIRE STORM by Christopher Rice writing as C. Travis
Rice
A Sapphire Cove Novel

ATLAS: THE STORY OF PA SALT by Lucinda Riley and
Harry Whittaker

A SOUL OF ASH AND BLOOD by Jennifer L. Armentrout
A Blood and Ash Novel

START US UP by Lexi Blake
A Park Avenue Promise Novel

LOVE ON THE BYLINE by Xio Axelrod
A Plays and Players Novel

FIGHTING THE PULL by Kristen Ashley
A River Rain Novel

A FIRE IN THE FLESH by Jennifer L. Armentrout
A Flesh and Fire Novel

VISIONS OF FLESH AND BLOOD by Jennifer L.
Armentrout and Rayvn Salvador
A Blood and Ash/Flesh and Fire Compendium

On Behalf of Blue Box Press,

Liz Berry, M.J. Rose, and Jillian Stein would like to thank ~

Steve Berry
Doug Scofield
Benjamin Stein
Kim Guidroz
Tanaka Kangara
Asha Hossain
Chris Graham
Chelle Olson
Kasi Alexander
Jessica Saunders
Stacey Tardif
Jeanne De Vita
Dylan Stockton
Kate Boggs
Richard Blake
and Simon Lipskar

Made in the USA
Columbia, SC
16 September 2023